"No," she whispered as he pulled her to him with feverish desire. . . .

But even as she spoke, every nerve in her body began to throb. She moved her hand from his neck and, hesitantly, brushed his cheek. He picked her up, carried her to the bed and laid her down. Barbara stared at him with enormous eyes. His bare chest and shoulders were so strongly muscled. The bed shook a little as it took his weight. She lay back against the pillows while he kissed her throat and the deep hollow between her breasts. She buried her hands in the soft blackness of his hair and felt his mouth move from her shoulder to her breast. Barbara inhaled sharply. She was beyond thought, beyond all but the wild singing in her blood, the longing to feel his strong body against hers. Her whole being quivered as she arched up against him. . . .

The Rebel and the Rose

The Rebel and the Rose

JOAN WOLF

Ⓞ
A SIGNET BOOK

NEW AMERICAN LIBRARY

NAL BOOKS ARE AVAILABLE AT QUANTITY DISCOUNTS WHEN USED
TO PROMOTE PRODUCTS OR SERVICES. FOR INFORMATION PLEASE
WRITE TO PREMIUM MARKETING DIVISION, NEW AMERICAN LIBRARY,
1633 BROADWAY, NEW YORK, NEW YORK 10019.

Copyright © 1986 by Joan Wolf

 SIGNET TRADEMARK REG. U.S. PAT. OFF. AND FOREIGN COUNTRIES
REGISTERED TRADEMARK—MARCA REGISTRADA
HECHO EN CHICAGO, U.S.A.

SIGNET, SIGNET CLASSIC, MENTOR, PLUME, MERIDIAN and NAL BOOKS
are published by New American Library,
1633 Broadway, New York, New York 10019

First Printing, July, 1986

1 2 3 4 5 6 7 8 9

PRINTED IN THE UNITED STATES OF AMERICA

I

An American in London

Spring 1773

One

Lady Barbara Carr, halfway up the majestic staircase of Bridgewater House, was standing alone waiting to be rejoined by her mother. She stood with perfect assurance, her small powdered head held high, her figure in its rich blue ball gown turned a little to the stair rail to discourage anyone from speaking to her.

Unselfconscious as she appeared, she was still in the awkward position for a young lady of being obviously alone, removed as she was from both the domed hallway below and the great gallery above. She was letting her gaze move idly over the crowd below her when suddenly she had the distinct sensation of being looked at. She raised her eyes to the source of that sensation, the gallery that ran along the top of the staircase.

A man was standing there, as solitary in his position as she was in hers. He was leaning his hands against the broad balustrade and, like her, watching the crowd below.

He was a young man, instantly noticeable by his unpowdered black hair. He seemed, even from a distance, to be very tall. His profile, which was all she could see of his face, was distinguished by a high-bridged and imperious nose. He was not now looking at her, but what had drawn her eye was the distinct sensation of being watched.

"Here I am, my love," said her mother's voice. "Forgive me for keeping you standing like this, but I did want to make certain Frederick got into the carriage safely."

"I'm perfectly all right, Mama," Barbara replied. "Poor Frederick. I hope he feels better."

"A good night's sleep is all he requires," Lady Abingdon said briskly. "I fear you and I will have to make shift this evening without a male escort. Neither of your other brothers can be expected at this particular affair."

The occasion was a great official ball given by the Earl and Countess of Bridgewater. It was the full flush of the London spring season and the state rooms of Bridgewater House were filled with various members of social and diplomatic London. Lady Barbara floated through the crowded rooms in the magnificent wake of her mother, smiling and chatting easily with the great and eminent men who invariably gravitated to Lady Abingdon's vicinity.

"Barbara! I've been looking for you," said a familiar male voice at her elbow, and she turned to look into the blue eyes of her cousin, Lieutenant Henry Wharton.

Barbara smiled. "Harry. I didn't know you would be here tonight."

"I was supposed to be on duty, but I changed with Edwards." He gazed at her in unabashed admiration. "You looked dashed lovely tonight, Barb. New dress?"

Barbara's long lashes lowered fractionally. "Yes." The material had actually come from an old gown of Lady Abingdon's, but Barbara did not give away secrets like that.

"Come along and I'll get you some punch," her cousin suggested.

Barbara put a light hand on Lady Abingdon's arm. "Mama, Harry and I are going to the refreshment room."

Lady Abingdon's shrewd hazel eyes looked appraisingly at the young lieutenant for a brief moment. "All right," she said then, crisply, "but don't detain Barbara for too long, Harry."

Very faint color had risen under the young man's fair skin. "I won't, Aunt Elizabeth."

The two young people crossed the room, passing directly under the glittering chandelier.

"Don't let Mama upset you," Barbara said softly when they were seated side by side on little gilt chairs drinking champagne punch.

"She's trying to marry you off and she's afraid I'll get in the way," Harry said in a queer, abrupt voice. "That's it, isn't it?"

"Well, she is certainly trying to marry me off," Barbara replied tranquilly, "but she isn't having much success." Barbara shrugged slim, graceful shoulders. "My portion is gone, you know."

"I know." Harry's eyes were focused doggedly on the floor in front of him. "God, Barbara, if only I had some money!"

Barbara sighed. "I know. But 'some' money won't do, I'm afraid. A great deal of money is what is needed."

"We could elope," Harry said in the same abrupt voice. "Go up to Scotland and get married."

"That would ruin you with your regiment and then where would we be?" Barbara asked practically.

He didn't answer, for the simple reason that there was no answer—as they both knew. Barbara sipped her punch and glanced around the room. Her eyes stopped as they encountered the stranger from the gallery.

"Who is that man?" she asked Harry suddenly, and her cousin's fair powdered head rose. "The black-haired man," Barbara elaborated. "Over there."

Harry followed the line of her eyes to the tall dark man on the far side of the room. "Oh, that's the son of the American who inherited Hexham Castle. You must have heard about it—old Maxwell left the property and the fortune he made in India to his great-nephew, a fellow from Virginia. Evidently the new heir was very happy to turn his back on the colonies and come home to England. Well, it stands to reason, don't it? Old Maxwell was rich as Croesus, I understand." There was a distinct note of envy in Harry's voice. "That's the colonial nabob now," he added as an older gentleman came up alongside the man they were both regarding.

The younger man had bent his head to listen to what his father was saying. An American, Barbara thought. That must be what accounted for his looking so out of place. He was the tallest man in the room. His eyes lifted suddenly and, across the width of the floor, met hers.

If Barbara were disconcerted, she did not show it. She held his dark gaze for the barest fraction of a second before allowing her eyes serenely to move away from him and drift along to the chubby young man standing directly before the punch bowl.

"He looks like a barbarian," Harry was saying next to her. "He's burned as dark as an Indian."

A barbarian? Barbara thought, startled. No, not a barbarian. But what?

The chubby young man, as if sensing her gaze, looked around at her. Barbara smiled. "Here comes Mr. Fox," she said gently to Lieutenant Wharton.

In a moment Charles James Fox, younger son of Lord Holland, was bowing gracefully over Barbara's hand.

"I should have thought an entertainment like this far too slow for you, Mr. Fox," Barbara said with the faintest lift of her winged brows.

Mr. Fox gave her his charming smile. "I was hoping to see you, Lady Barbara." Then, when Barbara merely looked amused, "And, as a very junior member of Lord North's government, I was expected to show my flag."

Barbara laughed. "I rather fancied that might be it. Papa is coming later, he said."

"Ah, but then Lord Abingdon is more than a junior member of the government."

At this moment Lady Abingdon, accompanied by the Earl of Newcastle, arrived in the refreshment room. Since Mr. Fox was quite as addicted to gambling as her husband and eldest son, she did not consider him a suitable candidate for Barbara's hand and in a very short time removed her daughter to the safety of her own circle. At one o'clock in the morning, ten minutes after her husband finally arrived, Lady Abingdon left for home with her daughter securely in tow.

*   *   *

Lady Barbara was awakened at the unusually early hour of six-thirty the following morning by the sound of someone hammering on her door.

"Wake up, Barb!" came her brother William's voice through the thick mahogany. "Do you want to go for a ride?"

Barbara sat up in bed and yawned. "Yes," she called back.

"Be downstairs in half an hour. I'll have the horses saddled."

Barbara got out of bed and rang for her maid.

In half an hour she was downstairs dressed in her favorite riding habit, a blue double-breasted jacket, tan waistcoat, and blue skirt. It was a more tailored habit than most of those seen in Hyde Park at the fashionable hours, but Barbara was fussier about her riding clothes than about her gowns, and this one had been made to her exact specifications. Her only concession to feminine frivolity was the small jockey cap she wore perched on her smoothly drawn-back hair.

Her brother grinned at her. "Only girl I know who could get dressed in half an hour."

"Only man I know who would include his sister in his morning gallop," Barbara returned.

"Ah well," said William as he held the door for her, "after me you're the best damn rider in London."

Barbara laughed at him over her shoulder as she went down the front steps.

It was a foggy and damp April morning and neither brother nor sister spoke as they walked their horses through the London streets to Hyde Park. Once they were in through the gates they moved into a brisk trot, then proceeded rather quickly into a canter and then to a gallop. When they finally pulled the horses up, Barbara's fine skin was flushed with exercise and glistening a little from the fog.

"That was splendid," she said to William.

"You should have been a boy, Barb," her brother said.

"Yes," she responded instantly. "Then I could have gone off to boxing matches with you instead of attending dreary receptions with Mama. Is that where you were last night?"

His hazel eyes, so like their mother's, glinted with humor. "Yes."

"Ugh. I'll take the receptions, thank you."

"Have you . . . er . . . met anyone you particularly like?" William asked tentatively.

"Oh, I've met a quantity of people I really like," his sister returned cheerfully. "None of them, unfortunately, has any money."

"What does Mama say?"

"Mama says she will contrive."

Harry suddenly stopped his horse and, surprised, Barbara followed suit. "Listen, Barb, don't you go and marry anyone you don't like. I mean that. It's not up to you alone to rescue Papa from debt." He stared at her, his face very serious. William was four years older than Barbara, the closest to her in age of all her three brothers, and they were extremely fond of each other.

Barbara bent her head a little and did not reply.

"Do you love Harry Wharton?" William asked after a moment.

"I suppose." Barbara's voice sounded slightly muffled. "There isn't any point in belaboring that issue, though, William."

"No, I suppose not. Harry needs to marry money almost as much as you do. *Damn.*"

Barbara touched her heel to her mare's side and began to walk forward again. "We must deal with realities, William," she said a little wearily.

"Papa ought to be horsewhipped," William said.

A very faint smile touched Barbara's lips. "Perhaps," she said. "But it isn't just a question of Papa. There is Mama to consider too."

There came to their ears the definite sound of drumming hooves. "Someone's coming," said William. "Get over to the side of the path."

They had just moved their horses to the edge of the grass when a big bay came galloping out of the fog. Horse and rider flew by them, kicking up mud in their wake.

"Good heavens," said Barbara as she brushed

mud off the skirt of her riding habit. "Who was that?"

"I think that was Danby's bay," William returned. "The one that tossed him into the Serpentine the other day. Danby wasn't riding him, though."

"I must apologize for almost running you down like that," said a deep, drawling voice, and both Barbara and William turned to look at the man riding toward them. "I had no idea anyone would be out in the park this early."

"Well, at this hour the only people you are usually likely to find are my sister and me," William returned. "We heard you coming, however, and got over to the side. No harm done."

Barbara straightened up from brushing at her skirt and met a pair of very dark eyes. "I muddied your skirt, ma'am," the stranger said. "Brigadier and I are deeply sorry."

"Brigadier. So that is Danby's horse," William said before Barbara could reply. "I thought I recognized him."

"I bought him from Lord Danby," the stranger said. "He seemed anxious to be rid of him."

William gave a crack of laughter. "I wonder why?" He gave the man and horse an appraising look. "He's a good-looking brute, but vicious."

The big bay was standing quietly. "I reckon he just needs a certain kind of rider," the other man said with slow amusement.

"I say, you must be that fellow from Virginia," William exclaimed with sudden enlightenment.

The stranger's amusement seemed to deepen. "Alan Maxwell, at your service, sir," he said.

"William Carr," William responded readily. "And this is my sister, Lady Barbara Carr."

"Mr. Carr." The deep voice was slow and lazy with its distinct Virginia drawl. The dark eyes moved to Barbara. "Lady Barbara," and he took off his hat, baring soot-black hair.

Barbara looked gravely back. She had recognized him instantly, the dark suntanned face, the aquiline nose and hard-looking mouth. It was the American from the Bridgewater ball last night.

"How do you do, Mr. Maxwell," Barbara said calmly. "Are you enjoying London?"

He smiled and his face was instantly transformed. "It's been interestin', Lady Barbara," he said.

"Indeed," Barbara replied a little faintly. She had never encountered a smile quite like that before.

"Your father inherited Hexham Castle, didn't he?" asked William.

"That is correct, Mr. Carr. We are just arrived from Northumberland, in fact." The big bay began to sidle and Barbara watched as the American's long booted legs closed around the horse's sides. "Whoa," he said authoritatively, and the horse quieted.

"William," Barbara said softly to her brother, "we should not be keeping the horses standing."

"Quite right, Barb," he replied. "Do you care to ride back with us, Maxwell?"

"I was planning to gallop."

"So were we," Barbara informed him serenely and, moving forward, put her mare into a canter. She heard the two men come up behind her and let the mare's stride lengthen into a gallop. In a moment the American's horse was alongside hers and, stretched out, the two of them flew along the path side by side, with William only slightly behind them.

Finally Barbara sat back and, closing her fingers on the reins, brought her mare down to a walk. The man next to her followed suit. Involuntarily they looked at each other and the American flashed her his extraordinary, disarming grin.

"Do all English ladies ride like you, Lady Barbara?" he asked.

Barbara smiled back. It was virtually impossible not to. "No," she replied simply and truthfully.

William came up on the American's other side. "You should see her in the hunting field," he boasted.

The American looked surprised. Then, "I should very much like to," he replied, and Barbara, for some odd reason, felt slightly flustered.

"Do you hunt in Virginia, sir?" she asked.

"Do we breathe in Virginia?" he replied humorously.

"What kind of hounds do you use?" William

asked curiously, and for the remainder of the ride the two men discussed the breeding of hounds, a subject on which the Virginian appeared very knowledgeable.

As they separated at the park gate, Alan Maxwell looked directly at Barbara. "Are you going to Lady Darcy's drum this evening?" he asked.

"Why, yes," Barbara replied.

"Perhaps, then, you would honor me with a dance."

"I should be happy to, Mr. Maxwell," Barbara replied, and wondered why the prospect of seeing him again should produce in her such an odd feeling of exhilaration.

"A good fellow, Maxwell," William pronounced as they rode homeward together. "Even if he is a colonial."

Two

"This is just the sort of affair I wanted Alan to attend," Mr. Maxwell said to Lord Peter Crashaw as they passed into Lady Darcy's ballroom. "It was damned good of you to secure us invitations, Crashaw."

Lord Peter was the younger son of a duke and in his early twenties he had been wise enough to marry an heiress from Yorkshire. The heiress had died in childbirth, leaving Lord Peter with a son and a great deal of money. Lord Peter always remembered her with great affection—she had proved herself a perfect wife. He had never remarried (there had been no need) and enjoyed a very pleasant life as one of London's most well-liked bachelors.

Maxwell had been a friend of the duke's son both at Eton and at Cambridge, and when he had arrived in London he immediately wrote to his old comrade.

Lord Peter adored arranging the lives of others and had immediately taken the two Americans in charge. Under his auspices doors were opened to the Maxwells that would otherwise have remained firmly shut—even considering the nabob's fortune that reposed so comfortably in Mr. Maxwell's pocketbook.

In response to Mr. Maxwell's words, Lord Peter smiled deprecatingly and waved a graceful hand. "The Darcys always do a first-rate job," he agreed. He looked up at his friend's extremely large son. "Is this at all like the colonies, Mr. Maxwell?"

"Oh, the London stage far surpasses us in elegance, sir," Alan replied agreeably.

Lord Peter smiled. "Yet I understand that, unlike your father, you are going to return to Virginia."

"That's right." Alan gave his father a distinctly sardonic look. "Papa was quite *insistent* that I accompany him on this trip, but I will be going home in June."

"Well, we must endeavor to make your sojourn here a pleasant one."

Lord Peter had reminded Alan of something ever since he had first met the elegant aristocrat. Now

Alan realized what the resemblance was. Lord Peter's round, alert, inquisitive face reminded him of a squirrel.

"Thank you, sir," Alan replied with admirable gravity. "You are very kind." He was afraid he was staring at Lord Peter's face, so he moved his eyes away to circle the ballroom. They stopped, arrested, at the doorway.

His father's eyes followed his. "What a lovely girl," Alan heard Mr. Maxwell remark beside him to Lord Peter. "Who is she?"

"Lady Barbara Carr, Lady Abingdon's daughter. That is Lady Abingdon with her now—and her brother William."

"Abingdon," said Alan. "Isn't there a Lord Abingdon in the government?"

"Yes. He has the privy seal. The earl is Lady Barbara's father."

Alan removed his eyes from Barbara and looked at his father's friend. "Yet you identified her as *Lady* Abingdon's daughter," Alan remarked on a note of inquiry.

"Oh well." Lord Peter made a graceful gesture. "In that family, it is Lady Abingdon who counts. Her husband is in the government because of his wife's exertions. She is a very clever, very influential woman. Half the fashionable world of London congregates daily at Abingdon House in Berkeley Square."

"I see. And how old is Lady Barbara?" Alan

asked casually, his eyes once again on the girl in question. She was crossing the room on the far side of the floor, she on one side of Lady Abingdon, her brother on the other.

"Eighteen. She was presented earlier this month."

"Well, I reckon the young men are queuing up for her hand," Mr. Maxwell said humorously.

"Ah . . . well, no," replied Sir Peter gently. "There is the slight problem, you see, of the family finances."

Alan raised a black eyebrow. "Broke?"

"Shot to pieces," Lord Peter returned bluntly. "Lord Abingdon is a great trial to his family." Then, as Alan continued to look inquiringly, "Gambling, you know."

"I see," said Alan.

Lord Peter sighed. "So many great families have been brought to ruin due to the Fatal Tendency. Look at the dear Duchess of Hampshire."

Alan continued to listen to Lord Peter's gossip with half an ear. His real attention was on the girl across the room.

It was halfway through the evening before he claimed his dance with Lady Barbara. Lord Peter had been assiduous in introducing his Americans to various members of the assembled company, and his hostess, Lady Darcy, had been equally assiduous in presenting Alan to several hopeful young ladies, whom he had, with impeccable manners, asked to dance.

Barbara, he noticed, had been out on the dance

floor for every set. As they stood side by side waiting for the music to start, he asked pleasantly, "Are you enjoying the evening, Lady Barbara?"

She looked up at him. She was so slender, so finely made, that she appeared taller than she actually was. The top of her powdered head just cleared his shoulder. Her eyes were a remarkable deep dark blue.

"Very much, Mr. Maxwell," she replied tranquilly. "And you? Have you many acquaintances in London?"

"My father has friends from his school and university days. He was educated at Eton and Cambridge."

"Oh? Was he born in England, then?"

"No, like me, he was born in Virginia."

"But you did not attend school in England?"

"No, Lady Barbara. I attended the College of William and Mary in Williamsburg."

The music struck up and she put her slender hand into his big one. They bowed to each other. She was the most graceful woman he had ever seen—her every gesture was slow, fluid, and elegant. Her waist was long, fine, and flexible—like the stem of a flower.

He accompanied her back to her mother and was welcomed enthusiastically by William. Lady Abingdon was temperately kind and after a moment William took Alan away to present him to a group of his friends.

William's friends were pleasant-enough fellows, clearly members of that London set Alan had heard designated as "bloods." They were all mad on sport and were politely interested in the kind of hunting one could get in Virginia. As he spoke to them, Alan was aware of Barbara dancing with the extraordinarily handsome young man he had seen her with the previous evening. When the dance was finished the young man joined William's group and was introduced as his cousin, Lieutenant Harry Wharton.

"Maxwell here has been telling us about hunting in Virginia," William said to his cousin. "It sounds splendid fun."

"I always thought Virginians were gentlemen," Thomas Wellbourne, a rather florid young man in a pigeon's-wing wig, remarked kindly. "A vastly different breed from that rabble in Massachusetts."

"Ah." Alan's dark eyes narrowed slightly. "Have you many acquaintances from Massachusetts, Mr. Wellbourne?"

Mr. Wellbourne looked astonished. "Of course not."

Alan stared at him, and the other young men were all of a sudden uncomfortably conscious of his superior height. "Of course not," he echoed evenly. "I myself have never had the pleasure of meeting anyone from Massachusetts, and so I refrain from making judgments that can be based only upon conjecture and not upon evidence."

Mr. Wellbourne's florid face grew even redder. "There's evidence enough that Massachusetts has little respect for the king's law," he said sharply.

"As to that, Mr. Wellbourne, respect is a two-way street."

"I say, are you fellows still fretting about Townshend's taxes?" William asked with an attempt at humor.

"I reckon we are," Alan drawled in reply.

William looked a little bewildered. "I thought that was all settled when Parliament repealed the bill."

Alan's face was inscrutable. "Parliament repealed part of the bill. It left the tax on tea."

"I think it only just, Maxwell," came the clipped voice of Harry Wharton, "that you colonials shoulder some of the burden of your own defense. There are several thousand troops stationed in America."

"We have a perfectly adequate militia, Lieutenant Wharton," Alan replied. "We do not require nor did we request the presence of British troops on American soil."

There was a moment of rather tense silence as the American planter and the British officer stared at each other. Neither pair of eyes gave way and William said, a trifle nervously, "Dash it all, Maxwell, but you colonials ought to pay some taxes. We pay enough of them in England, by God."

"You are also represented in Parliament," Alan

replied pleasantly. "We, unfortunately, are not." He looked around the circle of high-bred, aristocratic faces and then, slowly and quite deliberately, he smiled. "So you see, Mr. Wellbourne," he said to that young man, "we Virginians can be just as obstreperous as our Massachusetts cousins."

The smile, more than the words, disarmed the men who were listening to him.

"We'll patch it up, I'm sure," Thomas Wellbourne said magnanimously. "A family quarrel, that's what it is. We're all Englishmen, after all."

"Certainly, Wellbourne," Alan replied in his slow Virginia drawl. "As you say, we are all Englishmen."

Alan rode early in the park the following morning but he did not meet either William Carr or Lady Barbara. Later in the day, Sir Peter took Mr. Maxwell and his son to Brooks's, the club most heavily patronized by London's upper-class males. They played cards for a time, and after he relinquished his place to a newcomer, Alan fell into talk with a bushy-browed young man who had introduced himself as Charles James Fox.

For almost the first time since he had come to England, Alan found himself thoroughly enjoying a conversation. It was not until he discovered that Mr. Fox held a minor place in Lord North's government that Alan felt the first note of discord.

"So you are a member of the government, Mr. Fox?" he said pleasantly, slowly revolving his glass of burgundy and looking at the other man out of suddenly hooded eyes.

"Do I detect a sudden chill in the air, Maxwell?" Mr. Fox asked humorously. "Yes, distinctly there has been a lowering of the temperature. Is the government so unpopular in America, then?"

"The news can't come as any great surprise to you, Mr. Fox," Alan said bluntly. "There have been enough protests, surely, from the various colonial legislatures to have informed his majesty's government of the unhappiness of his subjects in America."

"Yes. One has wondered, however, how widespread that unhappiness is."

"Quite widespread," Alan replied briefly.

"The problem is that America quite simply refuses to shoulder its share of the national defense." The voice was a new one and Alan turned to look at the man who had joined them.

"I am afraid you have the advantage of me, sir," Alan said slowly.

"May I introduce Mr. Thomas Whately, Maxwell," Charles Fox said. "Mr. Whately was secretary to the treasury in Lord Grenville's government."

There was a brief pause. "Then I have the pleasure of talking to the author of the Stamp Act," Alan said. His arrogant nose had appeared to sharpen.

"You have, sir," Mr. Whately replied strongly. "And I still say that Parliament has the right to tax its colonies—particularly when the tax money is going for the defense of those very colonies. And you are scoundrels, sir, if you refuse to accept that right."

"We are not scoundrels, sir," Alan replied, and now his drawl was very pronounced. He spared a brief glance for his father, who had come up beside him before turning back to Mr. Whately. "We are, thank God, British subjects who were born to liberty and who know how to prize it highly. We have always been in possession of the constitutional right to grant our own money. We would be slaves did we not have this right. And we will allow no one— certainly not Parliament—to deprive us of one of the essential rights of the British constitution."

"All British subjects are virtually represented in Parliament," Mr. Whately began. Alan made an angry, impatient gesture and Mr. Maxwell put a hand on his son's arm.

"Do not speak to me of virtual representation, Mr. Whately," Alan said. His voice was calm but his eyes were narrow and cold. "America has no representatives in Parliament. And I tell you now the Parliament of Great Britain has no more right to put its hand into my pocket, without my consent, than I have to put my hand into yours."

Several other men had gathered to listen to the debate and now the Marquess of Rockingham, leader of the opposition to the present government, put a hand on Alan's other arm. "Come along and have a glass of wine with me, Mr. Max-well. I think we may have a great deal in common."

"Thank you, my lord," Alan replied. Mr. Max-well took his hand off his son's other arm and Alan glanced down at his father's worried face. He gave Mr. Maxwell a faint, reassuring smile before he allowed the Marquess of Rockingham to lead him off. Mr. Fox, after a brief comment, left to join the card game. Mr. Maxwell looked at his old school friend.

Lord Peter had a very speculative look on his face. "My, my," he said softly. "Your son is a bit of a firebrand, is he not, Maxwell?"

The worried look on Mr. Maxwell's face deepened. "I'm afraid you're right, Crashaw."

Lord Peter looked from Alan to Alan's father. "He doesn't resemble you at all, my friend. You're tall enough, but your Alan is quite a giant."

"He resembles his mother's family in both height and coloring."

"And temperament too, I should imagine," Lord Peter murmured.

Mr. Maxwell smiled ruefully. "True." There was a pause and then he went on, more slowly, "The situation in Virginia is far more unsettled than anyone in England appears to realize, Crashaw. And Alan, unfortunately, appears to have come under the sway of our more radical citizens. One of the reasons I was so insistent that he accompany me to

England was that I hoped the visit would mellow him a little."

"Well, he agreed to come. That is certainly something."

Mr. Maxwell cast an ironic look at Lord Peter that made him look suddenly quite like his son. "He came because I promised to deed Newland—our plantation—over to him if he would."

Lord Peter raised his well-tended eyebrows. "Ah. And are your other children of the same persuasion as Alan?"

"Helen, the eldest, is married to a sensible man who is as uncomfortable as I with this spirit of radicalism in the country. And Robert and Libby are too young to take much notice. No, it's Alan who worries me."

"Well, association with the Rockingham Whigs won't mellow him, my friend." Lord Peter looked at Mr. Maxwell curiously. "Just what are you afraid of, Maxwell? You don't really think anything is going to come of this situation, do you?"

"I don't know," Mr. Maxwell replied unhappily. "But things are unpleasant enough to cause me to desire to leave."

Lord Peter looked very thoughtful. "I see."

"I do not want to see my son hanged for treason," Mr. Maxwell said suddenly and explosively.

"Good God. Certainly not." There was a pause and then Lord Peter asked tentatively, "You don't think, then, you ought to remain in Virginia to . . . er . . . keep an eye on him, as it were?"

"If I thought it would do any good, I might. The sad truth is, Crashaw, that I haven't been able to get Alan to do what he didn't want to do since he was twelve years old."

The two older men watched in silence the man they were discussing. One or two others had joined Lord Rockingham and the Englishmen were paying close attention to the tall American. Quite suddenly Alan smiled and the warmth and good humor of that look reached all the way across the room.

"I have found him to be a most charming young man," Sir Peter murmured.

"Oh, he's charming," his father returned with the slightest edge of bitterness to his voice. "He's never defiant, Alan. He just—very charmingly—goes his own damn way. I wish to God there was someone sensible he would listen to!"

A perfectly vacant look descended over Lord Peter's face. It was the look that usually denoted he was thinking. "Someone he would listen to," he murmured. His eyes focused again. "Get him married," he said firmly.

"Married!" Mr. Maxwell echoed in astonishment.

"Certainly." Marriage had been so splendid an answer for him that Lord Peter tended to recommend it as a universal panacea. However, this was a fact of which Mr. Maxwell—buried all these years in Virginia—was unaware. "Wedlock to some nice sensible girl is what is required," Lord Peter said now positively.

"I don't know . . ." Mr. Maxwell murmured doubtfully.

"Take my advice, my friend. A good loyal English girl is what your Alan needs to bring him to his senses. Marry him off."

"Of course, we would also require Alan's consent," Mr. Maxwell said with irony.

The vacant look once again descended over Lord Peter's face. "Er . . ." he said after a moment, "I believe you have engaged to deed your plantation to him?"

"Yes."

"And he desires the plantation?"

"Very much. He has all sorts of newfangled things he wants to try."

"Well, then," Lord Peter said delicately, "I believe you have the . . . er . . . lever you require."

"Blackmail him, do you mean?"

Lord Peter smiled. "Precisely."

Mr. Maxwell looked at his son. The expression on his face was extremely doubtful. "Alan is not what one would call easy to handle, Crashaw."

"Resolution is all that is required, my friend," Lord Peter said firmly. "Now, come along. We need to put our heads together as to the question of the girl."

Three

"We have been invited to Chumley for Easter," Lady Abingdon said to her daughter. "The Lades are having a large house party and the Marquess of Derby will be there."

The Marquess of Derby was very wealthy and still unattached and had recently shown himself to be interested in Barbara.

Barbara put down the necklace she was holding. Lady Abingdon had come into her bedroom as she was dressing for the opera. Her mother was already magnificently gowned and elaborately coiffed and Lady Abingdon's handsome, carefully made-up face looked pleased at the prospect of the upcoming house party.

Barbara slowly turned to face Lady Abingdon. "Do you know, Mama, I don't feel at all comfortable with Lord Derby."

Lady Abingdon's eyes focused hard on her daughter's face. "Why not? What have you heard about him?"

"It's not so much what I have heard as what I myself feel."

"You will have to be more specific, my love," Lady Abingdon said patiently. "What does Lord Derby make you feel?"

Barbara flushed lightly. "I don't like him to touch me," she said.

There was a pause and then Lady Abingdon sat down. "You are a young girl, my love, scarcely more than a child. You have been very carefully sheltered. You are not accustomed to men other than your brothers. It is quite natural for you to feel shy with Lord Derby." Lady Abingdon's voice was good-tempered and eminently rational.

"I don't feel shy with him," Barbara said. "I feel repelled."

Lady Abingdon rose to her feet and began to pace the room. "Do you feel this way because of Harry Wharton?" she asked after a minute.

"I don't know, Mama," Barbara said unhappily.

"It is surely not necessary for me to tell you that a marriage between you and Harry is out of the question."

"No, Mama," Barbara said sadly. "You don't

have to tell me that. And truly, I do want to please you—only, not Lord Derby."

"There are not that many to choose from, my love," Lady Abingdon said wearily. "The state of your father's affairs . . . well, I won't scruple to tell you that we stand on the verge of utter ruin."

Barbara's blue eyes opened wide. "Mama!"

"We will have to let Carrington. If it weren't entailed it would have to be sold. We have only managed to keep the town house due to the generosity of Lord Newcastle."

"We are living on Lord Newcastle's money?" Barbara asked faintly.

Lady Abingdon looked at her. "Yes."

Barbara knew, had long known, what the relation between her mother and the Earl of Newcastle was, but never before had the subject been raised between mother and daughter.

"You needn't love your husband, Barbara," Lady Abingdon said practically. "One can be a perfectly good wife and still find ways to enjoy oneself. One must simply be careful to observe the conventions." Barbara's dark blue eyes remained fixed on her mother's face. "Then, too," Lady Abingdon continued, "there are your brothers to consider. Your father has cut their very future from beneath them."

"I will think about what you have said, Mama," Barbara said in a low voice, and Lady Abingdon bent to kiss her daughter's cheek.

"I know you will, my love. Come along down to dinner, now. You will have to wear your hair *au naturel* to the opera this evening. There isn't time to powder."

"Yes, Mama," said Barbara, and both she and Lady Abingdon went down to join her brother Frederick for dinner.

Barbara sat in Lady Abingdon's box in the King's Theater, oblivious of both the music and of the crowd of young gentlemen in the pit who ogled her so obviously. The only notice she appeared to take of her admirers occurred when she smiled briefly at Charles James Fox.

During the interval the opera house was ablaze with light and Barbara felt uncomfortably warm. "Would you like me to take you for a little walk, Lady Barbara?" said a light, familiar voice behind her, and Barbara turned to look into the dark blue eyes of the Earl of Newcastle. "You look rather pale," he said.

Barbara managed a smile. "No, thank you, my lord. I am perfectly fine, I assure you."

The slender, elegant nobleman, who was most probably her father, smiled back. "Very well. You mustn't overdo the parties, though, my dear. A first season can be very fatiguing."

Barbara bowed her head a little but did not reply, and in a moment she saw the earl bending close to say something to her mother. Barbara looked blindly out across the glittering opera house.

All of her life Barbara had adored her mother. Unlike many women in her social position, Lady Abingdon had always found time for her children. She had read to them, talked to them, written to them, brought them to town so they could be with her during the season, gone with them to Sir Joshua Reynolds' to have their portraits painted, listened to them, schemed and worried for them. It was her children, not her husband, who had received the brunt of Lady Abingdon's narrow and powerful affection. And her children, in return, loved her. Further, they were devoted to one another. Barbara had grown up in that most secure and reassuring of all social units, a strongly knit family group.

It was not until she turned sixteen that the first intimation that her life as she knew it rested on shaky foundations first struck Barbara. She vividly remembered the occasion. It was Christmastime and Harry Wharton had caught her under the mistletoe and kissed her. Later that evening her mother had taken her aside and explained, very gently, that she must not allow herself to become too fond of Harry.

Barbara sat now, gazing blindly out across the blazing opera house and listening to the low murmur of the Earl of Newcastle's voice as he spoke to her mother.

Nothing would ever be the same as it had been in her childhood. "You are a woman now," her mother had said to her. But I don't want to be a woman! Barbara thought passionately. I want to be a child again, playing at Carrington with William and Harry, wondering if there would be buns for tea. And instead she sat here, exposed to the knowing eyes of all these people—Lady Barbara Carr, for sale to the highest bidder. Oh, Mama, she cried silently, how could you do this to me?

But it was not Mama's fault. Mama had carried the family for years. It was time now for her daughter to lend some assistance.

Barbara drew herself up and took a deep, slow breath. The opera was preparing to begin again and as her eyes traveled back toward the stage they were caught by a tall, broad-shouldered figure in a box near the stage. Mr. Alan Maxwell was sitting with the Marquess of Rockingham, but now, almost as if he felt her gaze, his head turned and his eyes met hers.

It was the second time he had caught her staring at him, Barbara thought. He did not smile, nor did she, and the look they exchanged was an odd mixture of acknowledgment, wariness, and some other emotion that Barbara did not quite recognize.

The house party that collected at Chumley, country seat of the Earl and Countess of Lade, was large and glittering. The April weather was crisp, the gathering youthful and splendid, and the possibilities for new combinations of partners intriguing. Lady Abingdon was among the more mature of the guests and she was not one to be harshly judgmental as long as the proper appearances were maintained. It was a house party fraught with possibilities.

Alan Maxwell was there, invited at the request of Charles Fox. Mr. Maxwell and Sir Peter, being of more sober years and demeanor, had not been included in Lady Lade's splendid hospitality. Mr. Maxwell had urged Alan to attend. Chumley was one of the greatest country houses in England.

Alan could not help but be impressed by his surroundings. The house was more a palace than a home, with a grand high-ceilinged state room, two great staircases, and a plenitude of splendid wrought ironwork and exquisitely carved woodwork. The park, which had been laid out by Capability Brown, featured a deer park, a great sheet of artificial lake, and a waterfall.

The scale of everything was so different, Alan thought as he walked slowly about the garden on the afternoon of his arrival. The whole of Newland would fit easily into the reception rooms of Chumley. He was noticing a particularly pretty hedge when he rounded a corner and came upon Lady Barbara Carr sitting on a bench with a book in her hand. She was alone.

Alan stopped. She wore a simple dress of worked muslin with a tiffany sash around her waist. Her hair was dressed without powder and a quantity of shining dark brown curls were threaded by a blue ribbon and tumbled down about her shoulders.

"Good afternoon, Lady Barbara," Alan said.

She looked up from her book slowly. She never jerked or started, he had noticed, not even when she was surprised.

"Mr. Maxwell." Her voice was always more deeply pitched than he expected it to be. She closed her book. "Are you a guest this holiday also?"

He moved over to stand close to her. "Yes. Mr. Fox was kind enough to procure an invitation for me."

Barbara smiled. "If you are a friend of Mr. Fox's you will go everywhere."

He stood looking down into her face. Her skin, in the harsh afternoon light, was flawless as a baby's. Her face was delicately boned and utterly pure, except for the chin. It was a determined little chin, dented by a distinct and fascinating cleft. She was like a Renaissance painting, he thought, and she always provoked in him the same damn reaction.

"What are you reading?" he asked.

She held up her book a little so he could see the title. "*Robinson Crusoe*," she said. There was room on the seat beside her. "Do sit down, Mr. Maxwell. The sun is very pleasant here."

He sat down and stretched his booted legs in front of him. "What does one do on a country-house visit in England, Lady Barbara?"

She ran her hand lightly over the book in her

lap. "Very much what one does on a visit in Virginia, I suspect. One eats and drinks and makes music and rides horses." She looked up into his face. "Is that what you do in Virginia, Mr. Maxwell?"

"It sounds a familiar program," he replied easily. "We do quite a bit of boating, as well. All the plantations are situated on rivers, you see. One lives quite literally with the water at one's door."

A smile came into the dark blue eyes. "Carrington, my home, is on the water also. I have always been able to see the Channel from my bedroom window."

"Newland is on the James River. I can sit on my front steps and watch the boats from England dock right at my own landing."

Barbara's head tilted the slightest fraction. "Newland. Is that the name of your plantation?"

"Yes."

She ran her forefinger slowly along the binding of her book. Her hands were very slender, the nails immaculately manicured. "How did your family come to immigrate to America, Mr. Maxwell?"

He replied, his eyes on her hand, "My great-grandfather fought for the king during the English Civil War. After Charles's execution, he went to America to escape from the Roundheads. A great many Virginia families have similar origins."

"I did not know that. And will you be returning to Virginia, then, or are you planning to make your home in England?"

He moved his eyes from her hand to her face. Her eyes were a much darker blue than the afternoon sky. "I will be returning to Virginia, Lady Barbara. My father stays in England."

Barbara nodded and for a moment a wistful look flitted across her face. "It is hard to leave the home of one's childhood."

There was more seductiveness in the slow movement of her eyelashes than there was in the entire bodies of most other women he had known. She did not realize she was seductive, nor was she trying to attract him; it was just there, potent and dizzying and oddly at variance with the well-bred young lady she so obviously was.

She seemed to sense the vibration of his blood, for she drew a little away from him and then stood up. "I must be getting back to the house," she said. "Mama will be looking for me."

She bent to pick up her parasol and he noticed that her sash had become untied. He offered to tie it for her. She looked scandalized.

"Oh no." She was holding her book and her parasol and she looked around as if to put them down. "I'll tie it, thank you."

He put his hands on her shoulders and gently turned her. She could feel his hands close to her waist as he retied the sash. Her heart was hammering. "Thank you," she said breathlessly when he had finished and she turned to find him very close. His shoulders were so enormous they blocked out her whole view of the garden. "Mama will be looking for me," she repeated, and when he didn't reply, she added, "I shall see you at dinner, Mr. Maxwell."

"Until dinner, Lady Barbara," he repeated gravely, and stood watching her as she went down the garden path toward the house.

Barbara was preoccupied as she dressed for dinner. What was there about this big American that disturbed her so? He was not handsome—he was too dark, too hard-looking. Except when he smiled. His smile changed everything. He had not smiled at her this afternoon. She remembered the feel of his hands at her waist and a little shiver went all through her. It was not at all the same kind of shiver evoked by the thought of the Marquess of Derby.

The marquess was at Chumley and he took Barbara in to dinner. He was a dissipated-looking man in his early thirties whose reputation as a rake was well-deserved. He was reputed to be a charter member of the Hell Fire Club, a group famous for its unsavory sexual excesses. He was unmarried and, rumor had it, presently in the market for a wife. Despite his expensive dissipations, he was immensely wealthy.

Barbara could not like him. She behaved to him with perfect graciousness, but she did nothing at all to encourage his interest. She very much hoped he would transfer his attentions to some other prospect. There were two unmarried girls at Chumley besides herself, and both of them came from families that were notably solvent. She nodded her head when the marquess addressed a remark to her, and took a sip of her wine. She refrained, consciously, from looking down the table to where Alan Maxwell was seated next to Elinor Wells, one of the other unmarried girls.

She wished Harry was here. Or her brothers. She wished she did not feel so vulnerable, so dreadfully alone. She smiled slightly at something Lord Derby said and looked over at her mother. Lady Abingdon was talking to the Earl of Lade and did not notice her daughter's glance. Barbara straightened her spine slightly and this time answered Lord Derby calmly. She allowed no sign of relief to cross her face when Lady Lade rose to take the ladies into the drawing room, but she was careful to seat herself in a group around Lady Lade, who was seated at the harpsichord. When the gentlemen came in, Lord Derby had to take a chair next to Miss Wells, who looked disappointed and stared reproachfully at Mr. Maxwell. The faintest of smiles curved Barbara's lips before she turned back to urge Lady Lade to play another selection.

Four

The house party at Chumley did resemble, albeit on a much grander scale, the sort of house parties Alan was accustomed to in Virginia. The activities were similar, he found himself thinking; it was the atmosphere that was so different. In Virginia people were more informal, more comfortable, more friendly. The society was much smaller and so everyone knew everyone else. Most people were actually related in one way or another—society tended to comprise a host of one's cousins.

He remarked something of this sort to Charles Fox as they strolled through the gardens after dinner smoking cigars on the third night of their visit. It was a cool clear night and the stars above them were brilliant.

"Do I detect a note of nostalgia, my dear fellow?" Fox asked humorously. "Are you pining for the banks of the James?"

Alan grinned. "I reckon I am. My father finds me sadly provincial."

"I shouldn't call you provincial," Fox returned dryly. "Nor would the English ladies. You're the best advocate for America, Maxwell, who's ever graced our shores. You beat Dr. Franklin all to pieces. Why, I actually heard Maria Lade saying earlier at dinner that it was unjust of Parliament to tax the colonies without their consent." He gave his infectious chuckle. "I doubt if Maria ever heard of the colonies until you arrived."

"If I could change Lord North's mind as easily, then my trip would certainly be worthwhile," Alan retorted. "Unfortunately, Lady Lade is not in the government."

"Unfortunately? My dear fellow, we may be at odds, but certainly you wouldn't wish Maria Lade on us?"

Alan laughed. "You're not in favor of a petticoat government, Fox?"

"I don't say that. Lady Abingdon would certainly be an improvement on her husband."

"So I have heard. I understand the family has . . . ah . . . financial difficulties."

"Yes. And I don't like the way Lady Abingdon is

pushing Derby at her daughter. He may be rich as Croesus, but he ain't the man for a girl like Lady Barbara. I'm surprised Newcastle hasn't put a stop to it."

"Newcastle?" Alan echoed. "What has Lord Newcastle to do with it?"

There was a pause as Mr. Fox took a deep puff of his cigar. "Oh well, it's pretty general knowledge that Newcastle, not Abingdon, is Barbara's father. Not that Lady Abingdon ain't perfectly discreet. I suppose she won't let Newcastle step in—one thing one has to say for Lady Abingdon, she never puts her husband in an awkward position. She's always been very careful."

Alan stared at his friend's face. "And the other children? Lady Barbara's brothers?"

"Oh, Frederick, the eldest, is Abingdon's—trust her ladyship to do her duty that way. As to the others . . ." Mr. Fox shrugged slightly. "There are varying possibilities. But Newcastle has been her ladyship's most trusted adviser and chief lover for years."

"Good God," said Alan.

"Have I shocked you?" Mr. Fox asked curiously.

"Yes," Alan said. "You have." His profile looked hawklike in the dim starlight. "In Virginia," he added, "we expect our women to be virtuous."

"If you expect a woman to be virtuous," Mr. Fox replied, "you ought not to marry her to Lord Abingdon."

"What on earth is wrong with Lord Abingdon, besides the fact that he appears to be universally known as Lady Abingdon's husband?" Alan asked impatiently. "He gambles, of course, but so does half of London society from what I can see."

Mr. Fox appeared to consider the question.

"Is he as unfaithful to his wife as she is to him?" Alan asked.

"He's had scores of mistresses, dear fellow. A collection of shockingly dull and tedious women. I suppose, when one comes to think of it, that is precisely Abingdon's problem. He's dull. Lady Abingdon, for all her faults, is never dull."

"Dullness is hardly a sin," said Alan.

"It is in London, dear fellow. It is in London."

Alan gave his friend a skeptical look, but did not reply. After a few minutes Mr. Fox returned to the house, while Alan chose to remain out-of-doors.

He did not light another cigar but strolled along the stone terrace that flanked the south side of the house. There was a slight frown between his well-marked black brows and his face looked preoccupied. He paused outside the French doors that led to the orangery, and something, some flicker of movement, caused him to glance inside.

For a moment the scene that confronted his view confirmed his extremely cynical thoughts. Inside the orangery, silhouetted between two trees, were a man and a woman locked in a close embrace. It was a fraction of a minute before Alan realized that the woman was struggling.

He pushed open the French doors and strode into the room. As he put a hard hand on the man's shoulder to wrench him away, Alan realized that the captive girl was Lady Barbara Carr.

"*Damn* you," said the man. "What do you think you're doing?"

Barbara had backed away as soon as she was released. Alan could hear the small sobbing breaths she was drawing. He felt sheer cold fury sweep through him.

"What I will do in one minute is teach you not to take advantage of young girls," Alan said through his teeth. "Get out of here, you bloody swine." His voice, by dint of great effort, was low but at his sides his fists were slowly opening and closing.

The Marquess of Derby looked as if he were going to answer, and then, looking at Alan, thought the better of it. He shot a quick, angry glance at the girl and then turned on his heel and stalked out of the room.

Alan turned to look at the girl as well.

Her eyes were very dark in her pale face. "Are you all right, Lady Barbara?" Alan asked. His voice came out harsher than he intended.

She nodded mutely and her wide, frightened eyes lifted to him. He crossed the few feet that separated them. Close up, he could see she was trembling. The bloody swine, Alan thought again, and put an arm around her shoulders. "It's all right, sweetheart," he said soothingly, as he might have spoken to his younger sister. "You're perfectly safe now."

Barbara shivered violently against his arm and then, disarmed by the sudden gentleness in his voice, she turned her head into his shoulder. His arms came up to hold her lightly. The smooth flesh of her bare arms was like silk under his hands.

After a minute she drew a long, shuddering breath. Her eyes closed for a brief moment and then, resolutely, she stepped back from him. "I'm so sorry," she said. "What an unpleasant scene for you to walk into."

The light from the brazier fell on her face as she spoke.

"There's blood on your lip," Alan said abruptly.

Barbara's hand went quickly to her mouth. When she took it away she stared for a minute at the bright crimson drop on her fingers. Then she looked at the lace Alan wore at his throat.

"I'm afraid I've stained your shirt," she said in an unsteady voice.

They both stared for a minute at the telltale red mark on the frothy white lace. Then Alan's eyes, dark and intent, lifted and locked on her face. Her lip was indeed cut and a little swollen. He imagined the salty taste of that mouth under his own. Barbara looked back into the hard, predator's face that was so close to hers and her breath began to come more quickly. She felt caught, trapped, but in an entirely different way from what she had just experienced with Lord Derby.

"Barbara!" The voice came from the doorway, hidden from them by the trees. "Barbara! Are you in here?"

Barbara drew a deep breath and dragged her eyes away from the Virginian. "Yes," she answered a trifle huskily. "Yes, I'm over here."

There was the sound of steps and in a moment the Earl of Newcastle appeared. He looked at Alan and frowned.

"Lady Barbara was being made the object of some very unwelcome advances by Lord Derby when I happened by," Alan said crisply.

Lord Newcastle's frown became more pronounced. "Is this true, Barbara?"

"Yes, my lord."

The earl looked at her sharply. "Your lip!"

Alan handed Barbara a hankerchief. She gave him a swift, upward look and then held it to her mouth.

"Derby did that?" Newcastle asked in a hard voice. Barbara nodded in reply.

"It seems to me Lady Barbara's family ought to be more diligent in their care of her," Alan said. "I would not allow my sister to go off alone with a man of Derby's stamp."

"We *were* in a group," Barbara said in a muffled voice. "Then, somehow, we became separated."

"As soon as we saw your party return without you, my dear, your mother sent me to look for you," Lord Newcastle assured her. "Are you indeed all right?"

Barbara took the handkerchief away from her lip. "Yes, my lord, thank you."

"I think perhaps you had better retire upstairs. That lip . . ."

Barbara's face had taken on a cool and faintly remote expression. "Yes, my lord. I think I should like to retire."

Lord Newcastle offered her his arm. "I'll take you to the staircase." After Barbara had placed her hand on his, the earl finally turned to Alan. "Thank you, Mr. Maxwell, for your assistance to Lady Barbara. I need hardly ask you to keep this incident to yourself."

"No, Lord Newcastle," Alan drawled in reply, "you need not ask."

Lord Newcastle subjected the big American to a quick, hard scrutiny before nodding graciously. The earl's blue eyes were almost the exact shade of Barbara's. Alan did not wait for the two of them to leave before he himself turned and went back out the French doors to the terrace.

Alan was up early the following morning and spent the day in the saddle, exercising hard and at a safe distance from the house. He did not like the way his thoughts kept coming back to Lady Barbara Carr and he made a resolute effort the entire day to banish her from his mind.

He did not see her until later in the afternoon when the house party gathered in the great hall of Chumley before going up to dress for dinner. Her lip, from what he could see, appeared to be perfectly normal, and she was laughing and chatting lightly with Charles Fox and Miss Wells.

One by one people began to leave the room to go upstairs to dress, but Barbara lingered in her seat by the fire. Alan lingered as well and they so managed it that for a very brief period of time they had the hall to themselves before the army of rearranging, cushion-plumping housemaids descended.

"I don't believe I thanked you for coming to my rescue last night," Barbara said gravely.

He stood near her, his hands in the pockets of his riding breeches. "I was happy to be of assistance, Lady Barbara." He was looking at the tea table, not at her.

"What must you think of my behavior, allowing myself to go off alone with such a man?"

At that he looked down at her. "I don't imagine it was of your design," he replied briefly.

"No, it was not."

There was an unmistakable resemblance between Lady Barbara and the Earl of Newcastle. They had the same fine bones, the same high-bridged, straight nose. Alan was certainly not an innocent, but he found himself distinctly taken aback by the morality—or lack of it—that he had encountered among the English upper class. He found the arrangement between Barbara's mother and the Earl of Newcastle utterly scandalous.

"A man like Derby ought not to be allowed in decent society," he said now forcefully. "At home, I wouldn't entertain him in my woodshed."

A very faint flush came into Barbara's cheeks. "I will certainly take care not to be alone with him again," she said. "It is unfortunate that my brothers are not here."

Alan stared at her. She was sitting very quietly on her chair, her hands lying loosely clasped in her lap; there wasn't a sign of tension about her.

"I have had a great deal of practice at being an older brother, Lady Barbara," Alan said after a moment. His drawl was very pronounced. "Won't you allow me to substitute for yours?"

The look of relief on her face was brief but unmistakable. "I shouldn't like you to get out of practice, Mr. Maxwell," she said with a small smile.

"That would certainly be unfortunate."

She rose from her chair. "We will be late for dinner if we don't go and dress."

He bowed slightly and watched as she walked to the staircase. His eyes followed her until, with a simple, swift look round at him, she vanished.

God, he thought, what a family she must come

from. To think she was forced to ask a virtual stranger for protection. . . .

Alan went up to change for dinner, his face very grim.

Five

"What did you say the government is proposing?" Alan asked incredulously.

"They are proposing to give the East India Company a monopoly on the marketing of tea in America," Dr. Franklin repeated.

The two men were seated in the drawing room of the Maxwells' suite in the Clarendon Hotel. Benjamin Franklin, agent for the colonies of Pennsylvania and Massachusetts, had called on Alan as soon as he returned from Chumley.

"A monopoly," Alan said. "But why?"

"The East India Company has been riddled by financial scandal," Dr. Franklin explained. "Its stock has fallen prodigiously and any number of people have been forced into bankruptcy. The government is bound to do something to put the company on a sound financial basis. And it so happens that the company has sitting in its warehouses four million pounds sterling in tea."

"But America has been boycotting English tea for years," Alan protested.

"Precisely. The Dutch smugglers have been busily supplying the colonies, to the loss of Great Britain. If the government can open up the American market for English tea and give the East India Company a monopoly, the company's financial crisis would be solved."

Alan leaned back in his chair and stretched his legs in front of him. "Well, that should be easy enough," he drawled. "All the government has to do is repeal the Townshend tax on tea."

Dr. Franklin's lined face looked exceedingly grim. "That is precisely what I proposed to Lord North. Repeal the tea duty and the whole American market would become available to the company. Unfortunately, Lord North is in no mood to make concessions to America about the tea duty or anything else. The government is extremely annoyed at the petitions from Massachusetts urging the recall of Governor Hutchinson."

There was the sound of people in the front room and then Mr. Maxwell and Sir Peter Crashaw came into the drawing room. Both gentlemen greeted

Dr. Franklin courteously and Alan poured glasses of wine for his father and his father's friend.

"Dr. Franklin has brought us some strange news, sir," Alan said, once all the men were comfortable, and he proceeded to recount the situation.

"Well," Sir Peter said reasonably, "why should Americans start to buy English tea now when they have boycotted it for years?"

"Because, Lord Peter," Dr. Franklin explained, "the government is going to rescind the taxes payable in *England*. This will enable the company to sell tea at a price substantially lower than the smuggled article."

"Well"—Lord Peter shrugged—"how can you complain, Dr. Franklin? Economically, the colonies can only gain."

Alan stood up. "Gain, eh? I have to tell you that we in America are not fond of monopolies. Nor are we fond of clever schemes designed to undermine our liberties. There is no doubt that Lord North, by underselling Dutch tea, hopes to establish the Townshend duty as a precedent for further taxation." Alan turned to Benjamin Franklin. "This scheme must be stopped."

Dr. Franklin stood up as well. "Whom can you talk to?" he asked the young man who towered over him.

"Fox, to begin with," Alan replied. "Come along, Dr. Franklin. We'll see if we can catch him at Brooks's."

"Good day, Mr. Maxwell, Lord Peter," Dr. Franklin said courteously.

"I shall see you later, Papa," Alan said crisply. "Lord Peter, your servant, sir."

After the two patriots had left the room, Mr. Maxwell turned to Lord Peter. "Heavens," the Englishman said. "Such agitation about a three-pence tax."

"It isn't to be taken lightly, Crashaw," Mr. Maxwell said gloomily. "You heard Alan. The young men are so suspicious. Why, they have even threatened the king. Right in the House of Burgesses, Virginia's assembly, I heard Patrick Henry said, 'Tarquin and Caesar had each his Brutus, Charles the First his Cromwell, and George the Third—' God knows what he may have said next, but we all cried, 'Treason! Treason!' and he added, '—may profit by their example.' But *that* is the sort of man my son is listening to. A backwoods lawyer in homespun. The backwoods lawyers are becoming more and more influential—and none of them will like this new tea scheme at all."

"I have been giving a great deal of thought as to a girl who would be suitable for Alan, Maxwell," Lord Peter said after a minute, "and I think I have hit on the very one." He paused dramatically.

"Good God, are you still hot on that scheme?" Mr. Maxwell looked at his friend curiously. "Who?" he asked.

"Lady Barbara Carr."

"Lady Barbara Carr! That lovely girl? What on earth makes you think she would be willing to marry an American?"

"Her family badly needs money," Lord Peter said succinctly.

"Alan has noticed her," Mr. Maxwell said slowly. "He has certainly noticed her more than any other girl in London."

"There you are, then," Lord Peter said complacently.

"Not quite." Mr. Maxwell's voice was dry. "There's a vast difference between noticing a girl and agreeing to marry her."

Lord Peter pursed his lips. "You might at least make the acquaintance of Lord Abingdon."

"Well . . . I might do that."

"I'll arrange a card game at my house. That should provide you with an opportunity. Abingdon never refuses an invitation to play."

"Lady Barbara is certainly all that I could hope for in a wife for Alan. She is so perfectly an English lady."

"She's Quality, old friend. Definitely Quality."

"It certainly wouldn't hurt to play cards with Lord Abingdon."

Lord Peter looked as pleased as a cat with a bowl of cream. "Trust me, Maxwell," he said solicitously. "Trust me and all will be well."

*   *   *

On April 27 Lord North rose in the House of Commons and proposed that the East India Company be allowed to export tea directly to America. That evening there was a gala ball at the Duchess of Hampshire's and Alan attended in no good humor. The absolute indifference of the English government to all the colonies' claims angered him deeply. His father's efforts to point out the British side of things had done nothing to alleviate the blackness of his mood.

There was no trace of a smile on Alan's face as he stood talking to the Marquess of Rockingham on the edge of the duchess's ballroom.

"We will, of course, oppose it," Lord Rockingham said. "It will carry, though, I fear. North has a substantial majority."

Alan frowned.

"Do please erase that horrendous frown from your face, Alan," said Mr. Maxwell as he came up to them accompanied by a heavyset man dressed in pale blue satin and gold lace. "I have someone here I would like you to meet. Lord Abingdon, may I present my son, Alan Maxwell."

So this was Barbara's father, Alan thought as he shook hands with the genially smiling man. Or, not her father but . . . "How do you do, my lord," he said pleasantly, and unobtrusively scanned the other's face.

Lord Abingdon wore a wig but his skin and eyebrows were fair. Alan had heard so much in his disfavor that it was difficult to believe that this perfectly innocuous-looking man could be the villain he was painted. Of course, his villainy appeared to consist largely of innocuousness.

"What are you scowling for so harshly, Mr. Maxwell?" Lord Abingdon asked jovially. He had pale blue, light-lashed eyes. "Have you lost your plantation at cards?"

"No, my lord, but I might lose it in Parliament if things continue on their present course," Alan said.

Lord Abingdon's pale eyebrows rose. "Dear me. Surely not. What has happened to so distress you, Mr. Maxwell?"

Alan favored the earl with a dark, incredulous stare.

"The East India tea monopoly, Abingdon," murmured Lord Rockingham.

"Oh yes. That. Quite, quite."

Alan looked sardonic. "It is of some importance to us Americans, my lord."

"Of course. Of course." Lord Abingdon hastily changed the subject. "Are you enjoying your visit to England, Mr. Maxwell?"

Alan was aware that his father was regarding him anxiously. "Yes, thank you, my lord," he responded slowly, and looked at his father.

Mr. Maxwell's light brown eyes did most certainly look anxious.

"How are you, Abingdon?" asked a light, well-bred voice, and the Earl of Newcastle joined them.

"Ah . . . Mr. Maxwell and Mr. Alan Maxwell. How are the Americans in our midst these days?"

Both Maxwells responded politely and Alan found himself the target of Lord Newcastle's dark blue gaze. "You won't be able to partake of the joys of the London ballroom for much longer, I understand, Mr. Maxwell. When do you return to America?"

"In June, my lord. But we have some very enjoyable ballrooms in Virginia." Alan spoke pleasantly but there were faint lines of temper about his mouth.

"You have an active social life in Virginia, then?"

The temper flashed now in Alan's dark eyes. "Yes. And we sit down to table to eat and refrain from scalping our neighbors—at least on Sundays."

Lord Newcastle smiled. "Forgive me. Was I patronizing you? I did not mean to, I assure you. Merely, I was curious."

The line between Alan's brows smoothed out slightly. "Forgive me, my lord, if I snapped at you. The truth is, I am in no good temper and ought to have stayed at home."

"Nonsense," the earl replied. "But certainly you ought not to stand around glowering at our young ladies. You will frighten them."

"Indeed, indeed." Lord Abingdon seemed to have a habit of repeating his phrases. The music stopped and he beckoned to a couple on the floor. Barbara and Harry Wharton approached the group together. "Barbara," said Lord Abingdon, "I believe you know Mr. Maxwell and his son, Alan."

"Yes," said Barbara. "Indeed I do, Papa." She smiled at the two Americans.

"Lady Barbara. Lieutenant Wharton." Alan nodded. All it needed, he thought sardonically, was Lady Abingdon and this strange ménage would be completed. Lord Newcastle addressed a remark to Lord Abingdon, who answered pleasantly. Alan was beginning to find the situation humorous when a newcomer approached their oddly assorted party.

"May I have the honor of this next dance, Lady Barbara?" asked the Marquess of Derby.

"Lady Barbara has already promised the next dance to me," Alan replied instantly.

Lord Abingdon looked surprised.

"I'm afraid I *have* promised this dance to Mr. Maxwell, Lord Derby," Barbara said gently.

Very briefly Alan met her eyes. "We had better take our places." As he glanced around the group to excuse the two of them, he was aware of a swift flash of varying emotions. Harry Wharton looked suspicious, the Earl of Newcastle thoughtful, and Lord Derby angry. His father looked pleased. And Lord Abingdon's pale eyes regarded him blankly and steadily before they moved—assessingly—to Barbara.

Alan also looked down at the powdered head moving along so gracefully at his shoulder. He had the sudden feeling that he was being caught in a whirl of different currents and that it behooved him to be very careful if he wanted to keep his head above water.

Barbara raised dark blue eyes to his face. "Thank you," she said softly.

Alan's face remained preoccupied, even remote. "Not at all. It is always a pleasure to dance with you, Lady Barbara."

The music started and they took their places in the set.

"Abingdon has had the most extraordinary offer for Barbara," Lady Abingdon said to the Earl of Newcastle. It was a week after the Duchess of Devonshire's ball and the two of them were sitting in her ladyship's morning room at Abingdon House, Berkeley Square.

"Oh? From whom, my dear?"

"From Mr. Maxwell, the American who inherited the Hexham estate "

Lord Newcastle looked astonished. "From the *father?*"

Lady Abingdon moved her hands restlessly. "From the father on behalf of the son."

"The younger Maxwell does not appear to be a man who needs his father to speak for him," Lord Newcastle commented.

"The younger Maxwell knows nothing about the offer."

There was a startled pause. "This is all very peculiar, my dear. Enlighten me, if you please."

"It is all very tortuous, Richard. Maxwell senior would like to see his son married to an English girl—an English *lady*. Like so many colonials, he is extremely conscious of the superiority of the mother country in everything. He would be willing to pay handsomely—very handsomely—for Barbara. But he does not wish to broach the subject to his son unless he is certain that a Maxwell would be acceptable to a Carr."

"How handsomely?" asked Lord Newcastle.

Lady Abingdon told him.

The earl raised his eyebrows. "What does Abingdon say?"

"Oh, he is ready to jump at the offer, of course. It would solve his financial problems."

"And yours."

"And mine. I don't scruple to admit that. We have always known that Barbara must marry money. But I never intended she should be transported, Richard!"

"Virginia is a very pleasant place, I understand."

"It's a colony. She would be buried alive. And it is three thousand miles away!" Lady Abingdon was clearly distressed.

"Lizzie, my dear," Lord Newcastle said patiently, "I think this may be the very thing for Barbara. She likes Mr. Maxwell, you know. And, after all, what is the alternative? Derby?"

"Derby is no paragon, I grant you that. But at least Barbara would have a title and a good income and the freedom to go her own way. She would still have her family, her friends. She would not be banished."

Lady Abingdon rose and began to pace agitatedly up and down the room. Lord Newcastle watched her in silence for a few minutes before he spoke, gravely and thoughtfully. "Barbara is not like you, Lizzie. She doesn't have your . . . resilience. I think marriage to a man like Derby would destroy her."

Lady Abingdon stopped. "Nonsense," she said abruptly.

"It is not nonsense, my dear," Lord Newcastle replied serenely. "I think Abingdon ought to tell Mr. Maxwell he will consider his offer very favorably."

Lady Abingdon returned to her seat. "What if the son refuses?"

Lord Newcastle shrugged. "I don't think he will. He is not unaware of Barbara's charms."

"There is all this unrest in the colonies," Lady Abingdon said, beginning to waver.

"Nothing will come of it. The colonists will fall into line, mark me. They will have no choice, really. They cannot possibly expect to seriously challenge the most powerful nation in the world."

Lady Abingdon sighed. "I suppose not."

"Let this matter take its course, my dear. Trust me. I have Barbara's best interests at heart."

"Very well," said Barbara's mother. "I will speak to Abingdon this afternoon."

Mr. Maxwell cleared his throat. "Sit down, Alan. I must talk with you."

"Certainly, sir." Shortly after their arrival in London, Lord Peter had invited the Maxwells to stay with him. Father and son were presently in the drawing room of Lord Peter's London house and Alan moved to sit down in the largest wing chair. By unspoken consent, his family always granted Alan the largest chair in any room.

Mr. Maxwell sat down as well and regarded his son with the worried expression that had become so familiar over the last year or so. "I have not been arguing with any government members lately, Papa," Alan said humorously.

"Well, that is certainly good news." Mr. Maxwell tried to match his son's tone but failed sadly. He cleared his throat again. "You cannot be unaware, Alan, that I have been gravely concerned about your . . . ah, political inclinations."

The expression on Alan's face was perfectly courteous. "Yes?" he said softly.

"There is simply no way the colonies can win in this tug-of-war so loudly encouraged by the Sons of Liberty and their ilk. We can only petition and hope that, eventually, Parliament will redress our grievances."

Alan looked down at his boots and then up

again at his father. "We have spoken of this so often, Papa. I believe it is a subject on which we must agree to disagree."

Mr. Maxwell smiled a little crookedly. "Do you know, my son, I often look at you and wonder how on earth I got you?" At Alan's quick, startled glance, he laughed. "And I am not calling your mother's honor into question." He sobered. "No, it's just that I look at the burning life of you, the concentrated energy . . . You command attention just by being there."

"Well," drawled Alan with absolute good humor, "it would be hard to miss me, Papa."

Mr. Maxwell did not smile in response. "It isn't just your size. It's something in you. One has only to see you to know, instantly, that you are a leader." He sighed. "And that, precisely, is what I'm afraid of. When the British come to pick the victims for the hangman, you are certain to be among their number."

Alan frowned. "Nonsense, Papa."

"It's not nonsense, and you know it." There was a pause. "If this . . . family quarrel should come to war, would you take up arms against Britain?"

There was silence for so long that it became an almost tangible presence between them. Then, "Yes," said Alan very quietly. "I would."

Mr. Maxwell let out a long breath. "I thought so." His voice was equally quiet. "Then I must take what precautions I can to protect you."

"Papa," said Alan wearily, "leave it. There's nothing you can do."

"On the contrary, Alan. I am going to insist that you marry."

Alan straightened his spine and stared at his father. "I don't believe I heard you correctly, sir."

"You heard me. You will marry an English girl, someone who has connections with the government, someone who will be able to act as an advocate should the worst befall."

Alan's dark eyes held the glitter that always made his father nervous. "Oh?" he said with deliberate irony. "And am I to go down on my knees to anyone in particular?"

"Yes, as a matter of fact. Lady Barbara Carr."

It was a surprise. Mr. Maxwell watched his son with interest. "You are ridiculous, Papa," he said at last. "Lady Barbara Carr is not at all suited to life in Virginia."

"Her mother and father do not agree. In fact, they have said that an offer from you would be very welcome."

Alan looked as if he had been hit between the eyes. "Are you saying you have broached this matter to the Abingdons behind my back?"

Mr. Maxwell cleared his throat. "Yes."

Alan swore. Mr. Maxwell pretended not to notice.

"Well, I won't do it," Alan said curtly. "I'm sorry to have to disappoint the lady, but I won't do it."

"The lady knows nothing about all this."

"Well, thank God for that at least."

"You see, Alan," Mr. Maxwell went on, "if you don't agree, I am going to refuse to deed Newland over to you."

Alan pushed himself out of his chair with such force that it rocked. "What! You promised, sir!"

"And I am reneging on that promise." Unable to sustain his son's blazing look, Mr. Maxwell looked away. "I'm sorry, but there it is, Alan. And I mean it."

The force of Alan's motion had carried him to the fireplace and now he turned to stare into the grate. The logs were neatly laid, waiting to be lit. "And if I still refuse?"

"Then I shall hire an overseer to run the plantation. You may live there, of course, but you will have nothing to do with the operation of the farms."

"I see." Alan's back was not noticeably taut, but his white knuckles on the mantelpiece told another story.

"I'm sorry, Alan. I do this for your own good. I simply cannot bear the thought of you being hanged for treason."

"It would not be treason." Alan's voice was toneless.

"The British would certainly view it as such."

Alan turned and faced his father. There was a white line around his mouth. "There are worse things, Papa, than dying for one's country."

"No! You won't talk me out of this, Alan." Mr.

Maxwell stood up. "If this causes a rift between us, I'm sorry for it, but I stand on what I said. If you want Newland, you will marry Lady Barbara Carr." He walked to the door and paused to look back at his son. Alan had turned once more to the fireplace and his face was hidden. Mr. Maxwell left the room.

*   *   *

"Sit down, my love," Lady Abingdon said to her daughter. They were in the morning room that had been the scene several days earlier of her conversation with the Earl of Newcastle.

Barbara obediently sat down next to her mother on the blue brocade sofa.

"Your father received a call from Mr. Alan Maxwell this morning," Lady Abingdon said slowly. She picked up her daughter's fine narrow hand and held it in her own larger grasp. "He wishes to marry you, my dear."

"Marry me!" Barbara stared at her mother, dumbfounded.

"Yes, marry you. He will be calling later today to speak to you himself."

"But has he changed his mind about returning to Virginia?"

"No, my love. If you marry him, you will go to Virginia with him."

Barbara pulled her hand from her mother's. "Go to Virginia! But that is impossible, Mama."

"I am very much afraid, darling, that it is not

impossible. I wish you will give this offer serious consideration."

Barbara stared at her mother's grave face. "Mama," she whispered. "Do you wish to see me go to America?"

"Of course I don't, darling. But you understand your father's financial situation. Mr. Maxwell's father has agreed to a very handsome settlement if you accept his son's offer."

"I see," said Barbara on a thread of sound.

"Late yesterday Lord Abingdon received another offer for your hand. From the Marquess of Derby."

Barbara could feel the blood drain from her face. She shuddered. "Oh no, Mama. I could not marry that man."

"Darling," Lady Abingdon said very gently, "you must marry someone."

Barbara bent her head. "Yes."

"Mr. Maxwell is a colonial, true, but he is the kind of man who knows how to make a woman happy."

Barbara's head rose sharply and she looked at her mother's face. Lady Abingdon was smiling faintly and her hazel eyes were slightly narrowed.

"What do you mean, Mama?" Barbara asked.

"Haven't you sensed it? That hidden, arrogant power? You've been around him enough."

Barbara felt her cheeks grow warm. She raised her chin a trifle. "He has always seemed a gentleman to me."

Lady Abingdon looked amused. "I did not say he wasn't a gentleman. I said he has tremendous sexual power. The one does not preclude the other."

Barbara looked down at her own loosely clasped hands. "What you are saying, Mama, is that if I don't take Mr. Maxwell, then I must take Lord Derby."

"You don't lack for other admirers, Barbara, but none of them have sufficient money."

Barbara nodded. She knew her voice would break if she tried to speak again. And so, her body held stiffly, she leaned toward Lady Abingdon until her lips touched her mother's smooth cheek. Barbara's body did not relax as she felt Lady Abingdon's arms enfold her. After a minute she rose and went up the stairs to her room.

She had never felt so bitterly alone. They were going to send her to America—to a place thousands of miles away from her home and family. She would go to live with the tall dark stranger who had been looming so large in her life and her thoughts these past weeks.

Sexual power, her mother had said. A hidden and arrogant power. Was that what it was?

Why did he wish to marry her? Surely there were plenty of American girls to marry him. Why must he wish to uproot an English girl, a foreigner to the sort of life he must lead on his Southern plantation.

Were there Indians?

Her alternative was the Marquess of Derby.

Barbara drew a deep, steadying breath. She would prefer Indians to Lord Derby any day.

Her mother had said Mr. Maxwell was coming to speak to her this afternoon. With a ramrod-straight back, Barbara went to her wardrobe to choose a gown.

He came at precisely three o'clock, driving his own chaise. Barbara let the curtain fall back over her window and went to look once more in the mirror.

Her hair was unpowdered and arranged flatteringly in soft ringlets threaded with a blue ribbon. Her dress, an open robe of figured blue silk with a pure white stomacher, was becoming. Yet she looked too pale, she thought, and pinched her cheeks to give them a little color.

There came a knock on her bedroom door. "Lady Barbara," said one of the maidservants, "his lordship requests your attendance in the small saloon."

Barbara walked quite steadily down the stairs and only paused when she came to the massive mahogany door that led to the small saloon. Then, with a gesture of determination, she pushed the door open and walked into the room.

He was there, standing next to her father, looking very big and very formidable.

"Barbara, my dear," Lord Abingdon said without preamble, "Mr. Maxwell would like to speak to you."

"Yes, Papa," Barbara said, and was relieved to hear her voice sounded normal.

"I will leave you two young people for a few moments then," Lord Abingdon said, already moving toward the door. He passed by Barbara, avoiding her eyes, and went out the door, closing it behind him.

Barbara looked at the tall American.

"I reckon you know why I have come, Lady Barbara," he said in his deep, drawling voice.

Barbara nodded.

He crossed the room until he stood beside her, dwarfing her with his height. He looked down, his eyes hooded and inscrutable, his mouth faintly bracketed by two fine lines of what looked like temper. "Will you marry me, then?" he asked.

Barbara searched his face as if trying to find an answer to his question in the hard hawklike features above her. "I . . ." she began, faltered, and looked away. She was holding herself very straight.

Will you marry me, then?

I will not cry in front of him, Barbara said to herself fiercely. She swallowed hard. I will not cry!

Beside her the American swore. Barbara raised brilliant, startled eyes and saw, astonishingly, that he was smiling at her. "It's not as bad as all that, sweetheart," he said gently. "If you don't want to marry me, just say so."

He looked so different when he smiled.

"Do you want me to leave?" he asked.

Barbara shook her head.

He took her hands in his. His grasp was warm, comforting. "Will you do me the very great honor of accepting my hand in matrimony?" His Southern voice was soft and oddly gentle.

"Yes," said Barbara, "I will."

His face became serious again, but not, this time, intimidating. "You will have to come to Virginia, you know."

"Yes, I know that."

"Do you also know that there is serious discontent in America with the British government?"

"Mama said something," Barbara replied vaguely. "Do you have many Indian attacks, Mr. Maxwell?"

At that he laughed, his teeth very white in his tanned face. "Tidewater Virginia is perfectly safe from the Indians, Barbara, I assure you."

Barbara smiled up at him. "You are laughing at me, Mr. Maxwell. You will have to tell me all about Virginia. I am very ignorant, I fear."

"I will be happy to teach you—a great many things," he replied. He was still holding her hands and now he raised them and kissed the insides of her wrists—first the right and then the left. Barbara could feel the pulses in those wrists begin to race. He dropped her hands but did not move away from her. "I leave for Virginia in early June. That means we must be married within the month."

"You must make whatever arrangements you wish, Mr. Maxwell. I am at your disposal," Barbara said with dignity.

Just for a second, as he looked at her, Barbara glimpsed a curious expression in his eyes. But then he gave her his disarming grin. "My name is Alan," he drawled.

"Alan," repeated Barbara experimentally.

"Well, my love," said Lady Abingdon's brisk voice behind her.

Alan bowed to Barbara's mother. "Lady Barbara has done me the honor of accepting my offer, ma'am."

Lady Abingdon smiled and crossed the room to kiss her daughter's cheek.

Six

Two days after her engagement to Alan Maxwell, Barbara and her mother returned to Carrington, the Abingdon estate in Sussex, where all the Carr children had grown up. Lady Abingdon had invited a party of people for a visit to formally introduce Barbara's fiancé, and the two ladies were going down early to see that all was in readiness.

Barbara felt a lump in her throat as the carriage drove through the Sussex countryside on the approach to Carrington. There was not a square foot of land she did not know, not a field she had not ridden across, not a hedge or fence she had not jumped.

The carriage entered the beech woods of the

South Downs and began to climb. Up and up it went and Barbara found herself, as she always did, peering out the window for the first sight of the house.

When finally it came into view she felt the familiar rush of comfort the sight of it always afforded her—that comfortable, welcoming old house whose red brick had been transmuted by time and weather into a mellow, silvery pink. It was not until one walked around to the other side of the house that one realized how high up it was—right on top of the downs, with the rolling green turf all around it and the sea in the far distance.

Home.

Was this the last time she would ever see it?

This marriage.

It was not possible that this was happening to her, that she would be going three thousand miles away, across a vast ocean, to live among strange and foreign people.

Even her own people seemed foreign to her now. Her mother, her brothers, they had all acquiesced in this marriage.

Her mother had betrayed her.

She was alone.

She was alone and standing in front of a great door that opened into unfathomable darkness. She was afraid. Afraid, but determined to let no one see that fear—not her mother, her brothers, Harry.

Most of all, not Alan Maxwell, for he was the greatest and most frightening unknown of all.

Barbara sat at the dinner table, graciously listening to her cousin Harry and unnervingly conscious of her fiancé seated on her other side.

The scene was so familiar. Candlelight gleamed on the long, highly polished mahogany table. The footmen made their rounds with the silver salvers. The company glistened with jewels and lace and satin.

"I want only one thing," Harry was saying to her with great intensity. "To have one hour alone with you. That is all. Barbara . . ."

She turned and looked into his blue eyes. They were lighter than hers, the color of the sky. His beautiful chiseled face was urgent-looking.

"I am going to ride out tomorrow morning," Barbara said softly. "At seven."

His face lightened at her words and she smiled at him. Next to her, Alan was conversing with her mother. Lady Abingdon appeared to be enjoying their conversation enormously. So, apparently, was Alan, for he favored her mother with one of his beguiling smiles.

Barbara ate a small bite of dessert.

"You aren't hungry?" asked the deep Virginia drawl.

Barbara gave him her serene smile. "I have never had a very large appetite."

His eyes flickered over her long bare throat. "I can see that."

She felt the color come into her cheeks. "Is your home at all like Carrington?" she asked.

He took his time before he answered. "No American house is like Carrington, Lady Barbara. This kind of scale simply doesn't exist at home." He looked around the dining room, with its beautiful seventeenth-century paneling. "You could fit three of the rooms at Newland into this room," he said, and looked at her again.

There was nothing but gracious interest on Barbara's face. "But you have the river at your door."

He grinned. "But we have the river at our door."

"I thought you planters lived like nabobs, with slaves to wait on your every step." It was Harry Wharton, and the look in his celestial-blue eyes was distinctly hostile.

"We live like gentlemen," Alan replied impeturbably.

"*English* gentlemen?" Harry's tone of voice was an insult. Barbara looked at him, a faint frown between her brows.

Alan's expression hardened slightly. "Like English gentlemen," he agreed.

"English gentlemen don't object to paying their debts," Harry said. "Americans appear not to feel that necessity."

"I am afraid I do not understand you, Lieutenant Wharton," Alan said slowly.

"I am talking about the debt good sons owe to their mother country, Mr. Maxwell. You Americans want to take everything and give nothing in return."

Alan's dark eyes were hard on Harry's face. As Barbara watched, his mouth grew narrow and straight-lipped. "We pay our debts—more than our debts, by God—to the mother country," Alan said. "Plantation goods like tobacco, indigo, and rice give English merchants commodities in considerable demand throughout Europe. American iron is the raw material most used in British foundries. Almost one-third of all British merchant vessels are American-built. And the colonies are unsurpassed as a market for English goods.

"We are the sons of England, Wharton, not the bastards. And you need us more than we need you. It is a thing your government ought to remember when it goes about trying to bail out the East India Company at American expense."

Before Harry could reply, Lady Abingdon cut in. "Gentlemen! You are frightening Barbara with this altercation."

Two pairs of eyes, blue and dark brown, looked at Barbara. She smiled at her mother. "Dare we retire, Mama, and leave them alone?"

"I believe we may," Lady Abingdon replied. She rose, and Barbara and the other ladies rose with her. "Don't keep the gentlemen for too long, Abingdon," Lady Abingdon said pleasantly.

"Yes, my dear," her husband responded, and

the ladies passed out of the dining room and into the saloon.

The saloon at Carrington was a large, high-ceilinged room with five long windows looking out over the downs. Barbara went now to one of the windows and stared out into the gentle evening sunlight. Behind her she could hear her mother talking to her cousins and her aunt. No one disturbed her and she was still at the window when the gentlemen came into the room.

Her fiancé came over to her immediately. "Would you enjoy a stroll outdoors, Lady Barbara?"

He was standing slightly behind her and she turned her head slowly and tilted it up to look at him. She smiled. "That would be very pleasant, Mr. Maxwell," she replied composedly.

As the two young people left the room, their respective parents looked after them with complacent satisfaction. "Your son is a charming young man," Lady Abingdon said to Mr. Maxwell.

"Thank you, Lady Abingdon. And may I say that he is fortunate indeed to have secured your daughter for his wife. She is a rare young lady."

Lady Abingdon looked at Mr. Maxwell, and her expression became serious, even somber. "She *is* a lady, Mr. Maxwell. She is, profoundly, a lady. They are far rarer, even in the highest circles, than one would suspect. I hope they have the astuteness in Virginia to appreciate that."

"Lady Barbara will be appreciated, Countess.

Society in Virginia is not that provincial." Mr. Maxwell smiled. "Although I verily believe you could put Lady Barbara down in the middle of the Western wilderness and even the red savages would recognize her for what she is."

Lady Abingdon smiled her acknowledgment. "I am relieved to hear that, sir." She plyed her fan for a minute and then said, "Your son is a very determined American, is he not?"

"He was born and bred in Virginia, ma'am."

"As were you, I believe?"

"Yes. But I was educated in England. The young men who have never left the colonies are the hottest in defense of American liberties."

Lady Abingdon nodded graciously. "Well, I am certain it will all resolve itself amicably, Mr. Maxwell. These things always do."

"Yes," replied the American resolutely, "they do, don't they, Lady Abingdon?"

"Why are you so angry at the East India Company?" Barbara asked Alan as they walked along the terrace.

"Parliament is proposing to give the East India Company a monopoly on the tea market in America."

"Oh," said Barbara doubtfully, "I see."

He smiled down at her. "Do you?" he asked humorously.

"Well . . ." Barbara laughed. "No."

"Do you know, I think I ought to explain it to you. It is a matter of great importance to Americans."

"I have never been a great follower of politics, Mr. Maxwell . . ."

"Alan," he corrected her gently.

"Alan." For some reason she found it difficult to look at him and so she turned and rested her hands on the stone balustrade of the terrace. "But I will do my best to understand," she continued.

He moved to stand beside her. "The argument," he began gravely, "concerns the right of Parliament to lay taxes on the colonies when the colonies are not represented in Parliament."

Barbara listened to him talk, a small frown of concentration between her winged brows.

"So you are upset because of the threepence tax on tea?" she said when Alan finished speaking.

"It's not the money, Barbara," he said a trifle impatiently.

"No. It is the principle of the thing."

"Precisely." He grinned at her engagingly. "It is the principle of the thing. Taxation without representation."

"But what will happen if the tea is indeed shipped to the colonies?" Barbara asked curiously.

"I shouldn't be at all surprised if the warehouses holding it were burned."

"Good heavens," Barbara said, startled.

"Yes. It could well come to that."

There was a pause as they stood there, side by

side, facing out across the balustrade. Barbara looked at his hand where it lay so close to hers on the warm stone. For all its size and strength, it was a finely drawn hand. As she watched, that hand moved across the stone until it covered hers.

Barbara's throat felt tight. He picked her hand up and, turning her slightly, raised it to his mouth. He kissed first her palm and then each fingertip in turn. Barbara began to find it difficult to breathe. She looked up slowly. He was so very close to her.

"I am going to kiss you, sweetheart," he said in a deep voice, and suiting action to words, he pulled her against him, bent his head, and began to kiss her mouth. Barbara didn't struggle and after a minute he could feel her body relax, submit, and blend into his.

Finally he raised his head. She lay back in his arms; her eyes opened slowly and she looked at him through her lashes.

She had the most lovely neck, he thought, her breasts spilled so beautifully into the bodice of her gown. He imagined himself unhooking that gown and putting his hands . . .

She stepped back and away from him and, reluctantly, he let her go. He felt he had never wanted anything in his life as much as he wanted her at this moment.

"Alan," she said. He saw the wonder flicker in the dark blue of her eyes. And suddenly he felt himself on the verge of seeing her for the first time.

She had existed for him until now solely as a figure of carnal loveliness. But he looked now into the darkening blue of her eyes and saw there the mingled apprehension and fascination of a child poised on the very brink of womanhood.

A great wave of tenderness swept over him, banking for a minute the passion that their kiss had aroused. He cupped her face gently between his hands.

"Everything is going to be all right, sweetheart," he said.

Her bones were so fragile, so delicate. He smoothed his forefinger along her cheekbone. She looked up at him gravely.

"We are such strangers."

"I know." He gave her his most disarming smile. "But that is a situation that can be remedied."

An answering smile glimmered in her eyes. "Yes." The smile reached her mouth. "I reckon it can be," she said, with a fair imitation of his accent and, delighted, he began to laugh.

Long after Barbara had gone to bed, Alan stayed outside on the terrace, smoking a cigar and occasionally looking up at the windows that were closed against the evening air and wondering which one of them was hers. He imagined her lying in bed, her hair loose on the pillows. He took another puff of his cigar and stared out into the soft darkness.

He had agreed to this marriage because he wanted

Newland—or so he had told himself. Would he have agreed if the girl his father had named had been someone other than Lady Barbara Carr?

There was a wry look about Alan's mouth as he stared out across the darkened downs.

In truth, Newland had not been his object when he had agreed to his father's ultimatum. It was Barbara he had wanted. He had wanted her since first he saw her poised midway up the staircase of Bridgewater House, wrapped in the lovely serenity that was the hallmark of her personality.

He had wanted her, and so, when the opportunity had presented itself, when it seemed she was going to drop into his hand unsolicited, a pearl of exquisite quality and rarity, he had taken her. And now he doubted his wisdom.

She was a person. Not the mindless and beautiful figure he had desired. Her life was as important to her as his was to him.

He pictured in his mind the rooms at Carrington. How would a girl who had been brought up among such splendor ever adapt to life in Virginia? The mistress of a vast plantation had enormous responsibilities. She was expected to work, and to work hard—harder than the men most of the time.

How would this fragile English girl manage?

The heat would wilt her.

He had agreed to marry her so that he could sleep with her.

He had made a terrible mistake.

But as he stared with set mouth out across the darkened grounds of Carrington, Alan realized that there was no way he could back out now. The engagement had been published. He could not shame her in the eyes of her world by jilting her.

They would be married and go to Virginia. And God in heaven help them both.

Seven

Harry was at the stables the following morning when Barbara arrived, dressed in a well-worn riding habit. Her mare was ready and she and Harry mounted and moved out of the stableyard together, just as they had done a hundred times before.

They warmed the horses up at an easy trot and then, in mutual accord, let them stretch out into a gallop. They went along the top of the downs, Barbara moving easily with the motion of her horse, the two of them as smoothly integrated as a fine watch. This was heaven, she was thinking as she felt the rush of the wind around her. Here on top of the world, with a good horse beneath her, home and family to return to . . . How could she bear to leave it all?

"Let's pull up, Barb," Harry said and, reluctantly, she slowed to a trot and then a halt. Harry got off his horse and, holding his reins, came over to stand beside her.

"I'll help you down," he said.

Barbara nodded and let him lift her from the saddle. His hands lingered on her waist, but they did not produce in her the same sensations produced by Alan Maxwell's hands. Strange. She pulled her reins over the mare's head and turned to look out to the Channel.

"Oh," she said, and her voice was a cry of pain, "I shall miss this so!"

"Barbara." Harry's voice sounded strange and she turned to face him. He was so familiar, so dear, with his sun-blond hair and clear blue eyes. She felt so safe with him. There was no feeling of being out on an uncharted ocean, with its wild and dangerous currents and fierce and passionate storms. That was Alan. Harry was smooth and peaceful and secure. He was the home harbor, known, charted, sure. He picked up her hands and, bending his head, buried his face in them.

"God," he said into her palms, "how shall I bear it?"

"Oh, Harry. Don't." She felt a pain constrict her heart as she looked at the bright head bending over her hands. "There's nothing else I can do," she said helplessly.

He looked up at her, his blue eyes burning. "Elope with me," he said. "Now."

She slowly shook her head. "I can't do that. You know I can't."

"Barb . . ." And he pulled her against him with suddenly hard hands and kissed her.

He had never kissed her before. Strangely, Harry's kiss did not send her blood singing in her veins as Alan's had done. She put her hands on his shoulders and pushed, gently at first and then, when he paid no attention, harder.

"I'm sorry," he muttered when she finally pulled away. He was very pale.

Poor Harry, Barbara thought. And was dimly conscious that she had already left the safe harbor and ventured forth upon the ocean. "We must go back," she said gently and, wordlessly, he lifted her once again into her saddle.

"If only it weren't America!" Harry said fiercely as they approached the house. "In England, even if you were married, we would still see each other."

Yes, thought Barbara to herself, and if I were married to the Marquess of Derby, and were as miserable as I'm sure I should be, perhaps we should do more than just see each other. Perhaps I should end up just like Mama. And for the first time, hazily, she began to think that perhaps it was best that she was going away.

*   *   *

In the afternoon Barbara went for a ride with her fiancé. Instead of going along the top of the downs, she took him down the hill and through the countryside.

"Do you really ride to hounds?" Alan asked her after he had watched her effortlessly clear a five-foot fence.

Barbara looked surprised at the question. "Yes."

He grinned. "Your horsemanship is well up to it," he assured her. "I didn't mean to sound as if it weren't. It's just that at home women don't hunt."

"Not that many hunt in England, either," Barbara admitted. "But I have always ridden out. It comes, I suppose, of having older brothers."

"I reckon," he agreed amiably. "My younger sister has a very good seat on a horse. Perhaps you can persuade her to go out with you one day."

"That is your sister Libby, is it not?" Barbara asked.

"Yes."

They were walking their horses along a small rutted side road and at this moment they rounded a curve and saw a wagon in difficulty. As they came up to it, Barbara saw that the right rear wheel was stuck in a hole that the spring rains had created in the road.

"May I be of any assistance?" Alan asked the young farmer, who was vainly urging his team forward.

The farmer snatched off his cap. "Thank you, sir, but you see, I'm stuck."

Alan dismounted. "Perhaps if I put my shoulder to the wheel, it might help."

Both the young farmer and Barbara looked at him in astonishment as he took off his riding jacket. Members of the Quality in England did not assist farmers to move their wagons. Perhaps, if my lord were a particularly good sort, he would dispatch a servant to lend a hand. But to take a turn himself . . . Barbara took the coat Alan was holding up to her and then took his reins. He went over to the wagon and, bending, braced his shoulder. "Now then," he called, "start the team!"

The young man plied his whip, the team pulled, Alan pushed, and the wagon stayed stuck. Under his breath Alan expressed his feelings in a burst of language that made Barbara's eyes open very wide.

"Just a moment," Alan called then to the driver, and, straightening up, he unbuttoned his shirt at the neck and rolled up his sleeves. Once more he bent, once more the horses pulled, and this time, with a jerk, the wheel came loose. Alan lost his balance and almost fell as the support moved from beneath him, but as he regained his feet, Barbara saw that he was smiling.

"That's done it, then!" he called to the farmer, and the man jumped down from his seat to thank his rescuer. As Barbara watched, the two men shook hands. Alan stood for a few minutes talking, easy and comfortable, wearing only a loose white shirt and riding breeches. He towered over the burly young farmer.

"Your roads here are almost as bad as the roads in Virginia," Alan said to Barbara as he came up to her.

She looked down into his dark, hawklike face. The open collar of his shirt revealed the line of muscle that ran smoothly down the side of his neck into his shoulders. He began to roll down his sleeves, and the ripple of muscle in his biceps was evident. Barbara swallowed. He was so strong. She had not realized . . .

"Sorry to keep you waiting here," he said easily.

"I don't mind," Barbara replied. "It was very good of you to lend your assistance, but you might have hurt your back."

He looked amused. "Virginians are tough," he said cockily. His sleeves were rolled down but the shirt was still open at his throat. He reached up to take his coat from Barbara.

"Tough," she repeated. "And kind."

He paused in the act of putting on his jacket and looked up at her. For a long moment their eyes held and Barbara felt her heart begin to race inside her chest. Then he smiled and she had the oddest sensation that her heart had turned over.

"The class system in America isn't half so rigid as it is here in England," he said. "I reckon you might say the Maxwells are aristocracy in Virginia, but that doesn't mean the same thing as it does here. You will find yourself mingling with a far greater variety of people than you are accustomed to. I hope you will not be dismayed."

"Of course I will not be dismayed by any friends of yours," Barbara replied serenely.

He smiled again slowly. "So yielding you are, sweetheart, like silken reins under my fingers. Will you stay this way, I wonder?"

Barbara's chin rose. It was a very determined chin, softened only by that fascinating cleft. "I believe I will know my duty," she said with dignity.

"Well, that's good news," Alan replied cheerfully. He took his reins, held her hand, palm down, over his lips for one brief second, and then swung fluidly back up into his saddle. "Shall we proceed with our ride?"

"Certainly," said Barbara, and touched a heel to her mare's side.

The whole party returned to London after a few days' sojourn at Carrington. Alan was anxious to discover how matters were progressing with the East India tea monopoly and Lady Abingdon was anxious to shop with Barbara for her trousseau.

It seemed to Barbara in the busy days that followed their return that she scarcely saw her fiancé. He appeared to spend a great deal of his time closeted with Dr. Franklin and the group of Americans who acted as agents for the various colonies in London. The Americans were quite clearly more concerned about the tea issue than were any of the other people Barbara knew.

"Where have you been?" she asked Alan one night at Warrington House in Cavendish Square, where they were attending a ball together. She had not seen him in two days.

"I went down to Portsmouth to see our agent," he told her. They were standing in a group that included the Earl and Countess of Abingdon.

"I did not know you employed an agent in England, Mr. Maxwell," Lady Abingdon said pleasantly.

"I don't any longer." There was a look of grimness about Alan's mouth.

"Dismissed the fellow, eh?" Lord Abingdon asked genially.

"He's been bleeding us white for years," Alan said bluntly. "All Virginia planters depend upon English agents to sell their tobacco, and everyone I know is in debt to the bloodsuckers."

"Damn merchants," Lord Abingdon agreed feelingly. "When I think of the cheek of some of them! Do you know, Lizzie"—he turned to his wife— "Weston had the damn impertinence to send me *another* bill this morning?"

Not a flicker crossed Lady Abingdon's well-schooled countenance. "I will deal with them, my lord," she said.

"Well, I wish you will. It goes beyond the bounds of everything how, once the word gets out that a fellow has money, all his creditors start closing in. Bloodsuckers." He looked at Alan. "That's a damned good word for them, Maxwell."

Alan nodded gravely and turned to his fiancée. Her cheeks were faintly flushed. "Would you care to sit down with me, Lady Barbara, and drink some punch?"

Barbara nodded her agreement and in a few minutes they were sitting side by side on small gilt chairs sipping champagne punch.

"Your problems with your agent are not quite the same as Papa's with his tailor, are they?" Barbara asked after a moment.

He had been looking out over the dance floor but now he turned to her. "No," he said. "They are not."

"Is tobacco the main source of your income?" she asked.

"It has been." His dark eyes were hooded, unreadable. "Virginians traditionally grow tobacco and ship it to England to be sold. The English agent who sells the crop then purchases whatever luxury goods the planter may have requested—clothing, furniture, carriages, and so on." There was not a hint of humor about his mouth. "The problem with that system is that it leaves the American planter totally at the mercy of the English agent. The agent determines at what price he will sell the planter's tobacco and what price he will charge for the items he charges to the planter's account. It is a rotten system and I refuse to be caught up in it any longer."

Barbara smoothed her full silk skirt. "What then will you do?" she asked softly.

"I am going to emulate Colonel Washington and cut back on my tobacco crop. I could never convince my father to take this course, but now that Newland is mine, I can do as I wish. I am going to sever this irksome dependency upon foreigners and grow wheat and corn I can sell locally in Williamsburg, Jamestown, and York."

"Not foreigners, surely," Barbara said quickly. "Virginians are Englishmen too, Alan!"

He looked down at her in silence for what seemed to be a very long time. Then, slowly and deliberately, he smiled. "Of course we are, sweetheart." He took her hand. "Shall we have this dance?"

Barbara allowed him to pull her to her feet and take her out to the floor. It was difficult not to respond to that beguiling smile, but she was beginning to realize that he knew the worth of that look and was not above using it to achieve his own ends. She glanced fleetingly up at his face. He was nodding to Lord Peter Crashaw, and the look about his mouth was not at all genial. The music started and they bowed to each other. But neither the dancing nor Alan's returned smile was sufficient to quiet her apprehension.

*   *   *

"My mother has made light of the political tension between England and America," Barbara said to her prospective father-in-law later in the evening. "Alan does not seem to regard it as casually."

Mr. Maxwell sighed. "Come out into the garden with me, my dear. I think it is time we had a little talk."

When they were out of the crowded ballroom, walking in the small garden that lay hidden behind Warrington House, Mr. Maxwell looked soberly at the girl walking beside him, so straight, so slender, so ineffably graceful. "I do not think people here in England appreciate the seriousness of American feelings on this subject of taxation," he began.

Barbara looked up at him. "How do you feel, sir?"

"I do not think Parliament has the right to tax us. But I am an Englishman and, even if I disagree, I will bow my head if I must."

Barbara smiled faintly. "I do not think Alan is much in practice with bowing his head."

Mr. Maxwell laughed ruefully. "He has had no practice at all, my dear. Or yes—there is one person whom I believe he would readily bow his head to."

"And who is that?"

"Colonel Washington."

Barbara frowned slightly. "Isn't he the gentleman who has stopped growing tobacco?"

Mr. Maxwell grinned, and for a brief moment

Barbara could see the likeness to his son. "Among other things, my dear. Colonel Washington was the hero of Braddock's defeat. It was he and he alone who saved the remnants of the English army from the French and the Indians."

"Oh." She raised her lovely head and looked at the moon. Mr. Maxwell looked at her. She was such a perfect specimen of an English lady, he thought. There was such serenity about her, the effortless ease of one who has been born and bred a queen of her world. She was not haughty or arrogant, yet one never had any doubt when in her company of being in the presence of someone who stood very high in the world.

"What is going to happen, Mr. Maxwell?" she asked now, her eyes still on the moon.

"I don't know, my dear. I am very much hoping that *you* will be able to exert some influence on Alan."

Barbara turned her strangely dark blue eyes to him. "I?"

"Beautiful young wives do have an influence, you know," he said humorously.

"Do they?" Her eyes were unfathomable. "Whose idea was this marriage, Mr. Maxwell?"

There was an infinitesimal pause. "Why, Alan's of course!" His voice was hearty. Too hearty.

"I see." Barbara's narrow, faultless nostrils quivered slightly. "So I am to keep him loyal, then?"

"Alan *is* loyal. It is just that he's gotten in with

Patrick Henry and that crowd and they have exerted a very bad influence on him. I count on you, my dear, to counteract that influence."

"There isn't going to be a war, is there?" Barbara asked steadily.

"Good God, of course not! But I don't want to see my son arrested for seditious activity, Lady Barbara. There is a new law, you know, that says all persons involved in the burning of the English boat *Gaspée* last year are to be sent to England for trial. There is no reason why that law cannot be extended beyond the affair of the *Gaspée*." Mr. Maxwell's mouth looked grimmer than Barbara had ever seen it. "I do not think an American radical would receive a very sympathetic hearing on this side of the Atlantic."

"No."

"The Adamses, John Hancock, Patrick Henry—they may all end up at the end of a hangman's rope. I do not wish to see my son in their company!"

"Thank you, Mr. Maxwell," Barbara said with invincible graciousness. "I now see perfectly plainly the job I was hired on for. I shall do my best to fulfill my commission."

"My dear . . . I did not mean to frighten you."

The winged brows rose fractionally. "Frightened? I am not frightened, Mr. Maxwell." She put her hand on his arm. "Shall we go in? The air is becoming somewhat chill."

"Certainly, my dear," the American replied solicitously. "Let me take you to your mother."

Eight

Her conversation with Mr. Maxwell made it plain to Barbara that Alan had been pressured into this marriage quite as much as she. Nor did it take her long to determine what his pressure point had been—Newland.

She had wondered at his proposal. There had undoubtedly been a strong attraction between the two of them, but he had never said or done anything to indicate to her he was desirous of marrying her. Well, he was not desirous of marrying her. He was marrying her to get Newland—as she was marrying him to bail her family out of debt.

Barbara went home from the Warrington drum and, once inside the safety of her room, she cried.

When finally the tears stopped she lay awake listening to the silence of the house. She had never felt so absolutely alone.

It was all right for Alan, she thought bitterly. *He* was going home. Doubtless he thought she would serve as well as any other wife. He would have his plantation, his friends, his family, his politics. His life would not be greatly altered.

Whereas she . . .

She was going to a foreign country where she would be surrounded by black slaves and strangers. Indians lurked on the borders, and her husband—the only person she knew—would very likely be hanged for high treason against her country.

Barbara blew her nose and, lying back on her bed, looked at the ceiling. The crying bout had exhausted her and she felt curiously empty now, empty and passionless and clearheaded.

Her boats were cut and she was out on the ocean alone. Very well, Barbara thought, since that was the case, she would do everything in her power to make this marriage successful. She and Alan might deal very well together. They would have children. She would build a home for herself at this Virginia plantation.

She would not let herself be swamped in misery. She would get through. She was Lady Barbara Carr. She would survive.

*   *   *

Barbara and Alan were married on June 5. The ceremony was small and attended only by the bride's family and Mr. Maxwell. The newlywed couple were traveling immediately afterward to Portsmouth to spend their wedding night at the Golden Lion. They would take ship the following day for America.

Barbara wore ice-blue satin and looked cool and composed and beautiful. Alan looked splendid in dark green velvet with gold lacing. His hard, hawklike face, bronzed and arrogant, was as composed and unreadable as his bride's.

Lady Abingdon hugged her daughter tightly before Barbara got into the coach. "I shall write every week," Lady Abingdon whispered. "And remember, darling, you can come home anytime you wish."

"Good-bye, Mama," Barbara replied. She kissed her mother's scented cheek and smiled once more at her brothers and her father. Then Alan helped her into the coach and followed her himself. The horses started and they were away.

Barbara turned her head slowly and looked at her husband. He seemed enormous next to her in the confines of the coach. She hoped she did not look as frightened as she suddenly felt.

He gave her his disarming smile. "Your mother didn't cry," he said. "I thought all mothers cried at weddings."

"They must have a very poor opinion of the

bridegroom, then," Barbara replied. "Mama is evidently more sanguine about you."

He chuckled and tried to get a little more room for his legs. "I hate coaches," he said. "I never get in one if I can help it. I'd rather ride, no matter the season or the weather."

"Your legs are too long for a coach," Barbara said.

"I know." He shifted once again and Barbara smiled.

"Closed carriages always give me a headache," she confessed.

"Well, take your hat off, sweetheart. A contraption like that sticking into the head is bound to give anyone a headache."

"This hat is very à la mode," Barbara said with dignity.

"I didn't say it wasn't fashionable. I said it wasn't comfortable." His own tricorne was perched on the opposite seat. He turned his head to look at her. "Is it?"

"No."

"Well, take it off, then. We have a six-hour drive ahead of us." The carriage hit a rut in the road and Alan's head hit the roof. He cursed and Barbara bit her lip and tried not to laugh. She took off her hat.

They reached the Golden Lion in time for dinner. The ship they were to embark on the following morning, the *Duke William*, was docked in the harbor and loaded with all of Barbara's trousseau. The *Duke William* was owned by one of Alan's neighbors on the James, Mr. Benjamin Harrison, and the Maxwells were to be the only passengers on the return trip to Virginia.

Barbara's maid, Anna, was waiting for them at the inn. Anna was to travel to Virginia with them, with promise of a return passage if she so desired.

"I'm sure you want to change your dress for dinner, sweetheart," Alan said as they both came into the bedroom that had been allotted to them. "I'll just leave you to the ministrations of your maid while I have a quick look at the ship. We'll dine in half an hour?"

"That will be fine, Alan."

He flashed her a quick grin. "I've bespoken a private dining parlor. Be back in half an hour."

He was gone. Barbara looked from her window and in half a minute she saw his distinctive black head emerge from the inn. He walked purposefully toward the water, his stride long and lithe and energetic. The coach ride had been torture for him.

The ride had also left Barbara feeling slightly ill. She had never been a good traveler and hoped fervently that she would not be seasick.

"Get me out of this dress, Anna," she said to her maid. "And open the window, please."

Alan was back in forty minutes and they went down to dinner. Barbara's headache had gone but she found she had no appetite and merely toyed with her food while her husband ate heartily.

"The state cabin on the *Duke William* is very nice," he told her. "Quite large, really, and well-furnished. You should find it comfortable."

"I'm sure I shall," Barbara replied.

She asked him questions about Virginia and listened to his answers without really hearing them. Soon now, very soon, they would go upstairs. Barbara did not think she was afraid. She had been afraid, a little, when he had first gotten into the carriage next to her, but the feeling had soon gone.

"If you're finished, shall we go upstairs?" he asked.

"Yes." Barbara's voice was low and steady.

At the door of their room he halted. "Why don't I go smoke a cigar and give your maid a chance to undress you?"

"Yes." This time her voice sounded a little breathless.

Without another word he went back down the stairs.

For her daughter's wedding night Lady Abingdon had purchased a cream-colored lace-and-silk negligee. Barbara put it on, and the matching wrapper, and let Anna brush her hair until it hung like a mass of shining dark brown silk around her shoulders. Then she dismissed her maid, rose from her chair, and looked around the room. Ought she to get into bed? No. She did not want to get into bed. She was still standing indecisively in front of the mirror when she heard steps coming along the passageway. The bedroom door opened and her husband was there.

"Alan," she said.

The way it was said caught Alan by the throat. He closed the door behind him carefully.

"I hope you're not afraid of me, Barbara," he said slowly. "There isn't anything to be afraid of." He crossed the room toward her, moving slowly, and she watched him out of huge darkened eyes. "You are so beautiful," he said as he reached her.

Barbara had to tip her head way back to look up at him. "I don't think I'm afraid," she whispered.

He put his hands on her slender neck, his thumbs touching the front of it gently. He moved his thumbs caressingly and asked, "Do you know what the act of love is?"

"Yes." Barbara stood very still, feeling the warmth of his fingers on her bare flesh, aware of the sudden tumult of her heart. His eyes were so dark, the darkest eyes she had ever seen. With his thumbs he pushed her chin up a little and, bending, he kissed her.

Something in Barbara ignited in response to that kiss. As his arms came around her to pull her close against him, she reached her own arms up to encircle his neck. Her long hair streamed over his arm. It was he who finally broke the embrace, lifting his mouth away from hers. They looked into each other's eyes.

"Almighty God," he said, and his voice was husky, "how I want you."

At those words every pulse in Barbara's blood began to throb. She moved her hand from his neck and hesitantly brushed his cheek. He picked her up, carried her to the bed, and laid her down. He stripped off his coat and began to unbutton his shirt.

Barbara stared at him with enormous, dilated eyes. His bare chest and shoulders were so strongly muscled. He was so brown all over. How had he gotten so brown?

The bed shook a little as it took his weight. She lay back against the pillows while he kissed her throat and the deep hollow between her breasts. She buried her hands in the crisp blackness of his hair and felt his mouth move from her shoulder to her breast. Barbara inhaled sharply. His mouth was sending jolts of sensation searing up her nerve ends. She arched her back and pressed his head against her. His hands moved to caress the curve of her hip, the inside of her thigh. Barbara whimpered.

When he lifted her negligee, Barbara moved to accommodate him. She was beyond thought, beyond all but the wild singing in her blood, the longing to feel his strong body against hers. Her whole being quivered and arched up against him, and it was then that he came into her.

At first the pain was almost too great. But he held her and whispered to her and she stayed still and did not try to pull away. Then he began to move. The pain was still there, but the pleasure that blazed up became a part of it, until the shock waves of sensation that jolted through her were so intertwined one with the other that she could not tell the pain from the pleasure.

Then at last he was still, his breathing still coming hard and fast. Barbara lay perfectly quietly beneath him, afraid to move, afraid to speak. She did not think she had ever been so afraid in all her life.

What had he done to her?

She looked at the dark head buried on her breast, and realized that nothing would ever be the same for her again. She would never again be just herself. Now always, wherever she went and whatever she did, there would be this man—this man and what his touch could do to her.

There was the sound of someone walking down the passage and then a door slammed.

She was afraid to move. She felt terribly, terribly alone.

Alan spoke. "Am I crushing you, sweetheart?" He rolled onto his side and gathered her into his arms. "I'm sorry if I hurt you," he murmured into her ear.

"Oh, Alan." She pressed her face into the hollow of his shoulder and closed her eyes. He cradled her as if she were a child. "Everything is going to be all right," he said comfortingly. He leaned up and blew out the candle, and darkness enveloped them like a cocoon. Barbara could hear his heart beating strongly and steadily under her cheek.

She belonged to him.

He kissed the top of her head and she made a soft sound in response.

"Go to sleep, Barbara," he said, and his voice was heavy and dark with tenderness. Barbara fell asleep nestled against his shoulder.

He was dressed when she awoke the following morning. She pushed her hair out of her eyes and sat up against the pillows, holding the coverlet up over her naked breasts.

He grinned at her from where he stood by the window. "The weather is perfect. As soon as you've dressed and eaten, we can go on board." His whole tall, broad-shouldered figure was electric with energy. He turned back to the window and looked out toward the harbor. "In a few weeks we should be home."

Home. Barbara stared at his back. Home was this strange land across the ocean. Home was the Virginia plantation that called to him more strongly than she did. He turned back to look at her, then crossed the room until he stood beside the bed. Bending over, he kissed her long and lingeringly.

Barbara's lips parted sweetly under his and he braced both hands on either side of her on the bed. His face very close, he said softly, "We'll be at sea for at least five weeks. Just the two of us." He kissed her again and straightened up. From the way he looked at her, Barbara knew he was no longer thinking of "home."

"If I stay around here one more minute, we'll never get started," he said. "Get up, sweetheart. I'll see you down in the breakfast parlor."

Barbara smiled faintly. "All right, Alan." She watched him leave the room and waited for a minute before she rang for her maid.

At ten o'clock on the morning of June 6, Mr. and Mrs. Alan Maxwell boarded the *Duke William*. At ten-thirty they were under sail, heading for the colony of Virginia in British North America.

II

The Lord of the James

1773–1775

Nine

Barbara was seasick.

It started with a headache and progressed from there to shivering and nausea. Alan spoke encouragingly and sent her down to their quarters, where Anna undressed her and put her to bed. Once she had lost her breakfast, Barbara thought she would begin to feel better. She felt worse.

That was the first day out, when the sea was calm. The second day the wind blew up and the sea grew choppy. The third day they were in a storm.

Barbara had never been so ill. Her head ached, and just raising it off the pillow made her dizzy. She had long ago lost any food that was in her stomach, but her system did not seem to realize there was nothing left to bring up.

Anna was sick as well, so Alan came in periodically to take care of his wife. Barbara was dimly grateful for his concern, but there was little he could do.

He tried to get her to drink some water.

Just opening her eyes made her dizzy. She looked at him towering next to her, his body moving in effortless balance with the tossing of the boat. She closed her eyes again.

"I don't think I can, Alan," she said in a thin voice.

He sat on the side of the bed, slipped his arm behind her shoulders, and raised her. "Of course you can, sweetheart." He put the glass to her lips. Barbara obediently took a few sips, then lay back down.

But the effort of sitting up had disturbed her precarious equilibrium and now she stumbled out of bed to grab the bowl she had been using. Nothing much came up—just some yellow bile—but she was left both sweating and shivering from the bout.

"Oh God. Sweetheart, I'm so sorry." Alan picked her up and put her back into bed. He wiped her face with a cool, damp cloth. Barbara heard the sympathy in his voice and felt very slightly comforted. She closed her eyes and prayed for dry land.

During the following days, Barbara lost all sense

of time. All that existed was seasickness. She dreamed and awakened, only to be sick again. She could hear the waves crashing against the sides of the ship and thought, hopefully, that perhaps they would sink. Death seemed extremely attractive when the alternative was this utter wretchedness.

She dreamed she was a child at Carrington. Miss Nunley, her governess, had taken her and Harry and William for a picnic on the downs and the boys were rolling down a hill. Barbara, watching them, laughed and laughed.

She opened her eyes to find herself still in the stateroom of the *Duke William.* The motion of the boat was quieter than before, although still quite noticeable. Barbara, however, realized that she herself felt differently. She looked around the room, cautiously moving her head. The horrible, dizzying sickness did not come. The boat pitched a little, but Barbara's stomach remained calm.

Slowly, with infinite carefulness, she sat up.

Her head ached, she was violently thirsty, and there was a dreadful sour taste in her mouth. But her stomach was steady.

Barbara drew in a deep, slow breath. The sickness was going. Her body must finally be adjusting to the motion of the ship.

When Alan came in half an hour later, she was sitting on the edge of the bed drinking a glass of water.

The water helped the headache and after she had washed herself all over, Alan took her up on deck for some fresh air.

The ocean was still very choppy and Barbara grasped the rail and drew in deep breaths of the wet, salty air.

"I reckon you're going to live, sweetheart," Alan said next to her.

She looked at him. "How can one possibly be so ill, just from motion?"

"I don't know why it happens," he returned, "but you were a very sick girl. You had me worried."

"I was too sick to be worried. All I wanted was to die."

He looked down at her hand on the rail. The rings were loose on her thin fingers. "Do you think you could eat something?"

Barbara drew another deep breath. "Do you know," she replied in astonishment, "I do believe I could."

He chuckled. "You should be starving. You haven't eaten for days. Come along and we'll get you some food."

After that first week, the voyage changed radically for Barbara. Alan had been sleeping in the captain's quarters and now he moved back into his wife's bed and their married life resumed.

They had weeks to get to know each other. The long summer days followed one after the other in a haze of sun and fresh salt air. It seemed that all the bad weather had exhausted itself during that first week and now nature was going out of its way to give them a glorious honeymoon.

Alan knew a great deal about sailing and he spent many hours aloft or on the bridge with the captain. Barbara would watch him and write in the journal she had started to keep. Sometimes they just leaned side by side together at the rail, watching schools of dolphins playing in the sun. They would have a long, leisurely dinner in the stateroom, and after the meal had been cleared away, they would go to bed.

"Alan teases me," Barbara wrote in her journal. "He says all his family and friends will be impressed with his marrying what he calls 'a real English lady.' He says I will be a Personage for them, that I must cultivate some eccentricities so as not to disappoint my audience."

She looked up from her journal to watch for a moment the figure of her husband on the bridge. He had both hands on the rail and, eyes squinted against the sun, was looking out over the water. She heard someone call "Mr. Maxwell," and at the sound of his name he turned. A strand of black hair came loose and blew over his forehead in the wind. A sailor came up to him and said something. Alan answered and then he grinned. Barbara's fingers tightened on her pen and, slowly, she looked down once again at her book, at words she had written earlier:

Last night I dreamed of Carrington. Alan was there with me as I went around all the rooms, but for some reason I could not touch him. Mama and Harry and William were there also and they were talking and talking, and I was pretending to listen, but all the time I was trying to stretch out my hand to touch Alan. But I could not. I could not move my hand.

He was right there—so large, so blazing with life, that Carrington and all its inhabitants seemed pale and insignificant. He was real and they were not. But I could not touch him!

When I awoke my heart was pounding so. It was deep in the night. I could hear the creak of the ship. Alan was asleep next to me in the bed.

I lay very still, listening to my heart as it slowed, filled with wonder and with fear. How can it be that this has happened? How can it be that all my previous life now seems like a shadow—insubstantial, unreal. I have been married for exactly four weeks and my life has utterly changed.

I put my hand on Alan's back. Very lightly—I did not wish to wake him. His skin was smooth and warm under my fingers. The power of him. And yet he can be so gentle.

He stirred in his sleep and, rolling over, took me in his arms.

This is what it means to belong to someone. I don't think it even frightens me anymore. It is, quite simply, a fact of my life.

A fact of my life. Barbara gazed out across the sparkling water. Not something I decided upon, just something that happened.

Alan had gone up into the sails. Barbara watched him move aloft, surefooted as a giant cat. He did something to one of the ropes and then he was back on the deck again. This time he started coming over to her.

He was dressed in a white shirt which fit comfortably across the breadth of his shoulders and contrasted sharply with the bronzed column of his neck. He leaned against the rail and grinned at her engagingly. Barbara's eyes went slowly over him, over the narrow hips, flat stomach, and wide shoulders, up to his face. "I used to wonder how you got so sunburned," she said. "Now I know."

"Do you think I should wear a hat like yours?" he asked, referring to the wide-brimmed straw that shaded her own complexion.

She tilted her head to one side consideringly. "It might look very attractive."

A strong hand reached out and plucked the hat from her head. "What do you think?" he asked, perching it on his own black locks.

Barbara burst out laughing, he looked so funny. "I don't think it's your style. Too much brim."

One of the sailors gave Alan a startled glance. "What do you think, Smith?" he asked. "I think it's very stylish, but my wife says it's too much brim."

The sailor, who was an American, laughed. "I'd say your wife is right, sir. Too much brim—and too little crown."

"Ah well." Alan took the hat off. "We'll just have to choose a more suitable style. Come along down with me, Mrs. Maxwell, and we'll turn out my wardrobe."

"You haven't worn a hat in weeks," Barbara protested in bewilderment as he took her hand and walked her along the deck to the stairs.

"Ah, but I didn't come down here for a hat," he said as they entered the empty stateroom. He locked the door behind him and stood looking at her, his dark eyes filled with amusement and another expression that had become very familiar to her during the last weeks.

"Alan," Barbara protested feebly. "It's the middle of the day."

"What has that to do with anything?" He put his hands on her shoulders and turned her so her back was toward him. His arms went around her, and he bent his head and kissed the place where her neck met her shoulder. He undid the first hook on her bodice.

His touch had started her pulses pounding. "Alan . . ." she said.

She felt the fire of his kiss on her neck. All the hooks of her bodice were open now. He spoke in her ear. "I want to lie with you, and love you, and do terrible things to you."

She couldn't breathe. His hands were on her breasts and the nipples stood up taut against his palms. He slid her dress off and picked her up. He took her to the bed and laid her down. "It's even better than I had dreamed," he said. "Having you."

Her eyes were almost black in her faintly flushed face. Her hair had loosened and tiny ringlets clung to her neck. She reached for him and passion surged between them, swelling in a huge, towering wave, higher and ever higher, until it crashed all around them and they were left, spent and satiated, wanting only to be near each other and to be quiet.

"Aren't you going to put on a hat?" Barbara asked as they dressed again later.

His eyes lit with amusement. "Do you want me to?"

She looked up slowly, her disheveled hair falling out of her ribbon over her cheeks and shoulders. "It doesn't matter."

"No. I reckon it wouldn't fool anybody."

Barbara raised her hands to her hair and gave him a very faint smile.

"Christ, sweetheart," he said. "Whatever am I going to do with you in Virginia?"

She frowned very slightly. "What do you mean, Alan?"

He shook his head and didn't answer.

She regarded him thoughtfully. "You could always take a vow of chastity."

At that he grinned. "Not a chance, my dear, not a chance. And if you don't get up off that bed in ten seconds, you're going to find yourself lying back down on it again."

Barbara rose with ineffable grace. "It's almost time for dinner," she said serenely. "You can hook up my dress for me, Alan, please."

They went up on deck together and left the stateroom empty for Anna to set the table.

Ten

The James River was wide and imposing, a greater river than any Barbara had ever seen. Unlike the Thames, the shores of the James seemed scarcely to be touched by human habitation. Beyond Jamestown there was nothing but an occasional plantation house to be seen. For the most part the riverbanks were covered with forests.

"It's so . . . empty," Barbara murmured to Alan. "I had not realized how much land there would be."

Alan was standing beside her at the rail. "I know," he replied. "This is country you can breathe in." His eyes went up and down the wild shore. "Home," he said. There was great contentment in his voice.

It was a hot day but Barbara had to repress a shiver. Those great forests, this great river—how could this land ever be home to her? God knows what was lurking out there in that wilderness.

"Are you certain there are no Indians about?" she asked.

Alan chuckled. "Quite certain, sweetheart." He squinted upriver. "We should be at Newland in an hour."

It was in fact another hour and fifteen minutes before they docked at the wharf of Newland plantation. Alan helped his wife off the ship and onto the dock and Barbara gazed in wonder at the sight that met her eyes.

She might have been in an English garden. Between the river and the house lay a series of terraced boxwood gardens. Directly up the path that led through the terraces Barbara could glimpse a red brick house with a pediment roof. To her left, on a stretch of shaded lawn, was a graceful summerhouse with a bell roof and Chinese Chippendale railings. She looked up at Alan and smiled. "What beautiful grounds."

"My father had the terraces dug out," he told her. "The boxwood he brought over from England." He had been looking up the long graveled path that led to the house, and now a touch of humor softened his mouth. "Ah," he said, "here they come. I reckon the *Duke William* was spotted downriver."

Barbara followed his eyes and saw a whole party of people coming toward them from the house. Alan took her hand in his and began to walk up the path. The two groups met on the middle terrace and Alan kept his wife's hand in his large, comforting clasp as he introduced her to his sisters, his brother, his brother-in-law, his nephews, and an assortment of cousins and neighbors.

Barbara found all the people a bit overwhelming, although she smiled her serene smile and spoke pleasantly about her ocean voyage. She felt lost and afraid when they all repaired to the house and Alan loosed her hand.

It was a small red brick house built in a graceful Georgian style. The main house was flanked by two smaller houses made of the same brick, which Barbara knew from Alan's descriptions to be the kitchen and the residence for the house slaves.

The front door led into a wide center hall that ran from the river entrance to the carriage entrance of the house, and contained a pretty carved staircase and four doors leading into the four main living rooms of the house. The company went into the room on the left, the room Barbara had heard Alan describe as the Green Parlor.

It was an attractive room, with green-painted paneling and a graceful marble chimneypiece. The windows were hung with white dimity and green satin. It was, by Barbara's standards, an exceedingly small room, but two doorways on either side of the fireplace led into another parlor, which was painted blue. The two rooms together were an adequate size, Barbara thought a little doubtfully as she slowly looked around.

"I hope you are going to like Virginia," said a soft Southern voice, and Barbara turned to Alan's sister Helen. Helen was twenty-seven, a year older than Alan, and the mother of three children. She was much fairer than her brother, with light, sherry-colored eyes and medium brown hair.

Barbara smiled. "I'm sure I shall."

"I hope we haven't disconcerted you by this . . . vociferous welcome, but Virginians are a gregarious lot."

Barbara smiled again.

"You look a little pale, Lady Barbara." It was Helen's husband. "You're not accustomed to our Southern heat. Come and sit down and I'll get you a glass of cold lemonade."

"Thank you," Barbara said gratefully, and sat down in a Queen Anne wing chair.

"It takes a while to grow accustomed to the climate here," Edmund Brandon said when he had brought her the promised lemonade.

"We never get this hot in England," Barbara explained. "And there was always a cool breeze on board the ship." The lemonade tasted very good.

"I know." Edmund Brandon smiled at her. "I went to school in England and it took me a long time to grow accustomed to the damp."

"Where did you go to school, Mr. Brandon?" Barbara asked with interest.

"Eton and Cambridge. Then I studied law at the Middle Temple in London."

Barbara looked with increased interest at Alan's brother-in-law. Edmund, a slender, scholarly-looking man with spectacles, was in his early thirties. Like Alan, he wore his brown hair tied neatly at the nape of his neck.

"Do you practice law here in Virginia, Mr. Brandon?"

"I practice some law and try to run my plantation. Stanley is only a few miles down the river from Newland."

Barbara nodded and her eyes went involuntarily to where her husband was standing near the windows that looked out on the river. He was talking to a group of men who were listening to him intently.

A figure hovered on the edge of her vision and she turned to see Alan's brother, Robert. Robert was eighteen and looked very much like his sister Helen. He was to go to the College of William and Mary in September, Alan had told her.

He was regarding her now, evidently wishing to speak to her but feeling a little shy.

"Come over, Robert, and get acquainted with your new sister-in-law," Edmund said kindly.

"Yes, Robert," said Barbara. "Perhaps you can

tell me who all these people are once again. I'm afraid I've forgotten most of their names!"

Barbara was perfectly capable of dealing with a shy young man and putting him instantly and disarmingly at ease. In a very short time, Robert was laughing and talking as if he had known her for years.

Supper was served in the dining room at about eight-thirty. The dining-room windows, gracefully draped in white dimity and gold satin, overlooked the river, and the table was easily able to seat the ten people who joined them for dinner. There was room in the dining room, Barbara thought, for at least two dozen people to dine comfortably.

It dawned on Barbara about halfway through supper that all ten of her guests expected to stay the night. She made a great effort to hide her dismay as Helen competently arranged for beds. She had been so hoping to have her husband to herself.

She didn't get him to herself for almost the first week of their arrival home. Every day brought more people to welcome the newly wedded pair, more names for Barbara to remember, more men to take Alan aside to ask questions about the new tea bill.

"Doesn't anyone in Virginia ever wait for an invitation before coming to stay?" Barbara asked Alan one night as they were undressing for bed.

Late at night, in the privacy of their bedroom, was the only time she ever had his undivided attention.

"No." He grinned at her. "Virginian hospitality doesn't stand on ceremony, sweetheart. It's a rare day when someone doesn't come to visit."

Barbara's heart sank. "Oh."

"Of course, nothing quite equals the young cousin of the Stevenses' who went to pay a brief visit to friends and ended up staying ten years."

"Alan!" Barbara stared at him, horrified. "You're teasing me."

He had finished unbuttoning his shirt and now he tossed it on a chair. "I'm not." He came across the room to her. "Poor little girl. Are you finding all this company overwhelming?"

"So many strangers all at once . . ." Barbara murmured. His chest and shoulders looked enormous.

"It's gotten a little cooler," he said. "Tomorrow morning, do you want to ride around the plantation with me?"

"Yes."

He kissed her neck and she lay back against the pillows and waited for him to finish undressing.

Later, however, after he had fallen asleep, Barbara lay awake listening to the night sounds outside her window. Here with Alan she felt safe, but all the world outside this bedroom seemed a foreign territory.

She closed her eyes and imagined she was once

again at Carrington. She pictured her old bedroom and imagined she could hear her mother's voice. When she finally fell asleep, she dreamed of home.

As the weeks passed, Barbara's homesickness increased instead of abated. Nothing in Virginia was familiar and she longed, with an ache that brought a lump to her throat, to hear the crisp, clipped tones of an English voice. Everyone in Virginia spoke so slowly. The slaves' dialect was scarcely intelligible to her.

The plantation, despite the distinctly English look of the house and gardens, was nothing at all like a countryhouse at home. At home one had agents to run one's farms. One shopped in the village stores for one's necessities, or ordered them from London. Here there were no shops, and goods ordered from London took half a year to arrive.

Everything they ate and wore was made right on the plantation itself; Newland was virtually a self-sustaining unit. And Alan acted as his own agent. He personally supervised all the farmwork as well as the craftsmen such as the stonecutters, carpenters, blacksmiths, and saddlers.

The role of the mistress of a large plantation was scarcely less onerous than that of the master, as Barbara learned from Alan's sister Helen. The mistress was in charge of seeing that the thousands of pounds of pork produced on the plantation were properly cured and hung; that the fish taken from the James were salted down for the slaves; that ashes were collected for the soap; she was in charge of the fine sewing done in the house by the housemaids and she also was responsible for the supervision of the work done in the small houses where the spinners and seamstresses made the clothes for the hands. The gardeners fell within her domain as well, as did the health of all the slaves on the plantation.

Nothing in Barbara's background had prepared her to assume a position of such laborious responsibility. She had been reared as an English lady and as such she could order her immediate household and kitchen, knew how to entertain on a grand scale, and was versed in all the social niceties of the English aristocracy. She was lost in Virginia. She felt so fearfully alone.

She sat one hot afternoon at the pretty secretary in her bedroom, writing a letter to her mother. To Lady Abingdon she felt able to say the things she could not say to Alan. With her husband she felt obliged to keep up a pretense of capability, but to her mother she could pour out her loneliness, her fear of the slaves, her distress at the heat and the bugs, her horror at the sheer drudgery of the work she was expected to perform. All of the stifled feelings she had been diligently hiding from Alan and his sisters came tumbling out in this letter to Lady Abingdon. If she couldn't tell her mother, Barbara thought to herself as her hand raced across the page, then whom could she tell? Deep in her heart, although unacknowledged by her consciousness, Barbara was blaming her mother for pushing her into the situation she was now finding so distasteful.

It was almost time for dinner and Barbara put her letter away and went to the mirror to tidy her hair. Alan was downstairs in his office talking to Edmund Brandon. The master of Newland spent several hours every day in his office attending to the vast amount of paperwork required for running a large plantation. And since he was usually in the saddle by six in the morning to ride around the farms, Barbara rarely got a chance to talk to him before dinner, which was served at three-thirty in the afternoon.

Dinner was pleasant, with just her and Alan and Edmund Brandon. Barbara liked Alan's brother-in-law. He was more English than Virginian and consequently made her feel at home.

Later in the afternoon Helen and Libby and Helen's children came over to Newland and they all sat outdoors in the summerhouse watching the river. It was during a lull in the conversation that Alan turned to Libby and asked, "Aren't you ever coming home, Libby? Or are you planning to make your home with Helen permanently?"

Libby flushed and cast a quick glance at Barbara. "I thought you and Barbara would prefer to be alone," she said a little gruffly.

"One is never alone in Virginia," Alan answered genially. "I know you only planned to stay with Helen temporarily. Come on home. I reckon Barbara could use some help, and you know all about running the plantation."

Libby smiled with obvious pleasure. Barbara felt a distinctly nasty shock. As her husband and her sister-in-law continued to talk, Barbara sat perfectly quietly and tried to subdue her unquiet feelings.

Alan thought she wasn't up to running his home. That was why he wanted his sister to return to Newland, so she could do the work his wife was incapable of. Barbara took a deep, slow breath and deliberately relaxed her tightly clasped hands.

"I would like to come home," Libby was saying, "if it's all right with you, Barbara?"

Barbara looked into the dark eyes of her young sister-in-law. She and Libby had been polite but distant ever since they first met. Barbara had sensed that Libby did not like her, and that had caused her to assume her most aloof and regal air. But now she forced herself to smile and say pleasantly, "Of course you are welcome, Libby. Newland is your home, after all."

Libby's face lighted but she responded with a formal "Thank you." Then she turned to Helen and began to ask excitedly about packing.

"I did not realize Libby was desirous of coming back to Newland," Barbara said to Alan that night as they prepared for bed in their own room. "If I

had, of course I should have invited her myself."
She was sitting on the edge of the four-poster
brushing her hair. The air was heavy and still; there
was a thunderstorm building up, Alan thought.

He was unbuttoning his shirt and now he went
to the window to look out. "I thought at first it
might be a good thing to leave her with Helen, but
she can be a big help to you, sweetheart. She was
brought up here; you can leave a lot of the tasks
Helen has been telling you about in Libby's hands.
She is very capable."

Barbara stared at his broad back, and anger
began to stir in her heart. "I see," she said in an
expressionless voice. "And what do you propose *I*
should do with my day?"

He stripped his shirt off, and turning, tossed it on
a chair. "Whatever it is that English ladies do," he
replied. He smiled at her, consciously charming.
"Sew. Make music. Read."

Barbara didn't reply, but bent her head a little as
she brushed her hair. Alan looked at the long
lovely line of her neck, the luminous skin of her
bare shoulder and arm. "Take care of me," he
added, and at the changed note in his voice, she
looked up.

There came a flash of lightning from the window, and a second later they heard a rumble of
thunder. Alan promptly moved away from the
window.

"Don't you like a storm?" Barbara asked. Virginia's fierce electrical storms fascinated her.

"I respect them," he answered. He sat down to take off his boots. "Don't ever go near the windows in a lightning storm, sweetheart. It's not safe."

"Surely if one is in the house . . ." she protested.

"Ben Harrison's father was in the house. He had one of his little girls in his arms and the other by his side when he went to a window to close it in a thunderstorm. A bolt of lightning struck and they were all killed."

"Dear God." Barbara stopped brushing her hair and stared at him out of wide blue eyes.

He came across the room to stand in front of her. "I don't like to frighten you, Barbara, but lightning is a serious danger in this part of the world. Don't ever stay outdoors in a storm. Stay in the house and away from the windows. All right?"

She nodded in reply. The lightning flashed again and she jumped a little. He put his arms around her and held her against his bare chest. "Poor little girl," he said softly. "I've taken you so far from your home, to such a strange and different world."

These were precisely Barbara's own sorry-for-herself sentiments, but hearing them from Alan did not comfort her. Strangely enough, she began to feel irritated. "I'm not a child," she said tartly.

"Mmm. I never said that you were." He was running his hand caressingly up and down her narrow back. She could feel the sweet heaviness start to gather within her. He kissed her throat. "But I often think I was a selfish brute to bring you here," he murmured. "You weren't bred to this kind of life."

She tipped her head back to look up at him. Her hair streamed back from her face and over his arm. Her eyes were the color of midnight. "Are you sorry?" she asked challengingly.

He put his hands on either side of her face. "Not at all," he replied and, bending, began to kiss her mouth.

Later, long after he had fallen asleep, Barbara lay awake staring at the canopy over her head.

He had said he wasn't sorry he had married her. Was she sorry she had married him? If she could, would she leave Alan and go home to England?

The answer was immediate. No. As she lay next to the big strong body of her husband, she knew that no matter how difficult life in Virginia might be, still she would not wish to be anyone else's wife. To lie in another man's arms—no. No. No matter how hard the road, for her there would never be anyone but Alan. And if that was the case, then she must just learn to travel his road with him.

Cautiously she slipped out of bed and went over to the secretary where she had left the letter to her mother. How ashamed of her daughter Lady Abingdon would be, Barbara thought, as she picked up the pages. Lady Abingdon's road had not been an easy one either, but she had traveled it dauntlessly, her chin up, her courage always high. Barbara, at least, did not have to cope with a marriage that was dust and ashes in her mouth. She looked at the sleeping figure of her husband across the room.

She had so much more than her mother had ever had.

Slowly and deliberately Barbara tore her letter across once and then across once more. She would write a very different letter to Lady Abingdon tomorrow. And she would prove to Alan that he had married a woman every bit as capable as his sisters were.

On this heartening note, Barbara crept back into bed and went to sleep.

Eleven

As the cooler days of October set in, Barbara's energy increased and she began to take more of an initiative about her household. Shortly after Libby returned to Newland the two girls had a long talk. Barbara honestly confessed her own sense of inadequacy and asked Libby to help teach her the things she must know. Libby's initial hostility toward the English interloper disappeared and the two women found themselves actually becoming friends.

Tidewater Virginia was in general delighted that an earl's daughter had come to live in its midst, and in November the royal governor, Lord Dunmore, held an official welcoming ball at his residence in Williamsburg so that everyone of importance in the colony could meet Barbara. For the first time Barbara had a chance to meet many of the men whose names she had heard so often from Alan. She was the most curious about Colonel Washington. Alan always talked about him as if he were some sort of god, and Barbara had been prepared to dislike him on sight. She did not dislike him, however. As she said to Alan when he asked her her opinion, "He's not brilliant or amusing, yet there is something about him that is so impressive."

Alan had been gratified by her response. He did indeed admire Colonel Washington more than any other man he knew. He had also agreed to stand for his father's position in the House of Burgesses.

"I hope you don't mind," he said to Barbara. "It will mean our coming back to Williamsburg for the spring session."

Barbara was happy to reassure him that she did not mind at all. In her world, political office was an aristocratic responsibility. She would have found it odd if her husband had *not* run for the assembly that was to all intents and purposes the House of Commons for Virginia.

The Maxwells' brief sojourn in Williamsburg lifted Barbara's spirits and once they were back at Newland she threw herself into plantation work with an enthusiasm she had not been able to muster earlier. She set about training two of the housemaids to do fine sewing and put in hours of time in the cookhouse, an endeavor that resulted in a considerable improvement in their meals.

Her deepest concern during this period was the fact that she had not yet conceived. It was a worry she did not share with Alan, and he never reproached her, but when for the first time she was late with her monthlies and began to feel sick in the morning, she was delighted.

By Christmas she was certain she was with child. She harbored her secret zealously, her Christmas present for Alan, and as she went about her chores of preparing for a big Christmas house party of guests, her heart was lighter than it had been since first she arrived in Virginia.

They went to the small parish church in the morning and their guests started to arrive at Newland at noontime. Barbara had followed her mother's custom of decking the house with holly and, like Lady Abingdon, she had presented a small gift to each member of her household after church.

It was a clear, cold winter day and as she sat down to her enlarged dinner table, Barbara was happy. Her guests were relaxed and merry. She was finally going to have a baby. She met her husband's eyes across the length of the loaded table and smiled radiantly.

Once dinner was over, the entire party repaired to the Blue Parlor. The women had all clustered around the fire and the men around a bowl of hot punch, when the door opened and a newcomer

came into the room. Barbara recognized Will Mackenzie, one of Alan's seemingly endless stream of
cousins. Will was supposed to be having Christmas
at home with his large family, or so Barbara had
thought. She went over to greet him.

"But surely you brought your wife and the children?" she asked kindly.

"No, Lady Barbara." He looked at Alan. "I came
to give you a piece of news, Alan. I just got word
myself this morning at church."

"What?" Alan asked sharply.

"The Boston patriots dumped 3 whole shiploads
of English tea into the harbor. It happened on the
sixteenth."

Will had raised his voice slightly and now the
entire room crowded around him asking questions.

"It was the tea ship, *Dartmouth*," Will went on,
"and the two others that joined it. They had been
lying in the harbor for weeks. The Sons of Liberty
wouldn't let the tea land and Governor Hutchinson
wouldn't allow the ships to leave the harbor. The
customs officials, with the assistance of the Navy,
were going to forcibly land the cargo on the seventeenth. The night of the sixteenth a group of men
disguised as Indians boarded the ships and threw
all the tea overboard."

In the middle of the clamor around him, Alan
alone was silent. Gradually, as the talk died down,
the entire company turned to him.

"What do you think this will mean, Alan?" Will Mackenzie asked urgently.

Barbara glanced slowly around the group who stood waiting for Alan's reply. It was odd, she thought. Her husband was one of the youngest men present and yet they had all turned to him. She felt suddenly and profoundly uneasy.

Alan looked around the group of his friends and kinsmen as well. "I think," he replied very soberly, "that the time is coming when the rest of the colonies are going to have to stand behind Boston."

Barbara could feel herself stiffening. Beside her Edmund Brandon spoke up in his quiet way. "I don't see that at all, Alan. Just because an unruly mob has acted irresponsibly and destroyed the king's property is no reason for the rest of us to get involved in the quarrel."

"The confrontation was forced on Boston, Edmund." Alan's voice was quiet as well. "The governors of New York, Pennsylvania, and South Carolina, where the tea was also landed, did not insist that the duty be paid. Governor Hutchinson of Massachusetts did. It was a mistake on his part. He should have foreseen the outcome."

"Certainly he should have known the sort of men he was dealing with," said Edmund. "But one has to draw the line somewhere, Alan." Edmund looked around at the other men. "As a royal governor, charged with upholding the king's law, he really had no choice."

"The men of Boston had no choice either," said Francis Morgan, one of Alan's cousins, sharply.

"Francis is right." Alan's hawklike face looked grim. "A clash was inevitable. Now we must wait and see what Lord North's government does. The next move belongs to them." He met his wife's troubled eyes and his face relaxed into a smile. "Will you play for us, sweetheart?" he asked. "Let's all remember that this is Christmas Day."

Barbara moved to the instrument and in a short time the company had joined together in song. But a pall had been cast on the day.

That night Barbara lay awake by herself in bed. Alan and several other men had been talking quietly in his office for hours and still he had not come to bed. Barbara was seething. Here it was, Christmas Day, she was finally going to have a baby, and all he could think about was this wretched mob in Boston.

Damn Boston, Barbara thought crossly. And damn the tea, too. Between them they had thoroughly spoiled her Christmas.

She was asleep long before Alan came to bed.

In April Lady Dunmore and her six children arrived in Virginia to join the earl. All of the families who resided in the vicinity of Williamsburg traveled to the capital to welcome the royal governor's lady.

"I hope she's an improvement on her husband," Barbara remarked to Alan as they made ready to join the governor and his family at the palace for dinner.

"Well, we're among the first to get a chance to find out," Alan replied with slow amusement. "There are distinct advantages to having an earl's daughter for a wife."

"Who else will be there this evening?" Barbara asked curiously.

"The councillors and their wives. Peyton Randolph was invited as well." Peyton Randolph was the speaker of the House of Burgesses.

Barbara paused. "Aren't the Harrisons to be there? Or the Hills?"

"No."

"I see." Barbara clasped a necklace around her throat.

"Virginians aren't petty-minded, however," Alan said cheerfully as he put on his coat. "The House of Burgesses is going to vote to give a ball in Lady Dunmore's honor. After all, the governor gave one for you. These wives and daughters of earls, you know, demand a grand gesture."

"You're so amusing," Barbara said, half-laughing, half-annoyed. "Button your coat and we'll go and see this earl's wife for ourselves."

As the House of Burgesses was to begin its session in May, Barbara remained in Williamsburg. Alan traveled back to Newland a few times, but he wanted Barbara to do as little traveling as possible.

She was feeling well and still looking slim enough with her full skirts cut to hide her increasing figure, but he knew what a bad traveler she was under the best of circumstances.

Barbara found herself rather amused by the commotion Virginia was making over Lady Dunmore. For people who were always complaining about the English, she thought, they certainly made a fuss over a title. They loved using her own. "Lady Barbara" commanded far more attention and respect than mere "Mrs. Maxwell" would have done.

When the House of Burgesses formally met in May, the small capital became the scene of a busy social season. There were dinners and balls. The racetrack and the theater both opened and there were subscription dances held in the Apollo Room of the Raleigh Tavern.

The capital city of Virginia was a tiny little town that was like nothing with which Barbara was familiar. The Governor's Palace, the most imposing building in town, was smaller than Carrington and the homes of the townspeople and the planters were miniature cottages in Barbara's eyes.

But it was a pretty town, with its pink brick public buildings and its green-and-white wooden houses. The Maxwell house was typical of the usual architecture—it was long and low and the second floor was merely an attic with a series of dormer windows. The master bedroom was on the first floor, and Libby slept in one of the upstairs bedrooms under the roof.

Barbara was enjoying herself, however. Virginia hospitality had rather dismayed her when she first arrived in the colony, but she had come to appreciate the real kindness of the people among whom she had married. They were far simpler than their English counterparts. The women were interested in their homes and their children. There was virtually no gossip about marital infidelity.

She thought she was more of a mystery to them than they to her. She was, as Alan had once teased her, a Personage for them and as such she was accorded a certain degree of reverence. She was deferred to on social occasions and her opinion was often solicited in matters of taste.

Alan found this amusing. "The earl's daughter," he called her. Barbara, who was enjoying her pre-eminence, did not find him funny.

The date for the House of Burgesses' welcoming ball for Lady Dunmore was set, and Barbara, in her position as arbitress of what would be proper for an earl's wife, had been asked to head up the arrangements. She was happily submerged in her plans when news came from Massachusetts that as of June 1 the port of Boston was to be closed.

Twelve

It was called the Boston Port Bill and it had been signed by the king at the end of March. It mandated that the port of Boston be closed on June 1 until such time as compensation for the lost tea be paid to the East India Company.

"The whole port is closed," Alan told his wife and his sister as he made a brief visit home before repairing to an impromptu meeting at the Raleigh Tavern. "Even the ferries are shut down. The city can be supplied only across the narrow neck of land by Roxbury. I reckon the government thinks to starve Boston into submission."

"They never will!" said Libby fiercely.

But Alan was looking at his wife. "Five regiments of British troops are being sent to garrison Boston, and the fleet has been ordered to lie in the harbor."

Barbara was very pale. "I fear the government is serious about this tax on tea, Alan. If they are sending troops . . ."

"I believe they are very serious, Barbara. But then, so are we."

Barbara's white face set. "What can you do, Alan? If the king is prepared to commit troops to enforce the law? All you can do is continue to boycott the tea."

Alan's voice was gentle. "I reckon it's gone beyond that, sweetheart." He kissed her cheek. "I'm late. Don't wait up for me." He touched his sister's shoulder and was gone.

"They're fools if they get involved in this!" Barbara said to Libby. "What has Virginia got to do with Boston, for God's sake?"

"If it could happen to Boston, Barbara, it could happen to us." Libby's smooth olive face was very grave.

"Nonsense. Virginians aren't the Boston mob— masquerading as Indians! It's ridiculous."

"A whole town being deprived of its livelihood is not ridiculous, Barbara. It's tyranny."

Barbara drew a deep, slow breath. "Well, we aren't going to do any good just standing around here, Libby. I am going to see about the flowers for Lady Dunmore's ball. Do you wish to come with me?"

After a brief hesitation, Libby agreed.

The following day Barbara received a letter from her mother. Lady Abingdon wrote in great detail about the passage of the Boston Port Bill. It seemed there was also a series of other bills pending against Boston, of which the colonists were as yet unaware.

Lady Abingdon also had one other piece of interesting news. Lieutenant Harry Wharton was among the British troops posted to Boston.

"Harry has been fretting himself to death since you left," Lady Abingdon wrote. "There is no money to purchase him a captaincy, so he has determined the only way to win advancement is through active duty. I don't scruple to add that I think your being in America was an added incentive. Of course, Virginia is a long way from Boston."

Barbara sat smoothing the pages of her letter and staring into the fire. Her mother's words had only increased her uneasiness. It seemed to her that they had no idea at home of the temper of people in America. She looked down at her letter again.

"Lord Sandwich says that the colonies are the great farms of the public and the colonists our tenants. It is time, he feels, to keep them to the terms of their leases. And that, my love, is the prevailing sentiment in the government. This rash action of dumping the tea has put the king out of all patience. He means to bring Boston to heel."

Barbara folded up her letter and put it away in her drawer. She had no intention of showing it to Alan. The government was considering suspending Boston's constitution and putting it under the authority of a military governor. Good God—if Alan ever heard that!

"It's so stupid," Barbara said passionately, standing alone in her bedroom. "They are all being so stupid."

Barbara was visiting with Lady Dunmore on the afternoon of May 25. The two ladies were chatting comfortably over refreshments when the governor came into the room, visibly upset.

"They have gone too far," he said to his wife. "Really, this is just too much to bear."

"What has happened, my dear?" Lady Dunmore asked calmly. Lord Dunmore's face was as red as his velvet jacket.

"The Burgesses have just voted a day of fasting, humiliation, and prayer, to be observed throughout the colony on June 1—the day the Boston Port Bill goes into effect."

Barbara could feel herself go pale. "Surely that is not so very terrible, Lord Dunmore?" she asked gently. "A day of prayer, after all."

"Hah. And what is the purpose of this day of

prayer, madam? Here! Read it for yourself." And the earl shoved a paper into Barbara's hands.

"To implore the divine interposition for averting the heavy calamity which threatens the destruction of our civil rights and the evils of civil war," she read out slowly.

"Civil war! Did you hear that, Lady Dunmore?" her husband said indignantly. "They are trying to threaten me."

"I'm sure they don't mean to do that, Lord Dunmore," Barbara began placatingly, but the royal governor turned on her.

"I don't scruple to say that *your* husband has been one of the leaders in this ... this impertinence, Lady Barbara. Well, I won't have it. I tell you I will not have it. I have summoned the Burgesses to meet me in the council chamber."

"What are you going to do, my lord?" his wife asked placidly.

"I am going to dissolve them. That will stop any more of this nonsense."

The two ladies sat silently after the royal governor had left. Then Lady Dunmore said pleasantly, "What medicine do you find most efficacious for fever, my dear? I understand there is a great deal of it here in the summer."

Barbara replied automatically, but her mind was on the drama that was being played out across town in the council chamber of the capitol.

Would they accept dissolution? Of course, they

would have to, she told herself. They could not continue to sit in defiance of the governor's order. They had no quarrel with Lord Dunmore, after all.

Barbara was deeply disquieted when she returned home to find that Alan was not there. Nor did he come home for dinner. By then, of course, the entire town was aware that the House of Burgesses had accepted the governor's dismissal gravely and had retired to the Raleigh Tavern, where they were still in session.

Alan did not come home until very late that night. Barbara waited up for him, her heart heavy with unrest and fear. She sent the servants and Libby to bed and sat by the fire in the parlor, a piece of sewing in her hand. She had just put another log on the fire when she heard the front door open and Alan came in.

He was surprised to see her. "Barbara! Do you know how late it is?" He crossed to stand next to her by the fire.

It had begun to rain and his coat and boots were wet. He took his hat off and threw it on a chair. He did not look at all tired. Barbara felt suddenly overwhelmed by his vitality. How could she expect to keep him out of things?

"I might ask you the same question," she replied quietly. She was being very careful to keep her voice neutral. "I was with Lady Dunmore when the governor came in to say he was going to dissolve the assembly," she added. "He was exceedingly angry."

Alan smiled ruefully, sat down in a chair, and stretched his boots toward the fire. "I reckon he was."

Barbara looked down at her sewing. She had begun to embroider baby clothes. The child within her moved, as if sensing his mother's disquiet. She looked up again at her husband. His face was still tanned even though he had been away from the plantation for over a month. "What is going to happen?" she asked.

"I reckon you know we all met at the Raleigh." Barbara nodded. Alan's dark eyes were steady on her face. "Well, we will observe that day of fasting and prayer."

"I see."

"And we have adopted another boycott association. If the English merchants cannot sell their products to the colonies, they may well exert more pressure on the government to lift the tax than we can."

Barbara began to feel a spark of hope. "I've always thought boycotting was a very effective measure. It's legal and it's not violent. After all, no one can *make* you buy something you don't want to buy."

"That's true." Alan leaned over and took her hands. "You're freezing, sweetheart. You shouldn't be sitting here like this." He rose and pulled her to her feet. With his lips against her temple he murmured, "Come to bed."

She let him walk her toward the hall. "What about Lady Dunmore's ball?"

"We'll still have your ball." He sounded amused. "Having invited the lady, we can scarcely go back on our invitation now."

His arm was around her. Barbara relaxed into the strength of his body as he guided her across the hall. If they were going to have the ball after all, it couldn't be so serious a division.

Once in their bedroom she let Alan undress her and tuck her into bed. As she curled up on her pillow, she asked sleepily, "You didn't decide on anything else? Just the boycott?"

He was sitting on a chair pulling off his boots. "Well, we're going to call for a general congress of all the colonies to meet in September in Philadelphia. It's time we all got together to decide on a united course of action." Barbara's eyes opened wide. Alan's soft drawl came to her from across the bedroom. "It's not just Boston that has a stake in this situation, Barbara. It's all of us."

Barbara sat up. "I don't see that, Alan. There has been trouble in Boston for years. Now they want to drag the rest of the colonies into their quarrel. *They* destroyed the tea, let them cope with the consequences."

Alan came to sit beside her on the bed. "But don't you see, sweetheart, that is exactly the attitude Britain wants to arouse in us by this bill? They close Boston's port and hope that Providence and New York and Philadelphia will be delighted to steal some of her vast sea trade, that Salem and Marblehead will want to usurp her preeminence in government, that Virginia and Maryland and the Carolinas will denounce the New Englanders as hotheads and troublemakers."

"Well," said Barbara, "they are."

There was a thin deep line between his brows. "No. They are Americans. We are—all of us—Americans. And Britain's plan to divide and conquer will not succeed, Barbara. Already food is pouring into Boston overland from the surrounding area. Virginia has pledged to send food and clothing, as have most of the other colonies."

Barbara stared into her husband's dark, serious face. "I'm so afraid, Alan," she whispered. "What is going to happen?"

He took her into his arms and rested his cheek against her hair. His face, which she could not see, was bleak. We are all Americans, he had said to her. But Barbara was not an American. How could he possibly expect her to understand the forces that were at work now in the colonies? How could he expect her to travel his road?

He should never have married her.

He did not see how he could live without her.

She was six months gone with child.

He rubbed his cheek against her hair. "A united

front among the colonies is just what will bring the government to its senses," he said soothingly. "When Lord North sees that he cannot in fact divide and conquer, that he will have to deal with all of us, then we will be able to talk sensibly."

Barbara nestled her cheek into his shoulder. "Do you really think so?"

He did not.

"Of course I do," he replied. He put his hands on her shoulders and smiled down at her, his dark face suddenly brilliant with warmth and humor. "We wouldn't be giving a reception for the royal governor's wife if we were expecting any serious trouble, now, would we?"

The shadowed look around her eyes lifted. "I suppose not."

He kissed her temple and, standing up, began to unbutton his shirt. "How are the arrangements for the great affair coming along?" he asked easily.

Barbara responded and they continued to talk in low voices about the ball until Alan was undressed and in bed beside her. He blew out the candle and gathered her close.

She had surprised him this last half-year, this fragile-looking English girl he had married. After an initial period of adjustment, she had taken hold at Newland with amazing competence. Their life together had gone much more smoothly than Alan had ever anticipated. Barbara appeared genuinely interested in the running of the plantation and he often found himself discussing ideas for improvements with her and listening seriously in return to her own ideas and suggestions.

He did not think she fully realized the precariousness of the political situation. He felt her slender, light bones lying so trustingly against him and in the darkness his mouth had a distinctly grim set to it. He wanted very much to keep her safe and he was afraid that was going to prove impossible.

The ball for Lady Dunmore was successful in that everything Barbara had arranged went like clockwork. The food was excellent, the music lively, the company elegant and distinguished. The health of the king was drunk with perfect courtesy by all present.

Barbara was not dancing and spent the evening accepting the compliments of a vast number of people, all of whom had kind things to say about her arrangements.

"Lady Dunmore and her daughters are very pleased," Edmund Brandon said to Barbara as he sat down beside her for a moment halfway through the evening.

"I'm glad." Barbara looked gravely at her brother-in-law. "You look tired, Edmund," she said softly.

"It's this news from Boston. It has greatly discouraged me."

Barbara's mouth set. "I know. It's all so *stupid*, Edmund. All for a threepence tax. Why, at home the tax is a shilling! But one can't talk to Alan on this subject."

Her brother-in-law looked directly into her eyes. "I think you ought talk to him, Barbara. Perhaps he'll listen to you." Edmund smiled a little wearily. "He certainly isn't listening to me."

Barbara's dark blue eyes were troubled. "Why on earth would you think Alan might listen to me, Edmund?"

His thin face lit with its attractive smile. "Because he adores you, of course."

Barbara looked down at her hands in her lap. "Is there really cause for concern?"

"I think so. You must look out for your child's future, Barbara. Alan stands to lose a great deal if he takes the wrong side now." He stared out at the crowded dance floor. "It's all very well for fellows like Patrick Henry, who have no financial stake at risk, to go about making fiery speeches. But Alan is risking not only his life but also the impoverishment of his entire family."

"I hadn't thought of that," Barbara replied slowly.

"I don't wish to alarm you unduly, Barbara, but I do think it's time to exert your influence."

After Edmund had left her, Barbara sat alone for a few minutes, the serene mask of her face utterly at variance with the turmoil in her heart. She looked across the room to the corner where her husband stood talking to three other men. She had known immediately where to look for him. One always knew where Alan was in a room. What it was in him that drew one's attention, she didn't understand, but wherever he was, people turned to him.

There was a faint frown between her brows as she stared across the dance floor at Alan, and Helen, coming up to Barbara, asked with concern, "Are you feeling all right, Barbara?"

Barbara looked up at her sister-in-law and made an effort to smile. "I'm fine, Helen."

Helen sat down in the chair recently vacated by her husband. She was looking very charming in a purple *robe à l'anglaise* with a square décolletage and a flounced petticoat. "You *look* wonderful," she said now to Barbara. "You're blooming like an English rose."

Barbara smiled. " 'Blooming' is certainly the right word," she said, looking down at her figure ruefully. Her own dress was a discreet pale blue. "Helen, who is that man dancing with Libby? She seems to be spending a great deal of time with him this evening."

Helen looked out at the dancing couples. "Oh, that's George Wythe's new protégé. His name is Charles Dwight."

"Does he reside in Williamsburg?"

"At the present time, yes. He's originally from the western part of the state. He's studying law with Mr. Wythe. Edmund has met him several times and thinks he's quite brilliant."

Barbara looked with greater interest at the tall,

slender young man who was leading Libby down the dance. "Really? Is he a younger son or does he have prospects of coming into the family property?"

Helen smiled. "There is no family property, Barbara. Mr. Dwight's father came to Virginia as an indentured servant."

Barbara made a conscious effort to keep her face expressionless. "Indeed?" she said after a pause. "How interesting."

At that Helen laughed. "Edmund likes him. He says he will do very well at the law."

Barbara changed the subject. "Edmund seems to be worried about the political situation."

Helen suddenly looked five years older. "I know. He spent all the formative years of his life in England, Barbara. This . . . hostility is very hard on him."

"Oh, surely not hostility," Barbara said quickly.

"Not on the part of men like Peyton Randolph or Ben Harrison, certainly. But talk to Richard Henry Lee or Patrick Henry and it's quite another story."

Barbara forced herself to breathe slowly. "And where does Alan stand?"

"Alan stands with Boston. Unfortunately. He's younger than most of the men in the House of Burgesses and I hoped that would keep him out of a position of leadership. But they elected him to the Committee of Correspondence the other day. Colonel Washington proposed him—he thinks very highly of Alan."

"Well, Alan thinks Colonel Washington can walk on water," Barbara returned tartly.

"I know." Helen sighed.

"England is sending five regiments to Boston, Helen," Barbara said urgently. "They pulled troops out of Ireland to do it. My mother has written that the king is determined to make the colonies accept this tax."

Helen closed her eyes. "Men," she said. "How can they be so stupid?"

"I don't know," Barbara replied bitterly, "but it seems as if no one will listen to reason." She felt her child move restlessly within her.

"Here comes Lord Dunmore," Helen said, and both ladies rose to curtsy to the royal governor.

Thirteen

Barbara sat in the relative coolness of the Blue Parlor and sewed. Outside the house the humid August air hung heavy on the ground and Barbara felt herself to be as heavy and as leaden as the weather. Even the effort of pushing her needle through the fine material of the baby garment she was embroidering seemed too much.

She couldn't remember what it was like to be free and supple and light.

Soon now, she thought. There was not much longer to wait.

She rested her hands on her stomach and sat staring blindly in front of her.

Her whole family would be home at Carrington

for August. Barbara thought of the downs, of the cool rolling turf, the breeze off the Channel. She thought of her mother's hands—so much more capable than her own. She could see them quite clearly—Lady Abingdon's strong, well-tended hands, with the emerald ring she always wore on her little finger.

Mother. The ache in Barbara's throat was too great. She opened her eyes wide and forced back the tears.

The baby's coming was so close and Mother was so far away. Barbara got laboriously to her feet and went through the door to the Green Parlor that looked out over the river. She stared out the window at the James and imagined that a ship was pulling alongside the wharf, that Mother was getting off. . . .

"Lady Barbara." It was the rich, thick voice of Solomon, their butler. "Jassy's been took sick, ma'am. Seems to be the same thing what Betty had last week."

Barbara turned from the window. "Oh dear. Does she have a fever, Solomon?"

"I thinks so, ma'am."

Barbara moved toilsomely to the door. "I'll get out the medicine, Solomon. Come along. . . ."

Alan had been away in Williamsburg for over a week, attending a meeting of the dissolved House of Burgesses, which the members, sitting in defiance of the royal governor, had renamed the Virginia Convention. Edmund Brandon was the other delegate from Charles City County, and while the two men were gone, Helen had come to stay with Barbara.

As Robert had accompanied his brother to Williamsburg, Libby, Helen, and Barbara were the only three around the table for dinner at three-thirty that afternoon. After they had eaten, Helen insisted that Barbara lie down for a rest. She fell asleep on her bed and dreamed of home. She awoke at six with a pain in her back. The maid who had been attending her since Anna had gone home told her that the master had returned.

Barbara went downstairs to the Blue Parlor to greet her husband and Edmund and Robert. Alan smiled and kissed her cheek but the eyes that scanned her face were anxious. Solomon brought in some rum punch and Alan said, "There's a breeze off the river now. Let's go down to the summerhouse." He gave his wife his arm and they walked slowly down the graveled path toward the river.

"Well, what happened?" Helen asked after they were all seated. "Who is going to Philadelphia?"

"Whom you would expect, of course," Alan replied. "Colonel Washington. Peyton Randolph and Richard Henry Lee and Patrick Henry and Ben Harrison. Oh . . . and Edmund Pendleton too."

"Colonel Washington wanted to propose Alan's

name," Robert said. His fine-featured fair face was lit with adoration as he gazed at his big brother.

Barbara's fingers tightened on the arm of her chair and in a minute Alan's big warm hand engulfed hers in a comforting gesture.

"I said no. I wouldn't have been elected anyway—all those men are far better known than I. And besides"—he gave his wife his most engaging smile—"I have reason to want to be at home these days."

Barbara smiled back faintly and shifted slightly in her chair.

"Well, I will agree with this congress if the purpose is to petition the throne from the colonies as a whole," Edmund said. "Further than that I am not prepared to go."

"Oh, Edmund, we have been petitioning the king for years." Libby's vivid face was bright with impatience. "And to what end, after all? Has the king or his government ever once responded? You know they haven't."

"Still," said Edmund doggedly, "we must continue to try."

"General Gage has been ruling Boston like a military camp," put in Robert. "The citizens are forced to have foreign troops quartered in their homes. Their liberties and livelihood are under systematic attack. You know this is so, Edmund! How can you be so . . . so spineless."

"General Gage has been surprisingly moderate,"

Edmund said. He was speaking to Alan, not to Robert or Libby. "He could have had all the Massachusetts leaders arrested and sent to England for trial. He has not done that."

"General Gage does not want to provoke an outbreak of hostilities," Alan replied gently. "He has only five regiments in Boston."

"Only five! My God, Alan, five regiments of the best-trained troops in the world! What have we to oppose them with, for God's sake?"

"Gage asked for more." Alan's face was calm. "He asked for more—Mr. Fox wrote me the details. General Gage can't garrison America with five regiments, and he knows it."

"He can certainly garrison Boston."

"Yes, but that is just the point of this congress, Edmund. We must let Britain know that it is not just Boston she must deal with. It is our only hope of winning concessions from the government."

Edmund's thin, intelligent face looked very bleak. "And if we don't win those concessions, Alan? What then?"

There was a moment of heavy silence as they all looked at Alan. It was as if the fate of the world hung on his next words, Barbara thought a little hysterically. Suddenly the ache that had been in her back seemed to increase and concentrate and a hard pain shot all through her abdomen. She cried out in surprise and pain and instantly her family were on their feet and surrounding her. Alan picked her up and carried her into the house and Robert went for the midwife.

Five hours later Barbara's son was born.

From the moment they first placed her child in her arms, Barbara felt a peace and a joy that she had not known since her own childhood. The little downy head nestling under her chin was so tender, the little mouth against her breast sent such warmth into her heart. Her love for Alan had always been fraught with uncertainty and tossed with passion. But this little one . . . Holding him in her arms, nursing him, bathing him, watching him as he slept— for the first time since she had come to Virginia, Barbara felt as if she tasted real joy, real peace.

And her feelings for her child spread and encompassed the land into which he had been born. This plantation of Newland—his father's home, his grandfather's home, one day it would be his—sixteen thousand acres of fine Tidewater land. Centuries of dynastic instinct had been bred into Lady Barbara Carr and with the birth of her son that instinct, centered for so long on her own childhood home, changed its course and settled in Virginia.

The baby was christened Ian Richard George Maxwell and a week after the christening Alan received a letter from his father informing the family that he had married again.

Barbara was more interested in the details of her father-in-law's marriage than Alan. When she learned that Mr. Maxwell's new wife was but thirty-three and had two children from a previous marriage, her heart sank.

Alan couldn't understand why she was so distressed.

"But, don't you see, Alan," she said, "it's quite likely now that he'll have more children."

"Quite possibly." Alan was clearly indifferent as to whether he did or did not. "I think it's a good thing he got married, sweetheart. I think he was lonely in England. A wife will be good for him."

Barbara didn't reply. In the face of such generosity of spirit, what could she say? But she had hoped to see Mr. Maxwell's remaining fortune come into the hands of her son.

Unlike most of the other planters they knew, Alan was not in debt. His father had paid off their English factor and since they had returned to Virginia, Alan had had no dealings that were not local. They had an abundance of all that was necessary to live comfortably, but undoubtedly cash was short. Cash was always short in Virginia, Barbara had learned, which was why a little inheritance would have been so nice. But she was too happy to worry about Mr. Maxwell's new wife for very long.

Eight weeks after the baby was born, Alan went into Williamsburg to learn what news he could of the deliberations in Philadelphia. He was gone a week and Barbara found herself missing him fiercely.

They had not made love for months. The heaviness of the baby had drained all passion out of her, but now, in Alan's absence, she felt the longing in her body and blood begin to stir again.

It was after dark when Alan finally arrived home. There had been a fine mist falling for a half-hour and his coat and boots were damp. Barbara was sitting by herself in the Blue Parlor when he came in. He came over and stood before her chair. "Where's Libby?" he asked.

"Her stomach felt a bit upset this afternoon. She went to bed early." Standing in front of her like this, he blocked her whole view of the room. Her head tilted far back to look up at his face. "How was your trip?"

He shrugged. He had the widest shoulders. . . . "All right, I reckon. There isn't much news yet. How is the baby?"

"Very well."

He had not given her his usual kiss on the cheek. His eyes on her face were dark and hooded. "And you?" he asked.

Suddenly her whole body was trembling. She didn't answer but stared up at him, her own eyes a deep midnight blue. The air between them was charged with sexual tension.

He put his hands on her arms and drew her to her feet. He had not smiled since he came into the room. "Christ," he said, "but it's been a long wait."

She swayed slightly and his arms came around her. "Barbara," he said, and she raised her head.

His kiss burned her, scorched her, but the fire in her blood answered to it and she arched up against him, the whole length of her slender body pressed along his.

"Upstairs," he said in her ear, and she nodded.

He was so hungry for her. And that hunger awoke a like response in her. There had always been passion between them, but this went beyond anything they had known before. It seemed the more Alan wanted of her, the more she had to give. Deeper and deeper, stronger and stronger, until there was nothing left of either of them that did not belong to the other.

They fell asleep wrapped in each other's arms.

She had to get up at two oclock to feed the baby, and when she came back to bed, Alan was awake. He rolled over and buried his face in her throat. "The whole time I was in Williamsburg, I did nothing but think of you."

She put her hand on his bare shoulder and felt the hard muscle under the smooth warm skin. "I've not been much of a wife to you lately, have I?"

His black head moved in a negative motion. "I know it hasn't been easy for you—so far from your home."

She gazed over his head toward the window. "This is my home now."

He raised himself on an elbow to look into her face. "I wish you could really feel that, sweetheart."

"But I do." The rain had stopped and moonlight from the window dimly illuminated their faces. "It was having Ian, I think," she tried to explain. "It's as though now I too am linked to this place—this land. My blood as well as yours." She smiled a little ruefully. "Am I making any sense?"

"A little." A strand of brown hair had caught in her lashes and he brushed it away. She had put on her nightgown when she got up to feed the baby and her long slender neck looked like the fragile stem of a flower as it rose out of the fine white cotton. All he knew at the moment was that he had got her back, that there were bottomless depths of delight in her and that he could not get enough. Her loose hair was spilled over the pillow. Bending his head, he began to kiss her. When he felt her response, he groaned and rolled so that her body was underneath his. "Barbara," he said hoarsely, and she whimpered a little in response.

It was a long, mild autumn and Barbara was happy. She was no longer homesick. Newland was no longer a strange and frightening world; its gardens and flowers and teeming, busy houses were all familiar now, comfortable and ordinary. Libby and Robert were like her own sister and brother. She had her baby.

Most of all, she had Alan. All her thoughts and

joys and deepest emotions were bound up with him. She could feel her love for him flowing deeply, strongly, fearlessly, unimpeded by the wariness, the loneliness, the strangeness of her first year at Newland. She loved him with all the passion and the possessiveness that was inherent in her nature and she knew that his feeling for her was as deep. He was the very focal point of her existence.

The political situation seemed calmer to her than it had since she arrived in Virginia. The Continental Congress had done nothing more than send another petition to the king and resolve to widen its boycott efforts. Life seemed to be perfectly tranquil and so it came as a distinct shock to her when Edmund Brandon came to see them in December to tell them that he and his family were returning to England.

"Alan will understand," Edmund said, and turned to look at his brother-in-law. The three of them and Libby were seated around the fire in the Green Parlor.

"I am sorry, Edmund," Alan said simply. "I know this is hard for you."

"Yes." Edmund looked haggard but calm. "There is no place left for moderation, Alan, no place for the middle ground. The time has come to take sides—for survival one is being forced to take sides. I cannot join the cabal around Lord Dunmore, but neither can I follow you, my friend. So, like the Fairfaxes, I am returning to England.''

"But what are you talking about, Edmund?" Barbara's voice was higher than normal. "What is all this about choosing sides? Everything has been so quiet lately!"

Edmund looked at her. "Has it, Barbara? Do you know that your husband has been drilling militia over near Burton's Crossing?"

The blood drained from Barbara's face. She turned to look at Alan. His face was grim. He was not looking at her but at Edmund.

"Was that necessary?" he asked in a hard, clipped voice.

"How long do you think you can hide it from her, Alan? The whole county knows."

"Edmund, stop it!" It was Libby. Barbara realized, with painful astonishment, that Libby knew all about it. Without another word, she rose and left the room.

The three left behind sat in heavy silence for a minute, then Libby rose also. "I'll go make sure she's all right," she said, and left to follow Barbara.

"I'm sorry, Alan," Edmund said bleakly. "Perhaps I was wrong to say that. But you can't go on fooling her forever."

"She's been happy," Alan replied with equal bleakness. "God knows, the least I could give her was a few months of happiness."

Edmund stood up, paced to the fire and back. He did this twice before stopping at last and turning to look at his brother-in-law. "You're a fool, Alan. I've seen that ragtag collection you call a militia. Do you really think that with fellows like that you are going to be able to fight the greatest nation and the best army in the world?"

Alan's face set. "If the mind of the country is behind us, yes."

Edmund swore.

Alan rubbed his forehead. "I'm sorry, Edmund. I'm sorry you feel you must go."

Edmund took a deep breath. "I feel so angry about all this. Angry and bitter and trapped. But I cannot stay here and swim against the tide. It's best that I go. Helen agrees with me."

"You will go to relatives?"

"Yes."

"I shall look after Stanley for you, Edmund."

"Thank you, Alan." He gestured toward the door. "I'm sorry about Barbara."

Alan sighed. "No, you were right. She had to find out sometime." He rubbed his temple as though there was a pain there. "I think she'll understand. But it will make her unhappy."

"This whole situation is just *bloody*." There was concentrated passion in Edmund's voice and Alan went to his brother-in-law and reached a quick, hard arm around his slender shoulders.

"Let me know what I can do."

"Yes. I will. Good-bye, then, Alan. I'd better get home to Helen."

Alan stood at the bottom of the stairs for a long minute before he squared his shoulders and went on up to his wife's room.

Fourteen

Barbara was standing at the window, her back to the room, a slender, delicate figure in her full blue skirt. His two hands could span her waist, Alan found himself thinking. She appeared to be looking out at the river. Poor little girl, he thought pityingly, how can I make this easier for her?

"Barbara?" he said softly.

She turned to look at him and Alan instinctively took a step backward. He had been prepared for pain and sorrow. Barbara's face was wild with anger.

"How dare you do this to me?" she said. Her low voice was shaking. "How *dare* you? Go behind my back like this—the whole county knows, Edmund said! But not your wife."

Alan realized his mouth was open. He closed it firmly and came into the room. "Sweetheart," he said. "I didn't want to upset you."

"Upset me? Are you insane, Alan? Did you think I would never find out?"

The transformation of that serene face utterly astounded him. "You were so happy," he said. "I didn't want to take that away from you."

Barbara's narrow, elegant nostrils were white with temper. "Drilling militia," she said. "You fool."

Alan began to feel his own temper rising. "It is merely a precaution," he said in a consciously quiet voice. "Given the circumstances, it's well to be prepared."

"Prepared for what?" Barbara flashed. "War? Do you really think you have a prayer of defeating the British Army, Alan? You're a planter, not a soldier. Soldiering is a profession—and it's not yours. Nor is it anyone's profession in this colony. What do you expect to do, you and your fellow farmers? What in God's name do you expect to do against the best-trained troops in the world?"

There were two thin lines at the corners of Alan's mouth. Barbara saw them and knew he was getting angry. "We expect to beat them," he drawled.

There was a tense pause while they both stared at each other. Then, "Do you know what *I* expect if this should ever come to pass?" Barbara asked bitterly. "I expect you to be either killed or arrested for treason. Either way, my son will have no father and I no husband. This plantation will be lost . . ."

Her voice had begun to shake and she turned away abruptly to look out the window. "Have you thought about what you are risking?" she asked him over her shoulder.

"Yes." His voice was very steady. "And I have thought, too, that the most important thing I can do for my son is to safeguard his liberties."

"Liberties!" Barbara angrily dashed a tear away and turned back to face him again. "We're not talking about liberties, Alan. We're talking about a bloody threepence tax on tea!"

"You don't understand," he began patiently.

"No, I don't. I'm only a simple woman, thank God, who doesn't think it necessary to take up guns for the 'principle' behind a little tax."

"Barbara, you're not being reasonable."

"Get out!" She stamped her foot. "Get out of here, Alan Maxwell, before I say something I might regret."

After a brief hesitation, Alan went.

Downstairs he met his sister. "How is Barbara?" Libby asked cautiously.

"I thought she was about to throw something at me, so I got out," Alan replied with an attempt at humor.

"I've never seen Barbara angry," Libby said in an awestricken voice. "She is always so . . . controlled."

"Well, on the subject of my drilling militia she is not controlled at all." Alan sighed. "I reckon it's unreasonable for us to expect her to have the same view of things we do, Libby." He patted her shoulder. "I'm going out for a while."

"But, Alan, it's raining."

Alan shrugged. "I'll be back later." He grinned. "Give Barbara a chance to settle down."

Libby laughed. "Yes, I see what you mean."

As Alan rode down the muddy road toward Moreland, however, his thoughts were not at all humorous.

Christ, but she had been angry!

He had not expected that from her. He had not expected ever to have her oppose him, really seriously oppose him. His Barbara—so serene, so gracious, so yielding.

She had shouted at him.

Alan pulled his hat down further over his forehead and hunched his shoulders against the cold rain. How was he going to convince her to see things his way?"

It was late in the evening when Alan returned to Newland. Barbara was in bed when he came in, dripping wet.

She looked up from her book. "You won't last to be cannon fodder if you stand around like that," she said. "Pneumonia will get you first."

He stared at her. Her smooth brown hair was

done in a thick plait that lay over her shoulder. Her face was like a Madonna's. "I never knew you could be such a shrew," he said.

Her dark blue eyes blazed at him. "I never had cause before," she replied shortly, and went back to her book.

Alan began to undress in front of the fire. He pulled off his boots and looked over at his wife. She appeared to be completely absorbed in her book. He unbuttoned his shirt and laid it on a chair. Then, bare-chested and in stocking feet, he went over to the bed.

"Barbara, you're being foolish," he began.

She looked up at him. "Don't touch me."

Quite suddenly he was angry. "What do you mean, 'don't touch me'? You're my wife." He sat down on the bed. Barbara moved as if she would get up, and his hand shot out to grab her arm.

"Are you contemplating rape?" she asked coldly.

His hand dropped. She looked over at him and saw how pale he had become. There was a line of pain about his mouth.

Quite suddenly Barbara began to cry. She cried exactly as she had done when she was a small child, weeping with great shuddering, gulping sobs.

"Oh, sweetheart." She was in his arms, held against his great strong chest. "Don't. It's not as bad as all that, truly it's not. The drilling is only a precaution. It doesn't mean we are going to war."

Barbara clung to him and wept and when he

bent his head she raised her mouth and kissed him wildly and there was the taste of salt in both their mouths.

"I love you," he said. She was kissing him frantically—his mouth, his face, his shoulders. He suddenly felt himself on fire for her. He pushed her back on the bed. "I love you," he repeated. "Barbara. Sweetheart. Angel. Love me. Show me how much you love me."

Her nails dug into the bare skin of his back as he stripped the covers off and pulled her nightgown up.

"What else are you doing besides drilling militia?" Barbara asked, much later.

"Nothing else, sweetheart. I swear it."

"You promise you'll never keep something like that from me again?"

"I promise."

From the dressing room next door came the sound of a baby crying. "I have to feed Ian," Barbara said softly, and reluctantly Allan rolled away from her.

Barbara got up, put on her nightgown and a shawl, and went next door to the room that had become a temporary night nursery. She picked the baby up and sat down to nurse him by the fire. By the time she returned to bed, Alan was asleep.

*   *   *

Barbara sat with Ian on her lap, gazing from the summerhouse out across the James. The March afternoon was so fair. The river before her was bright and still. It had rained earlier in the morning and the smell of the earth was in her nostrils.

She should be so happy. Spring was coming. The baby was bright and active and healthy. They had made good profits on their crops in Jamestown and Williamsburg.

But she felt so unsafe. The political situation was like the river, she thought. On the surface, all was calm and smooth, but under the surface—unseen but always present—the current ran swift and wild and perilous.

The general election in Britain last summer had produced a House of Commons solidly behind Lord North's government. And Lord North's government was determined to subdue Boston.

Speaking in favor of the series of bills aimed at bringing Boston to heel—acts called the Coercive Acts in Britain, the Intolerable Acts in America—Member of Parliament Mr. Van had said, "The town of Boston ought to be knocked about their ears and destroyed. Great Britain will never meet with that proper obedience in the colonies to the laws of this country until we have destroyed that nest of locusts."

Dr. Franklin had kindly passed that quote along to his comrades in Boston, who promptly channeled it through their Committee of Correspondence to all the other colonies. Alan had been furious when he heard it.

Charles Fox had left the government over its handling of the American situation and gone over to the Rockingham Whigs.

"The temper in England is running very strongly against Boston, my love," Lady Abingdon had written her daughter recently. "According to your cousin Harry, the citizens there are a nasty, rebellious lot. It might be wise for you to consider coming home until this unpleasantness is resolved."

Barbara had no intention of returning to England. She would stay where she was and exert whatever influence she had to keep her own family safe.

If it came to a clash of arms in Boston, it should be over very soon. The Massachusetts militia would be soundly defeated and Alan and his friends would see the futility of any opposition in arms.

Let them continue to boycott. Barbara had been very happy to lock away her tea, and gladly would she refrain from buying any English or East Indian goods. Lord Dartmouth might say that everyone who signed the Boycott Association Agreement was guilty of treason, but England could not indict an entire people. No, the boycott was safe.

Then why did she feel so uneasy?

Ian waved his fists and began to talk. Barbara laughed and lifted him so she could see his face. He had Alan's coloring, but his eyes were going to be blue. "This is all going to be yours someday, lovey, and Mama is going to make certain it's here for you to inherit."

He looked at her, suddenly serious, his clear blue eyes wide and solemn. Barbara caught him close to her. Never would she fail this little one. Never.

Without benefit of governor or council, the House of Burgesses had constituted themselves as a governing convention and were to gather in Richmond in late March. Alan was attending with Francis Morgan, who had been elected to replace Edmund Brandon as a representative for Charles City County.

Alan rose before six to ride down the river to meet Francis. They were to travel together. Before he put on his coat he went over to the bed to say good-bye to his wife.

She was asleep, her hair in loose strands over her eyes, her face as perfect and as still as one of Raphael's Madonnas. He looked at her and felt desire stir.

She had been up several times last night with the baby, who was cutting a tooth. He should let her sleep.

He bent over her and kissed her throat.

Her eyes fluttered open. "Alan?" she said sleepily. "Are you leaving now?"

"Mmm." He kissed her breasts.

Still half-asleep, she moved toward the center of

the bed to make room for him. He stretched out next to her and ran his hand over the curve of her waist and hip. "I'll miss you, sweetheart," he murmured.

He caressed her until he felt her begin to tremble. "Christ, Barbara," he muttered, "but you are so sweet. . . ." She was rippling around him, as warm and as sweet as honey. There was nothing like this anywhere else in the world. He felt such tenderness for her. How could such tenderness coexist with such passion? he wondered. He kissed her throat and then her eyes and her mouth. Never would he be able to get enough of her.

"You beast," she said when finally he sat up once again on the side of the bed. "You didn't even take off your boots."

He grinned at her, cocky and irresistible. "I couldn't help myself," he growled.

Barbara laughed and yawned. The baby, hearing his parents' voices, began to cry. Barbara sighed.

Alan immediately felt contrite. "I should have let you sleep."

Barbara stood up and reached for a shawl. "It's a little late to think of that now." Then, because he was going away and she would miss him, she leaned over and kissed the top of his head. "I'm glad you didn't."

He stood up as well. "I'd better be on my way. Francis will wonder what's keeping me."

"Don't tell him," Barbara said warningly, and Alan grinned once more.

His thoughts as he rode down the drive of his plantation were not of his wife, however, but of the upcoming meeting.

Since the royal governor had dissolved the House of Burgesses last May there had been in effect no official government in Virginia—except that symbolized by his lordship, isolated in his palace in Williamsburg. No courts had met, no law-enforcement officers had been appointed, no representative legislative body had sat.

And yet life in Virginia had proceeded smoothly enough. At the county level, the large landowners had formed committees to control affairs. There had been no increase in crime, no violence. And all over the colony local militias had been formed.

The second meeting of the Virginia Convention was being called to set forth measures to deal with their ambiguous political situation and to select and instruct delegates for the Second Continental Congress in Philadelphia.

It was afternoon when Alan and Francis rode into the little city of Richmond. They took rooms at a tavern and repaired the following day to the only public building in the city—small white-framed St. John's Church.

Peyton Randolph was once again presiding, and crammed into the narrow pews in front of him was a collection of Tidewater aristocrats in European-made clothes, and upcountry representatives in homespun and buckskin. Alan and Francis found seats beside a thin, wiry westerner in buckskin. In front of them sat the massive bulk of Ben Harrison, and across the aisle was Colonel Washington. Toward the back of the church were Patrick Henry and Richard Henry Lee.

There was not enough room for Alan's legs. As a series of innocuous resolves was read aloud by Peyton Randolph, Alan shifted and tried to find a comfortable way to sit. Out of the corner of his eye he could see that Colonel Washington was having the same problem.

Peyton Randolph was reading a resolve to express gratitude to the Jamaica Assembly for its efforts to restore harmony between Britain and her colonies. "We wish to assure the people of Jamaica," the chairman intoned, "of the most ardent wish of this colony to see a speedy return of those halcyon days when we lived a free and happy people."

There was a murmur of general approval and Alan stifled a yawn. They had to go through all these motions, he supposed, but it was extremely tedious. He shifted his legs again and the man in buckskin next to him smothered a grin.

Alan's attention focused sharply on the proceedings, however, when Patrick Henry, cutting through all the pious mouthings, rose to propose that Virginia be immediately put into a state of defense.

Alan forgot his cramped legs and listened attentively as speaker after speaker protested the rashness of Mr. Henry's proposal.

Mr. Bland argued that such a threatening tone would undo all the progress made by the hitherto gentlemanly statements of their demands.

What progress? thought Alan.

Ben Harrison was afraid that such action on the part of Virginia would vitiate any effect on the British merchant class of the boycott of British goods.

The British merchant class is not going to defy British public opinion over the colonies, thought Alan.

Mr. Carter feared the consequences should Great Britain take their actions seriously. What would happen should England send her established armies and navies against a scattering of unarmed people without military organization or the stores of war?

They cannot garrison America, Alan thought. We are too widespread and too numerous.

He listened and knew that what these gentlemen of property were arguing were the very arguments he would hear from his wife. These were men with everything to lose and very insubstantial things to gain. But he could not agree with them. All he knew was that they were wrong. He shifted his weight once more.

There was a pause as the last speaker resumed his seat. Then, slowly, Patrick Henry once again approached the front of the church. He began to speak quietly. He mentioned the most recent petition the colonies had laid before the king. "Ask yourselves how this gracious reception of our petition comports with those warlike preparations which cover our waters and darken our land," he said pleasantly enough. "Have we shown ourselves so unwilling to be reconciled that force must be called in to win back our love? These are the implements of war and subjugation—the last arguments to which kings resort."

Alan's jaw hardened. At last someone was saying the things which must be said. Mr. Henry looked around the church. "We have done everything that can be done to avert the storm which is now coming on. We have petitioned, remonstrated, supplicated, prostrated ourselves before the throne. In vain, after all these things, may we indulge the fond hope of peace and reconciliation. There is no longer any room for hope."

A deep hush had fallen over the small church. All the representatives crammed into the little pews sat as if mesmerized. The speaker's voice bugled out now above the quiet: "If we wish to be free, we must fight! I repeat it, sir, we must fight! An appeal to arms and the God of Hosts is all that is left us."

They were words that no one in that church had ever expected to hear. But they had been said. And more. They had no choice, the impassioned speaker shouted: "Gentlemen may cry peace, peace, peace—but there is no peace. The war is actually begun! The next gale that sweeps from the north will bring to our ears the clash of resounding arms."

He flung his arms aloft and, burning with revolutionary intensity, cried: "Is life so dear or peace so sweet as to be purchased at the price of chains and slavery? Forbid it, Almighty God. I know not what course others may take; but as for me, give me liberty or give me death!"

There was profound silence in the church as he walked back to his seat The assembled representatives were perfectly motionless, as though transfixed. The trance was broken only when Richard Henry Lee arose to speak in support of Patrick Henry's resolution.

Fifteen

66 "I am one of the delegates selected to go to Philadelphia," Alan told his wife shortly after his return home.

Barbara's face hardened.

"It was a surprise to me," he assured her. They were talking in the privacy of his office and he paced to the window and stood there, looking quickly at his wife's face and then away again. "I'm not much of a one for talking—in fact, I say very little at these sessions."

He didn't understand his own power, Barbara thought. He didn't go around shouting and making speeches, so he didn't think of himself as a leader. He didn't realize the mysterious, effortless ability he had to inspire admiration and confidence just by sitting there.

"You should have heard Patrick Henry, Barbara," he said now, turning to her with sudden enthusiasm. "By God, he was splendid. 'Give me liberty,' he said, 'or give me death!' "

Barbara could feel a dull ache begin behind her eyes. She stared at the tall figure of her husband.

"Perhaps there are some outrages that demand such sacrifices," she said in a low voice, "but this quarrel between the colonies and Britain is not one of them. Alan, think. What has England done that is so dreadful? She wants us to pay a threepence tax on tea. Is that worth going to war over? Is that the principle Mr. Henry is willing to die for?"

"The principle, Barbara, is that we have no voice in the British government and yet that government is forcing measures on us which are abhorrent to us. If they succeed in making us accept this tax, what will be next?"

Barbara made an impatient gesture. "George the Third is not Alexander the Great, Alan. He is not out to conquer the world."

Alan's dark face looked distinctly saturnine. "No. He is just out to conquer America."

The ache behind her eyes had become a steady throb. "Oh, I can't argue with you. I'm only a woman and have no vocabulary of political catchwords. But I know this, Alan. War means that men are slaughtered, children are starved, and homes are ruined. It's not the great, glorious enterprise your Mr. Henry would have you think it is. War doesn't build anything up. It destroys."

He was looking at her with an odd, grave curiosity. "This isn't a national thing at all with you, is it, Barbara? You aren't feeling loyal to King and Country. You just can't bear the thought of anyone fighting."

"I can't bear the thought of *you* fighting. I can't bear the insecurity of wondering if my son will have a home next year, or the year after that. If there is fighting in Massachusetts, Alan, and if you are one of the delegates in Philadelphia supporting that fighting, what will happen? The entire congress may well be arrested for treason!"

He shrugged.

She thought she would scream with the pain in her head. "Do you know what happens to men who are accused of treason? They lose their property, Alan. Don't you understand that? They could take this plantation away from us. If you don't understand that, I do. I understand very well what it means to grow up with the knowledge that one's father has thrown away one's future. And I won't let that happen to my son. I won't!"

He stared at her pale face and felt himself on the verge of understanding her, of understanding the fear that was driving her. He crossed the room and, sitting down in his big desk chair, drew her into his lap. "Sweetheart," he said very gently, "this country is not like England. We are not all crowded together here into a small, cramped island. The possibilities for expansion are endless in America. There will always be a future here for our son. There is no need for you to be so careful for him. There is more to the new world than Virginia."

She sat stiffly on his lap, resisting the pressure of his hand on her waist. "You did not think so once," she said bitterly. "You married against your inclination to get this plantation you are so quick to scorn."

He put his hands on her shoulders and made her turn to look at him. His hands were not gentle; they bit into her flesh through the fabric of her dress. His face was as hard as his hands. "Is that what you think?" he asked.

"It's true, isn't it?" she asked defiantly. "Our marriage was your father's idea, not yours. You only agreed so you could have Newland."

He looked at her through a long hard moment's silence. Then, "I didn't marry you to get Newland," he said. "I married you so I could lie with you."

They were so close together, in a position of such intimacy, and the emotion crackling between them was sheer hostility.

"Well, you got what you wanted." Barbara's voice was low and trembling with anger. "You got me into your bed and you gave me a child. And now you are ready to toss us both into the river for the sake of some misconceived idea about 'liberty'!"

He put her off his lap, slowly and deliberately, and got to his feet. He towered over her, but Barbara would not allow his size to intimidate her. She was right and he was wrong.

"If that is what you think, then there is nothing more I can say on the subject." He spoke in a flat voice that seemed to come from a great distance. He walked to the door. "I'm going out," he said, and left.

Barbara came downstairs after putting the baby into his cradle for a nap. Libby was sitting in the Green Parlor sewing and Barbara joined her young sister-in-law. Alan was in Williamsburg, where Governor Dunmore had recently seized the colony's powder from the town's magazine. Alan had almost forcibly restrained the local militia from marching on the town to demand its return, and he and a few other planters instead sent a formal protest to the governor. He was in Williamsburg now to try to make Lord Dunmore come to his senses.

Barbara went to the window and looked out at the April afternoon. It had been raining for hours, and the color of the rain, the color of the air, of the mud, of the river, of life altogether, seemed to her an unutterable dirty brown.

For weeks now she and Alan had lived in the house together as though they were separated by a wall of ice. They went about their usual daily duties, but all the time, there between them was the wall—relentless, unbreakable, unbreachable.

He didn't care about her. He cared for nothing but this insane war that was hovering over them like a dark and threatening and ugly storm.

She wished she could say the same held true for her, that she didn't care what became of him, that she would turn her back on this strife-ridden land and go home to the safety of Carrington. But she did care. She cared desperately. When she thought of Alan she could almost feel the vibration of him in her bones. She saw him now as he had looked when he left for Williamsburg, riding, head up, a frown between his eyes. She was so afraid for him. What he was doing was so dangerous.

"Whatever was Lord Dunmore thinking of?" Libby asked for perhaps the tenth time that day.

"He wasn't thinking at all, obviously," Barbara replied impatiently. "That's just the problem in this whole situation. *No one* is thinking."

Libby sewed for a few minutes in silence. "It's different for you, Barbara, I understand that. You're English."

"That has nothing to do with it," Barbara replied sharply. "Alan understands that at least, if he understands nothing else."

"He's not a radical, you know, Barbara," Libby said to her sister-in-law with frowning intensity.

Barbara laughed shortly. "If he isn't, then I should like to know who is." She turned to face Libby.

"Do you know what I can't forgive about all this, Libby? It's the fact that it could so easily be avoided. We are going to war over a threepence tax on tea!"

Libby looked at Barbara's lovely flushed face. "No. It's more than that, Barbara. The tea is merely an excuse—you're right about that. The issue is quite something else." She leaned a little forward in her chair. "I was talking about this with Mr. Dwight last week. Look around you here in Virginia, Barbara. We are all people whose families have been here for generations. The simple truth is that we have ceased to be English. We are Americans now. We are Americans and we want to be able to control our own destiny. It's as simple as that."

Barbara stared back at Libby out of stormy eyes. There was a long moment's silence; then Barbara paced again to the window. Libby sighed and once more picked up her sewing.

There was the sound of horses' hooves on the drive and Libby ran through the doorway to the Blue Parlor to look out the window. "Alan's back!" she called. Barbara could hear her go to open the door for her brother. There was the sound of voices in the hall and after a minute Alan and Libby came back into the Green Parlor to join her.

Alan came over to kiss her cheek. He had taken off his wet coat but his boots were splashed with mud from the ride. His kiss had been as cold as a knife. He went to sit on a sofa by the fire. Barbara remained where she was at the window.

"What happened?" she asked. "Did Governor Dunmore return the powder?"

"He said it had disappeared, but he sent us a bill of exchange for its value and he authorized the force to acquire more."

"Well," Barbara said flatly, "that should solve that then."

He was sitting quite still on the sofa, his ringless hands clasped together between his long mud-splashed boots. She could not see his eyes.

"Alan." It was Libby's voice. "Is something else wrong?"

He lifted his lashes and looked at his wife. "On April 19, General Gage sent a party of British troops out of Boston into the countryside. They were met by several thousand militia in the village of Lexington. There was a battle."

Barbara could feel the blood drain from her face.

"Who won?" asked Libby sharply.

"There was no clear-cut victory. There were casualties on both sides. The troops are back in Boston and the Massachusetts militia are forming around the town."

"Oh my God," breathed Barbara through blood-less lips. She sat abruptly in a chair.

"Yes." Alan's face was hard as nails. "It has finally come."

War. She had feared it for so long and now it was among them. "Harry," she said out of a constricted throat. "My cousin Harry's regiment is in Boston."

"I don't have any names, Barbara."

She closed her eyes. She could hear the guns roaring—or was it the blood pounding in her head?

"Barbara!" It was Alan's voice, sharp with fear. His hand was on her arm and then she knew nothing.

When she awoke she was lying on her bed. She looked around and saw Alan standing in front of the window, his head pressed against the glass. He heard her moving and turned.

How could there be such strife between them? Barbara thought. When people loved each other as they had, how could they come to this?

He came across to the bed. "You fainted." He put an impersonal hand on her forehead. "Are you all right now?"

She took a deep, slow breath. "Yes. It was the guns," she tried to explain confusedly. "I thought I heard the guns in my head."

"Oh *God*!" Alan said. "Barbara . . ."

She looked up at him. "I know," she answered wearily. "There's nothing you can do. Don't worry, Alan, I'll be fine. I just need a little rest. I have a headache."

She lay back against the pillows and closed her eyes. After a minute she heard him go out of the room.

Several days later Alan was preparing to leave for Philadelphia. "Every member of that congress is living with a rope around his neck," Barbara said tensely as she watched him put papers into his portmanteau the night before he was to leave.

He turned to look at her. "I used to think you were so fragile," he said. "So yielding, so tender. But you're not fragile at all. You're like a rock—adamant."

She felt bitterness well up in her heart. "It's you that's made me this way."

The candlelight threw a shadow against his cheek. Barbara stared at the line of his hard mouth. "If that's how you feel, then there's nothing more to say, is there?" He closed the portmanteau. "I'll sleep in my office tonight so I don't disturb you when I get up tomorrow. I'll be leaving early."

He began to walk toward the door. Barbara watched his tall figure, moving with all its usual strength and grace and self-command. It had always been one of her greatest joys, to watch the way he moved. She would be able to pick him out from among a hundred men, she thought, just by the way he carried his head.

But the only emotion she felt now as she watched him open the door was cold, hard anger. He was jeopardizing everything in the world that she held dear, and he was doing it deliberately.

He turned to look at her once more. "Good night," he said.

He was waiting for her to relent, to call him back to his own bed, but she would not give in. Not over this. It was too important. "Good night, Alan," she answered coldly, and saw his mouth harden even more. He slammed the door behind him so hard that her bedside table shook.

She watched him ride down the drive the following morning from the shadow of her bedroom window, but he never turned around to see if she was there.

On June 14, 1775, the Second Continental Congress, meeting in Philadelphia, resolved to raise several companies of riflemen to be enlisted in the "American Continental Army."

On June 15 a bill passed Congress stating: "Resolved that a general be appointed to command all the continental forces raised or to be raised for the defense of American liberty." The Congress then proceeded to the choice of a general by ballot, and George Washington, Esq., was unanimously elected.

On June 16, Washington, solemn in his uniform, appeared before Congress and formally accepted the command.

The command, at this point, consisted solely of the New England troops gathered around Boston.

In effect, there was as yet no "Continental Army." There was, technically, no nation to fight for. There was only Washington.

When the new commander in chief left Philadelphia a few days later to take up his command outside Boston, Alan Maxwell was with him.

III

The Times That Try Men's Souls

1777–1779

Sixteen

In January of 1777 the American Army, buoyed from its recent victories at Trenton and Princeton, went into winter quarters at Morristown, New Jersey. Those victories had been sorely needed: the Americans had previously lost Boston, been driven from Long Island, and been defeated yet again at Harlem Heights, White Plains, and Fort Washington. The attack upon Trenton in the snow on Christmas Day and the subsequent rout of the garrison at Princeton had been, to the downtrodden Continentals, like manna in the desert.

"We are quartered here at Morristown for the winter," Alan wrote to his wife in mid-January. They had been corresponding regularly for the last year and a half, and on the surface, at least, their quarrel had been patched up. Both of them regretted the bitterness of their parting, although both of them still felt justified in the stands they had taken. They corresponded mainly about the plantation and the family.

Alan continued his letter:

> The ground is high and our presence should keep the land route to Philadelphia blocked. General Howe has withdrawn his army almost all the way back to New York and things look to be quiet for several months.
>
> Mrs. Washington, Mrs. Greene, and a number of other ladies will be joining their husbands here at winter quarters once again this year. I know what a bad traveler you are, and I know the roads will be wretched this time of the year, but I surely would like to see you, sweetheart. It has been such a long time since last we were together.
>
> Come to Morristown, Barbara. Nothing will happen with the war until spring, and I am comfortably quartered here in the farmhouse of a war widow. We would have a few months together before hostilities commenced again.

Alan put his pen down and looked around the bedroom in which he sat, frowning with thought. Outside he could hear the voice of Anthony Wayne calling to someone. Alan, still frowning, slowly finished his letter, sealed it, and went downstairs, where he met his hostess in the front hall. "Mrs. Thornton," he said civilly.

"Colonel Maxwell." Lucy Thornton's large brown eyes looked up at him and she smiled, showing a dimple in her right cheek. Alan had not mentioned to Barbara that the widow in whose house he and Anthony Wayne were residing was twenty-six years of age and pretty. "I would like it very much if you and General Wayne would join me for dinner this evening, Colonel," Mrs. Thornton said softly. "My cousin and her husband will be dining with me also."

"Thank you, Mrs. Thornton," Alan replied with alacrity. He was heartily sick of camp food. "It's very kind of you to show mercy to a hungry soldier," he added with a grin.

Lucy's eyes never left his face. "It is my pleasure. My husband was a Continental also and I should like to think someone fed him a home-cooked meal once in a while."

Alan felt a flash of pity. John Thornton had fallen at White Plains the previous year. Already this war had made so many widows.

Martha Washington duly arrived in camp, and Kitty Greene as well. A number of other wives also came, some of them accompanied by small children. It seemed, to Alan's sensitive and increasingly resentful eyes, that everyone's wife was at Morristown but his.

He did not hear from Barbara until February and

then she wrote to tell him that she could not come to New Jersey. There was an influenza going around the plantation, and although she herself was better, Ian and Libby were ill. A great number of the slaves were also down with the sickness. Under the circumstances, much as she desired to see him, she could not possibly leave Virginia.

Alan tried to be understanding, but deep inside he felt she was not coming because she was still angry at him for joining the army. He had been faithful to her since leaving Virginia—for almost two long years—yet still she was punishing him for doing what he knew was simply his duty.

Every time he saw the pretty domestic sight of Martha Washington sewing in front of her husband's fire, his resentment toward his own wife grew.

He dreamed of the river.

He had seen so many rivers since leaving home, the Charles, the Hudson, the Delaware—but none of them were like his river.

She was there with him. They were standing together in the summerhouse and before them the river sparkled in the sun.

Then they were on the river, on board a ship. It was their honeymoon. She was under him on the bed, her body soft and silken, her hair spilling over the pillows.

Alan woke up sweating, looked around his room,

and cursed. It was very dark and he could hear the sound of sleet against the windowpanes.

The ache in his loins was unbearable. *"Christ!"* he said forcefully, and got to his feet. He lit the candle next to his bed and started to get dressed. He would go downstairs and work on the supply lists he had been making. He had to occupy his mind, had to stop thinking . . . .

He was sitting at the dining-room table trying to concentrate on the papers in front of him when there came a sound and a flicker of light behind him. He turned quickly and found Lucy Thornton in the doorway, her hair in a thick brown plait over her shoulder. She wore a white cotton nightgown and she carried a candle in her hand.

"Colonel Maxwell!" she said in a startled voice. "What are you doing here?"

He stared at her without answering. Her nightgown was full and perfectly opaque, yet in his mind's eye he could picture the slender female body those white folds concealed. She was such a little thing, and so pretty . . . . He stood up.

"I'm sorry if I frightened you," he said. His nostrils flared as he took a deep, unsteady breath. "I couldn't sleep."

He noticed that the small hand holding the candle began to tremble. He crossed the room toward her, took the light from her unsteady hand, and set it on a table. Her head barely reached his shoulder. Actually, she was not that much shorter than Barbara, it was just that Barbara gave the appearance of being taller than she was. It was because she was so finely made . . . Damn Barbara, he thought with sudden violence. He was very close to Lucy Thornton. "I thought you were asleep," he said.

"I could not sleep either." Her voice was a thin whisper. Then, after a fractional pause, "It is not easy, being a widow."

So. Her need then was the same as his. Her head was tipped way back to look up into his face. Everything about her said she was his for the taking.

He bent his head and she raised her lips to meet his. He felt her arms go around him and under the pressure of his mouth her own parted. The feel of her breasts against him was exquisite. "Let's go upstairs," he muttered against her mouth, and felt the response in her yielding body and mouth.

She was the first woman he had had in a year and a half. He took her mindlessly, aware only of the softness of her under him and the urgency of his own driving need. He heard her cry out with pleasure and, somewhere in the deep recesses of his mind, was glad that she was satisfied too.

He lay beside her afterward, grateful to her for the peace she had given to his body and wanting only to be quiet. But he could not simply go to sleep; she was not a camp follower to be used and then ignored.

He made an effort and said, "I reckon we've both been alone for too long a time."

She sighed softly. "Yes. John was one of the first to volunteer from our area, and then he was killed at White Plains. It's been difficult here on the farm, with no man around. Difficult and lonely." She looked at her hands, clasped together above the coverlet. "We had no children," she said in a low voice. "It would be less lonely, with a child."

Alan felt an enormous sense of relief sweep across him. She was barren. That was all right, then.

"This war has left many lonely people," he said.

"Yes." She turned her head to look at him. "Your wife—she is not coming to join you?"

He kept his face expressionless. "No. There has been influenza on the plantation and she can't leave."

"Oh. That is too bad." She did not look at all sorry.

The first light of dawn had lightened the sky to a dull gray and Alan got out of bed. "I'd better get back to my own room before General Wayne arises," he said. "I wouldn't want to damage your reputation."

She stared at his bare shoulders as he reached for his shirt. "I am not sorry, Alan."

He came over to the bed and she smiled up at him. "Come again," she whispered, and as he bent to kiss her, he knew that he would.

They were in winter quarters until June and for four months Alan and Lucy Thornton maintained their liaison. Alan was never quite sure if anyone knew about it. Anthony Wayne, who shared the house with them, tactfully maintained his silence, and no one else in camp ever indicated there might be something more between Alan and his hostess than appeared on the surface.

Alan liked Lucy Thornton very much. He liked being around a woman again—not just sleeping with her, but talking to her, listening to the soft sound of her voice in return, watching the graceful gestures of her expressive hands. He was so weary of the endless masculinity of war.

She knew he had a wife and a son. Once or twice she tried to ask him questions about Barbara, but he cut her off with unusual curtness. He did not want to talk about Barbara to Lucy. He tried not to think about Barbara these days. He had forgotten his bitter feelings when he first learned that she was not coming to Morristown, and remembered only that she was coping with a plantation full of influenza and that she had been sick with it herself. Her letters came with unusual regularity that winter, and though she was determinedly cheerful, he could read between the lines. Things were very difficult at Newland; they had lost fourteen slaves to the influenza. Barbara had not been making excuses to avoid coming to New Jersey.

He tried not to think of his wife during the day, but at night he lay in Lucy Thornton's bed and he dreamed of her: Barbara as she looked poised midway up the Bridgewaters' staircase the first time he had seen her; Barbara on board ship; Barbara holding Ian in her arms; Barbara in bed, flushed with love . . . He woke up with a start.

"Alan, are you all right?" It was a moment before he realized it was Lucy beside him in the dark and not his wife.

He took a deep breath and forced his voice to calmness. "Yes. Was I restless? I'm sorry if I disturbed you."

She turned into his arms. "My sweetest love, you always disturb me."

His hands moved over her naked body and he sought forgetfulness in the assuaging of his body's needs.

At the beginning of June, General Howe moved into New Jersey in force. Washington's army held firm on the heights at Morristown and after a few feints Howe returned to New York and began to prepare to load his army onto ships. Washington broke up winter quarters and made ready to move.

It was only when he received the orders to march that Alan, feeling the relief flood through him, let himself realize how anxious he was to get away from this entanglement with Lucy Thornton.

He had been too fastidious to make use of one of the camp followers to fulfill his needs, and so he had turned to the respectable, lonely young woman in whose home he was residing. He had been selfish and despicable; the worst part of the whole affair, he realized in dismay, was the fact that Lucy loved him.

It was an impossible situation. He could not break with her while he was still living in her house; he could not possibly hurt and insult her in a such a fashion. Yet the longer he spent with her, the more deeply involved with him she became.

He tried to hide from her how relieved he was to say good-bye.

"You will be coming back to Morristown, won't you, Alan?" she asked.

He could not bear to see the anxious, fearful look in her big brown eyes and so he tried to be kind. "Of course we will be, Lucy. Morristown is one of our key positions." He bent his head and briefly kissed her lips. "Good-bye, my dear," he said, and turned away from her. From behind him he heard her say, "I'll write to you, Alan. Take care of yourself." He could hear the tears in her voice and, determinedly, he strode out of the confinement of the house and into the sunshine.

Seventeen

The Clove, New Jersey
July 24, 1777

My Dearest Wife,

I received your letters of June 18 and 25 and July 3 yesterday. This is all the reply I can manage at the moment, as we are to march for Philadelphia tomorrow. Word has just reached us that the British Navy took off most of General Howe's troops from New York, and General Washington feels their destination is the capital.

This letter should reach you without mishap, as one of my officers who is going home to recuperate from illness has promised to see it delivered personally. The erratic post from Virginia is very irritating— you are all so good about writing to me, and the letters arrive so irregularly. However, to answer some of the concerns in your last letters:

I was very pleased to hear that Libby desires to marry Charles Dwight. He always seemed to me an excellent young man and if he has the patronage of George Wythe he will be universally respected and esteemed. I know he is poor, but Libby has enough of a portion from my father to see them safely established. I also know Mr. Dwight's father was an indentured servant—but, sweetheart, so was Edmund Pendleton's, and there are few men more respected than he in all of Virginia. America is not like England. A man's parentage does not predestine him to a certain place in society here—there is plenty of room for him to rise by his own merits.

Speaking of merits, Congress has seen fit to raise me from the rank of colonel to that of brigadier general. If only they would cease to bombard us with swarms of French officers who insist they are entitled, because of their glorious records on European battlefields, to one of the very highest commands in the American Army. His excellency is weary of them and so are we all. Greene, Knox, and Sullivan actually threatened to resign if a Frenchman named du Coudray was appointed head of the artillery over Knox. All has been resolved for the present, however, and Knox is still our artillery commander.

As to Robert's desire to join the Continental Army—sweetheart, I can't stop him if that is what he wishes. I know he is in the militia, but there has been no fighting in Virginia since the war began. Please God, there will never be any fighting in Virginia. It's selfish of me, I suppose, but one of the things that sustains me is the thought of Newland, safe and secure and the same.

I fear there is no chance of my getting leave to come home for a visit. His excellency needs all the strong, steady support he can get. It is not easy, keeping an army in the field under the conditions that Congress imposes. I understand Mr. Adams wanted a new commander in chief to be elected every year! The man must be mad.

My Virginians have been splendid. When their terms of enlistment were up, two-thirds of them enlisted again. They are splendid fellows, but they need to see that I set the example. No, I simply cannot come home for a month or so, Barbara, much as I long to see you and Ian.

My best to Libby. Give Ian a kiss for Papa. And to you:

All my love,
Alan

Barbara read the letter through twice before she put it down. She was seated at the secretary in Alan's office and now she pushed the big chair back a little and stared blindly at the terrestrial globe which stood next to the bookcase in the corner.

He would not be coming home.

Two years.

Two years of working to keep the plantation going. Two years of working to keep them from going into debt, as she saw happening to so many other families whose husbands were away serving in the army or the government.

The war might not have physically touched Virginia, but they had felt the brunt of it in other ways. Barbara did not think that some of the plantations would ever recover from it. The British Navy had cut off much of the tobacco trade and British counterfeit currency had succeeded in devastating Continental money until it was nearly worthless. Newland had survived because it was largely growing food crops and because Barbara had rigidly cut all expenditures to the bone. She knew too well what happened to people who lived on their capital.

At first Barbara had been content to leave the management of Newland to Alan's cousin, Gavin Maxwell, whom Alan had asked to act as estate manager while he was gone. But gradually, during that first year of Alan's absence, Barbara had come to realize that Gavin, pleasant and agreeable though he was, was not the man to replace her husband. Under Gavin the economic mainstay of the plantation—the growing of crops and the transporting of them to market—began to fall off. Barbara, concerned for her family's security, began to look into areas that had always been Alan's responsibility.

She spent hundreds of hours in the estate office going over the books. It was a difficult task; she had never kept anything more than a simple household expense reckoning, but she persevered, and finally the numbers began to make sense.

Alan's bookkeeping was meticulous and she was able to see how he made his profits. It became equally and frighteningly clear that Gavin was falling dangerously below Alan's productiveness.

It was then that Barbara took all the bookkeeping into her own hands. It was the only way she could keep track of what was being grown and what was being sold and for how much. When production fell behind, she pushed Gavin, who, in turn, pushed the field workers, who had begun to take disgraceful advantage of Gavin's easy negligence.

Barbara was thinking about Gavin when his thin dark face appeared at the office door. "Barbara? We're about ready to leave for Williamsburg now."

Barbara smiled as he came into the room. "Good. The wagons are all loaded?"

"Yes. I went over them all with the inventory list you gave me, and everything is there."

"How many men are you taking besides the drivers?"

"Four."

"Not Henry?"

"Yes, Henry is coming."

"I have a job for Henry to do here," Barbara said pleasantly but decisively. "Take the three others. They should be enough."

"All right." Gavin's brown eyes were soft as they looked upon the beautiful face of his cousin's wife. "Do you have the bill for me?"

Barbara reached for a piece of paper. The desk was covered with piles of paper and account books, all neatly stacked. "Here it is. Do you see how I have charged for the wheat?"

Gavin bent his head close to hers. "Yes," he said after a minute. "I see."

"Very well." Barbara gave him a friendly smile. "Have a good trip, Gavin. We'll see you in a few days."

"Yes." Gavin's return smile was slightly wistful, but Barbara did not notice. "See you in a few days," he echoed, and turning, went out, closing the door behind him.

Barbara sat, a slight frown on her forehead, and stared at her loaded desk. So much work to be done . . . so much responsibility . . . how was she to manage if Robert went off to war and Libby got married?

This war. She had not believed it possible that it could continue for so long. First the Americans had lost Boston, then New York, then Charleston. Now it appeared General Howe was going to try to take Philadelphia, the fourth major American port city, the capital of the United States, and the second-largest English-speaking city in the world.

The terrestrial globe blurred before Barbara's eyes as she stared at it in trancelike concentration.

She had been furious when Alan rode to Boston with General Washington, furious and terrified. No one had been more surprised than she when word had come that the Massachusetts militia, standing solidly together under heavy fire, had succeeded in inflicting a great loss on the British Army before it retreated from Bunker Hill. Barbara had always assumed that there was no way in which an untrained force could stand against professional soldiers.

The war had not been quickly over, as she had assumed. Here it was, more than two years later, and still there was an American army in the field. They lost and lost and lost again, but still they were there, and the war went on. She had never dreamed, that morning she watched Alan ride down the drive on his way to Philadelphia, that she would not see him again for years.

There came a light knock on the door and a fair head looked into the room. "Barbara?" said her brother-in-law. "Solomon tells me you've heard from Alan."

"Yes. Come in, Robert." Barbara gestured him to one of the chairs that stood next to the small walnut table between the windows. She smiled into his golden-sherry eyes. "He was in a rush—the army was marching south to Philadelphia—so he didn't have time to write to you and Libby."

"Oh." Robert looked disappointed. "I wonder if he even received my last letter."

"I don't know, but he did receive mine." Barbara sighed. "It's your decision, Robert. If you wish to join the army, Alan says you may."

Robert's fine-featured face began to blaze. "By Jove, that's good news!" He jumped to his feet. "Didn't I tell you he wouldn't object?"

"You told me." There was a dry note in Barbara's voice and, hearing it, Robert grinned. There was a brief, fleeting resemblance to his brother, and Barbara's heart contracted.

"Did you say the army was marching to Philadelphia?" Robert asked now eagerly.

"Yes. Apparently General Howe has loaded his entire army on ship and disappeared into the Atlantic. Alan says they think he is heading for Philadelphia. He probably is. The British have captured every other American city of importance. Philadelphia must be next on their agenda."

Robert began to pace around the room. "If I left immediately, I could join the army at Philadelphia." He halted in his pacing and looked at his sister-in-law as she sat at her meticulously piled-up desk. "I want to go," he said a little gruffly, "but now that I know I can, I feel like a deserter."

Barbara didn't reply. She wasn't even looking at him. Instead she was staring at her desk with an abstracted look on her face.

Robert swallowed. "Before I go, I'll see our tobacco on board that ship at Portsmouth that's bound for France," he said heroically.

"Gavin can do that." Barbara's voice sounded distracted too.

Robert sat down. "Of course he can, so long as you prepare the inventory and the bill. You don't really need me. You do all the real work around here—you and Libby. Gavin and I are merely deliverymen."

His words pierced through her abstraction and she looked up sharply. "Is that why you want to leave, Robert? Don't I give you enough responsibility?"

He smiled at her warmly. "Of course that's not why I want to leave. You and I both know that I have no patience for account books—or for growing crops, either. I think a military life will suit me just fine. If I had been born in England, I should probably have followed an army career. A typical younger son." His fair, good-looking face was perfectly relaxed.

"You remind me of my cousin Harry," Barbara said slowly.

"The fellow who's with General Howe?"

"Yes." Barbara's lips suddenly compressed. "What is it about men that makes them want to go to war?"

Robert laughed. "I don't know, Barbara, but I assure you it's not to get away from *you*."

Barbara's face didn't change. "Well, even if it were, you wouldn't succeed. I am going to Philadelphia with you, Robert."

"What!"

"Yes. Since Alan can't come to see me, it seems I must be the one to go to him."

"You can't be serious, Barbara." Robert was

staring at her as if she had taken leave of her senses.

"I am perfectly serious. Alan wanted me to join him at Morristown and, with the influenza epidemic, I couldn't leave. There is no reason I can't leave now."

Robert stared at the desk. "But who will run Newland if you leave?"

"Libby—if I can talk her into delaying her marriage—and Gavin."

"Libby doesn't do the accounts."

"Well, she will have to for a while," Barbara snapped. "You and Alan seem perfectly able to walk away from this plantation. I don't see why I can't do the same."

Robert rose hastily from his chair. "Yes, of course."

"Will you find Libby for me, Robert? I want to talk to her."

"I believe she's in the tailor's cottage. I'll go fetch her for you."

"Thank you, Robert."

After her brother-in-law had left the room, Barbara began to work on one of her account books. She appeared to be totally absorbed in her numbers when Libby entered the office fifteen minutes later.

"Barbara? Robert said you had a letter from Alan."

"Yes." Barbara looked at the dark, vivid face of

Alan's sister. She and Libby had drawn very close over the last two years. "He writes he's delighted about you and Mr. Dwight."

"Does he?" Libby smiled and sat down in the chair recently vacated by her brother. "I gather he also wrote that Robert could join the army?"

Barbara looked down at her hands and then slowly up. "He's just a boy, Libby."

"There are boys younger than he serving."

"I know." Barbara looked down again. "I *hate* this war, Libby. I simply hate it. How many boys like Robert have been killed? How many wives have been made widows? How many children made orphans? And for what? So that Patrick Henry can sit in the Governor's Palace instead of Lord Dunmore?"

"If England would just take her armies and go home, there would be no more war."

There was a pause and then Barbara looked up again. "I am going to travel to Philadelphia with Robert. Did he tell you?"

"No." Libby's dark eyes, so like Alan's, widened. "No, he didn't tell me." She drew a long breath. "Is that where the army is now?"

"Yes, I think so. Alan wrote that he can't get leave to come home."

"I see. Why Philadelphia?"

"General Howe's army is heading there also. Presumably, Washington is going to try to keep the British from taking the city."

Libby frowned. "But what if he does take the city, Barbara? You don't want to be caught there."

Barbara shrugged slim shoulders. "I shall be perfectly safe, Libby. My cousin Harry is on General Howe's staff and General Howe is also a friend of my mother's."

"Ah." A little color crept into Libby's smooth olive cheek. "I forget, sometimes, how well-connected you are."

"Alan has been made a brigadier general," Barbara said flatly. "If we lose this war I may need all my connections to save his neck from the hangman. *And* to save Newland from confiscation."

"Mmm." Libby looked at her speculatively. "Do you know what you just said, Barbara? You said if *we* lose this war."

"Do you think I desire the British to win? All my interest lies with the American side. But I will do all that is in my power to protect my husband and my home in the all-too-likely event of a British victory."

"A brigadier," Libby said admiringly. "My, my, my."

"Libby," Barbara said, and there was an unusual note of urgency in her low voice, "will you remain at Newland while I am gone? I know you desire to marry soon, but I don't see how I can leave Gavin in sole charge here."

"Good God," said Libby. She pulled thoughtfully on a coal-black curl. "Charles is talking of joining the army too."

"What!"

"Yes. He has finished his studies, as you know."

"I thought he was to practice law in Williamsburg."

"He was. But like Robert, he is finding the militia to be dull stuff."

"So you are going to postpone your marriage?" Barbara asked hopefully.

"No. Oh no. I am going to marry him before he goes."

Barbara leaned a little forward. "Libby, do you think that is wise? You are so young . . ."

"You were my age when you married Alan."

There was a brief pause; then Barbara said, "It's not that I don't like Mr. Dwight. I do. But he has no prospects, Libby."

"I love him. That's prospect enough for me." Libby looked a little speculative. "Barbara, may I stay on here after I am married? Until Charles comes home from the war, that is."

"My dear Libby," Barbara answered fervently, "you may stay at Newland for as long as you desire. You *know* how much I rely on you."

Libby grinned. "I rather thought you might like to keep my company."

"Can you keep Gavin to a straight course while I am gone?"

"We'll keep Newland going, Barbara. How long do you reckon you'll be gone?"

"I don't know. A few months. I'll have to be home before the roads close for the winter."

"Charles and I will be married immediately, then. You won't mind if he stays here for a few weeks' honeymoon? I won't be able to hold him for much longer—he's been champing at the bit to join Washington ever since he finished at William and Mary last month. I insisted we wait to hear from Alan before we married. After all, Papa gave him control of my money—and Charles and I need my money. You're quite sure, Barbara, there will be no problem about that?"

"Quite sure."

Libby's smile was radiant. "Splendid. I'll send to Williamsburg to tell Charles the good news. We'll be married before you leave. You can arrange that, surely?"

Barbara sighed. "I suppose so."

"What about Ian?"

"I'm taking him to see his father." Barbara raised a winged eyebrow. "You don't want to be minding a three-year-old on your honeymoon."

"Four days in a coach with Ian! Are you certain you want to take him, Barbara? I don't mind if you leave him home, truly."

"No," Barbara replied, and Libby recognized the inflexibility in that soft, low voice. "Ian should see his father. He's coming with me to Philadelphia."

Libby cast her eyes upward. "All right. I'll get a letter off to Charles and tell him to come right out to Newland to be married."

Barbara smiled. "Are you certain he will agree?"

Libby grinned. "Quite certain, Barbara. Will you go and see Reverend Thorpe?"

Barbara went over and kissed Libby's cheek. "Yes, my love. I will go and see Reverend Thorpe."

The journey to Philadelphia was fully as dreadful as Libby had predicted. The weather was unbearably hot, the roads rutted and dusty, the taverns where they were forced to put up flea-ridden and uncomfortable. Ian was impossible in the coach and only quieted when Robert took him up before him on his horse.

They arrived in Philadelphia on the afternoon of August 21. Barbara was agreeably surprised by the elegance of the city. The stately three-story red brick houses and the gardens which surrounded them were reminiscent of England. The streets they drove through were all paved and lighted and the coaches that traveled them were smart and expensive-looking. The city was situated between two rivers, the Delaware and the Schuylkill, and there were groves and hills and ponds scattered here and there to delight the eye.

They drove directly to the State House, where Congress was in session. Barbara sent Robert in to fetch Ben Harrison, one of the representatives and their neighbor on the James in Virginia. By suppertime she and Ian were settled in a private house on Chestnut Street. The owners of the house were a Quaker family whom Congress strongly suspected of Tory sympathies. The Pembertons were pleased to welcome Lady Barbara; they were not as pleased when they learned she was in Philadelphia to meet her husband, an American brigadier general. However, Mrs. Pemberton gave her guest the entire second floor of the house, with separate bedrooms for herself and Ian and Robert.

The following morning Robert rode out of Philadelphia to join the American Army, which, they had learned, was encamped twenty miles north of the city. He carried a letter from Barbara to her husband.

Eighteen

Alan was with General Washington in the American camp some miles north of Philadelphia when word came to the commander in chief that the British fleet had definitely been sighted far up the Chesapeake Bay. All their uncertainty as to the enemy's destination was finally over; the British were indeed coming to Philadelphia.

"It's a damn circuitous route," Alan said to Anthony Wayne as they stood for a moment in the sunshine outside the farmhouse that served as Washington's headquarters. "The fleet was sighted off the Delaware at the end of July. Why didn't Howe just come up the river? Why take another three weeks to go round to the Chesapeake?"

General Wayne shrugged. "Perhaps the fortifications on the Delaware scared him off."

"If he wants to take Philadelphia, he will have to open up the river in order to supply his army."

"Well, whatever his reasoning, he's here now. Thank God. I was going nutty from all this inaction."

"I know." Alan squinted into the morning sun. "We'll have to cross to the other side of Philadelphia to head them off if they're coming up from Chesapeake."

"Better than marching all the way back to New York."

Alan grinned. "A damn sight better."

It was early afternoon when Alan was summoned by one of his majors. "There's someone here to see you, sir. I put him in your tent."

"Thank you, Woods," Alan replied, and turning his inspection chores over to Colonel Fredericks, he went down the hill to his temporary home.

Inside he found his brother, Robert.

"Let me look at you," Alan said after the first delight and surprise had been expressed. He held Robert away from him, his hands on the boy's shoulders. "You've filled out, gotten older-looking."

Robert looked gravely back at his brother. Alan's face was healthily tanned but the faint hollows under the cheekbones were new. The arrogant nose and straight, firm mouth were harder-looking than Robert remembered. Alan looked muscular, lean, and very, very tough. "Have you come to enlist?" he asked Robert now.

"Yes. Do you need new recruits, Alan?"

"We always need new recruits." Alan grinned and reached out to hug Robert once more. "Christ, but it's good to see you! Sit down. How are things at home? How is Barbara?"

Robert laughed. "Barbara is in Philadelphia, Alan. She traveled north with me. Ian too."

Alan's dark eyes fixed themselves on Robert's face intently. "Barbara is in Philadelphia?"

"Yes." Robert reached into his waistcoat pocket. "Here's a letter from her."

Without a word, Alan took the letter and, going to the door of the tent, stood and read it through. When he looked up, Robert could see that he had gone pale under his tan.

"The British may take Philadelphia," he said.

"I know. However, it appears Barbara's mother is friends with half the British command, so she should be safe no matter what happens."

The color had come back to Alan's face. "How was the journey from Virginia?" he asked.

"Wretched," Robert replied frankly. "Barbara was sick and Ian was abominable. I don't know which one of us was happier to see Philadelphia."

Alan laughed. His eyes looked brilliant in his sunburned face. "Come along, my boy, and let me introduce you to one of my colonels. I have someplace to go at the moment."

Alan suddenly looked much younger. Robert smiled. "Philadelphia?" he inquired.

"Philadelphia," came the firm reply.

General Washington gave Alan permission to go to Philadelphia.

"I've called Sullivan's division in from Morristown," he told Alan. "On Sunday the army will march through Philadelphia. Such a display of strength may well have a desirable effect upon the disaffected, of whom I understand there are many in the city."

"The Quakers, sir, have no love for war."

"Neutrality I can condone," Washington said a trifle grimly. "What I cannot accept is the communication of intelligence to the enemy."

"You are broader-minded than I, sir," Alan replied wryly. "I find I have a hard time condoning even neutrality."

At that Washington smiled. "You will never be a neutral, Alan. And I thank God for that. Go to Philadelphia and give my best regards to Lady Barbara. You can join your brigade before we march into the city."

Alan grinned. "Thank you, Your Excellency. And I will be sure to give your regards to my wife."

Washington looked at him for a moment and then sighed. "You and I, my friend, are nothing but two lonely planters longing for our homes and our wives." The two big men looked at each other in perfect sympathy; then the older man straightened his already erect shoulders. "However, we know our duty. We will see you, my dear general, at Philadelphia."

It was true what his excellency had said, Alan reflected as he rode toward the capital city an hour later. He had no great love for soldiering. He had a talent for leadership, and it had served him in good stead in his present situation, but the military life held no great appeal for him. He missed his home, his fields, his horses, his river. Most of all, he missed his wife.

She had actually come all this way to see him. Barbara. He was ashamed of his resentment at her absence from Morristown—better not think about Morristown, Alan caught himself up hastily. Think instead about Barbara and how it would be when they finally met. She must have forgiven him for joining the army. She would not have come all this way to see him if she still held that against him.

It was dark when Alan finally rode into the city. He had Robert's directions to follow and it was not long before he had located the prosperous-looking house where Barbara was staying. Trust her ladyship, he thought with a flash of humor, to find herself a luxurious billet.

The elderly lady who came to the door did not look pleased to see him. She cast a gimlet-eyed look at his shabby uniform and sent a maid to inform Lady Barbara that her husband had arrived.

"My horse is out front, ma'am," Alan said courteously. "Do you reckon there is someone who can see to it for me?"

"I'll send Davey," his soberly clad, sour-faced hostess said, and Alan, whose ears had been tuned elsewhere, caught the sound of a step on the stairs. He turned, looked up, and she was there.

For a long moment they said nothing, just stood and stared at each other. Then Barbara came slowly down the rest of the staircase.

"Have you met my husband, General Maxwell, Mrs. Pemberton?" she asked graciously.

He had forgotten how low-pitched her voice was. She was smiling at old sour-face, trying to smooth her obviously ruffled feathers. That damned aristocratic graciousness, Alan thought. He wanted her to look at him. Then she raised her eyes. So dark a blue; the darkest blue he had ever seen.

Mrs. Pemberton was smiling. She said something to him about food and he replied he was not hungry. Then, finally, the old harridan went away to the back of the house and they were alone together.

"Come upstairs," Barbara said softly, "to my room."

He followed her without a word. She entered the room first, he closed the bedroom door behind him, and they were alone.

For a long minute they said nothing, just stared at each other, neither of them quite sure what to say first. Their last parting was vividly present to both their minds.

"Your face is thinner," Barbara said at last.

"You are as beautiful as ever."

Barbara bit her lip. "Oh, Alan," she said, and it was as if that simple use of his name released the bonds of constraint. He reached for her.

Her own arms went tightly about his waist and he held her against him, his mouth buried in her hair. He closed his eyes and inhaled deeply. The wonderful scent of her.

"I miss you so much." Her voice was muffled by his shoulder. She stirred in his arms and leaned back a little to look up into his face. "Alan," she said again, and reached up to touch his cheek.

Blindfold him and put him in a room anywhere in the world, he thought, and he would know her touch. He stared down, eyes devouring that beautiful face. "I still can't believe you're here."

"I wanted to come to Morristown," she said, and a pang of guilt shot through him. The less said about Morristown, the better, he thought.

"Well, you're here now and that's all that counts," he murmured and, bending, he began to kiss her.

Barbara felt a wave of response begin to sweep through her body. Her lips answered to the urgency of his and they stood for a long moment, locked together in a passionate embrace.

He tore his mouth away from hers. "Come to bed."

She looked up at him, her blue eyes midnight dark. "All right."

He had a hell of a time getting his boots off and when finally he looked up she was just stepping out of her chemise. They lay down on the bed together and Barbara turned into his arms. How natural it seemed for her to be here, she thought. For over two long years her body had been asleep to passion. It was as if, away from Alan, that part of her went into hibernation. Yet now it seemed as if time had rolled back and it was only yesterday she had lain in his arms.

He was caressing her, and calling her love words, and she felt a flood of desire rising within her.

"Barbara. Love." The having of her. It was all that mattered, all he wanted. And the wildness in her flamed up in answer to his own desperate urgency.

He wrapped his arms around her and buried his face in her throat. He felt her narrow hand stroking his back.

After a long time she spoke in a low voice. "Is there going to be a battle, Alan?"

He kissed the fine bones at the base of her throat. "Don't ask me questions," he murmured. "Love me."

After Alan had finally fallen asleep, Barbara lay awake savoring the feel of his big body next to hers in the bed. How she had missed this. How weary she was of carrying on by herself. If only he could come home with her to Virginia.

The following morning Barbara went in to Ian while Alan finished dressing. She had the little boy dressed and ready for breakfast when Alan came into the room.

Ian stared wide-eyed at the big stranger in uniform who filled his doorway. "Papa?" he asked in an uncertain little voice.

Alan looked scarcely less astonished than his son. Was this well-grown boy the baby he remembered? The only familiar things were the curly black hair and the deep blue eyes.

"Ian," he said. "How you've grown!" He came into the room, crossed to where his son was standing by the tea table, and squatted on his heels in front of him. "I reckon you don't remember me at all," he said softly.

Ian stared with a child's unblinking gaze straight into his father's face. "Mama talks about you," he said at last. "And so do Uncle Robert and Aunt Libby."

Alan reached out a big hand to touch his son's hair. Barbara blinked back a tear and murmured, "I'll go see about breakfast," then slipped out of the room, leaving them alone together.

They spent the day shopping for Alan. Barbara had been horrified by the state of his boots and his shirts and he had cheerfully agreed that he needed a whole new wardrobe.

"But why ever didn't you replace your things before?" Barbara asked in bewilderment.

Alan lifted a black eyebrow. "It's been a trifle difficult to go shopping in New York or Boston lately."

"Oh," said Barbara blankly. "Yes, I suppose it has been. Well, you're in Philadelphia now, and the shops are very nice." She smiled with delighted anticipation. "It's been so long since I've seen any decent shops."

Alan looked at her lit-up face. He thought of fashionable Bond Street in London. Poor girl. Life these last few years had not been much fun for her, either.

Just how little fun it had been was made clear to him when they sat down in the parlor after dinner to talk about the plantation. For the first time Alan was made aware of how much responsibility Barbara had taken on.

He protested. It wasn't necessary. Gavin could see to all that.

She gave him the statistics of Newland's year under Gavin's stewardship and he was silenced. They could not go on like that, and he knew it. With those figures, the plantation would soon be losing money badly.

He listened to his wife as she talked, and watched the play of expression across her lovely face. "I had no idea you were doing all this, sweetheart," he said finally. "Why didn't you tell me in your letters?"

"There was no purpose in worrying you," she said. Her blue eyes held a challenge as she added, "Would you have left the army and come home if you had known how things stood with us?"

His mouth hardened. "No."

She didn't say anything, just continued to look at him out of those challenging eyes. He could feel his temper rising. She *knew* he couldn't come home.

"Well, we are managing," she said at last. "I must have more of Mama in me than I ever thought. She always contrived on her own."

He was angry. Angry because there was nothing he could do to ease her burden and angry that she should throw his impotence in his face like this. He was also guilty, and his guilt only fed his anger. While she had been working so hard, he had been sleeping in Lucy Thornton's bed.

If Barbara should ever find that out . . .

Barbara looked at his bleak face and felt her own heart soften. Poor darling, he looked so tired. And his face was too thin. She got up from her chair and went over to sit on his lap. "Let's not argue," she said softly, her cheek against his shoulder.

He cradled her against him.

"What time must you leave tomorrow?" she asked.

"Early. I want to join my brigade before they enter the city."

Barbara closed her eyes. "There's going to be a battle, isn't there?"

"I'm afraid so, sweetheart. His excellency feels he must try to protect Philadelphia."

The house was very quiet. It had begun to rain and the open window let in a wet night smell.

"I never thought the war would last this long." Barbara's low voice was muffled by his shoulder.

Alan sighed wearily. "I know, Barbara. But you see, that is our strength. We are going to win because we are prepared simply to wait them out."

"But how much longer, Alan?"

"I don't know, sweetheart. I just don't know." He put his mouth against her hair. "I'm so glad you came. The last time we saw each other . . ."

He could feel her stiffen slightly in his arms. "I know. Let's not talk about it."

"All right."

He held her on his lap and listened to the sound of the rain. The warm weight of her was so sweet.

"I love you so much," she said.

"Barbara . . ." When his mouth touched hers it was as though a hood came down over her mind and all she knew was the dark call of his body and the answering cry of her own.

He stood in her bedroom doorway the following morning, dressed in uniform, and she stood before him in her nightgown, her long hair hanging loose down her back. "Alan," she said in an unsteady voice, "please be careful."

"I'm always careful, sweetheart," he said reassuringly, and she looked up into his dark, vibrant face and did not believe him. She put her arms around his waist and clung to him. Against her cheek she could hear the steady beat of his heart.

She closed her eyes and tightened her arms. The power of him. The strength. Yet he was so fragile. One musket ball and all this splendid manhood would be gone forever.

How could she bear to let him go?

"I have to leave now, sweetheart," he said gently, and after a minute she loosed her arms and stepped back. This was sheer agony. He bent, gave her a quick hard kiss on the mouth, and was gone.

Nineteen

The rain stopped as Barbara and Ian were having breakfast. Ian could scarcely eat, he was so excited about seeing the Continental Army parade through the city. The pavement was still wet when Barbara and her son took up a position on Chestnut Street.

The streets were crowded although the mood of the city was scarcely festive. Barbara listened to the various conversations going on around her and diagnosed the temper of the people as nervous. They weren't here to cheer the army. They were here to assess how capable of protecting them that army was likely to be.

From up the street there came the sound of fifes

and drums and then, in the distance, there came into view a big man on horseback.

"It's General Washington!" Ian cried excitedly, and Barbara, afraid he was going to dash into the path of the parade, put a restraining hand on her son's shoulder.

It was indeed Washington and next to him rode a reddish-haired young man whom Barbara heard identified around her as the young Marquis de Lafayette. Ian was jumping up and down with excitement. Washington's face, as he rode past them, was magisterially calm.

Right after the commander-in-chief and his aides came the Philadelphia Light Horse. They, of course, were well known in the city and provoked a great cheer from the crowd surrounding Barbara. Then there was more light horse, and finally from up the street came the drumming noise of army feet and the steady rumble of artillery wheels. The infantry was coming.

Nathanael Greene was not present and so, leading his division, was one of his brigade commanders.

"That's Maxwell," Barbara heard a man behind her say to his friend. "The men call him Hawk. You can see why—look at that face."

"Papa!" Ian cried when Alan, riding his dark bay, was almost abreast of them.

Alan turned his head, looked, and saw his son. He grinned at Ian and the little boy waved back frantically. Alan raised his eyes and, for a fraction of a second, looked directly at Barbara.

Her heart lurched into her throat and began to race wildly, frantically, like a caged bird bettering for freedom in her breast. Her eyes followed him all the way down the street until he was out of sight. Ian spoke to her three times before she was able to answer.

Alan's brigade went by first, accompanied by their own guns. They marched twelve abreast and in every hat there was a sprig of green.

"There's Uncle Robert!" Ian shouted, and sure enough, marching with one of the companies, Barbara saw the fine-featured, handsome young face of her brother-in-law. He looked very serious, but when he saw them, he smiled.

Regiment after regiment of Virginians went by. Their arms were clean and shining but their clothing varied from faded uniforms of different cuts and colors to fringed brown hunting shirts. In the entire army Barbara doubted if there were a dozen decent pairs of shoes.

A big cheer went up all around her for Brigadier General Anthony Wayne, a Pennsylvanian leading a regiment from his own state. Barbara looked up at the new flag which floated above each regiment as it passed by.

Thirteen white stars on a field of blue. Red and White stripes. The United States of America. And how many of these young men would live to see

their homes again? How many widows and orphans would weep when this battle was done?

It wasn't worth it, Barbara thought bitterly. Nothing was worth this sacrifice. And what chance did
they have? The youngster passing in front of her
now was virtually barefoot. They're going out to
meet the British *Army*, she thought on a note of
near-hysteria. They must all be mad.

Ian grabbed her hand. "Isn't it splendid, Mama?"
he asked, his blue eyes shining. "I wish I were big
enough to be a soldier."

Barbara invited Richard Henry Lee, one of Virginia's congressional delegates, to tea the following
day. Ben Harrison had gone home and Barbara
wanted to discover what was happening with the
Continental Army. From Mr. Lee she discovered
that Alan was already at Wilmington, twenty-five
miles down the river. The reports were that the
British had landed at Head of Elk, in Maryland.

The succeeding days dragged unmercifully for
Barbara. Washington was in constant communication with Congress, and Richard Henry Lee, flat-
tered by Lady Barbara's attention and not unmindful
of the fascination of those dark blue eyes, proved
to be a ready source of information. But the British
troops moved very slowly. Word had it that they
were foraging the countryside for provisions after
their long journey by sea.

Washington had eleven thousand troops, includ-

ing local militia—eleven thousand half-trained in-
adequately equipped boys and men—to face a
mighty regular army of fifteen thousand. Barbara
lived in terror as each day brought them inevitably
closer to the time these two armies would clash in
battle.

On September 10, Washington decided to make
his stand behind the Brandywine River, which the
British would have to cross in order to reach
Philadelphia.

On the morning of September 11, Robert, along
with Alan's entire brigade, found himself stationed
in the American center—behind Chad's Ford, facing the main road along which the British were
expected to come. The day was already hot and
the heavy morning mist made the air lie heavy on
his skin. It seemed to Robert, as he grasped his
musket between surprisingly cold fingers, that the
entire world was holding its breath, waiting for
these two armies to meet. His eyes turned instinctively to the figure of his brother. Alan was walking
his bay horse up and down the line of Virginians,
speaking a word of encouragement to each group
of men as he passed. To Robert he looked amazingly good-humored.

Shortly before dawn the artillery began to boom.

Robert was still in his position facing the river
when word came at noon that they were to cross

the Brandywine and attack the British on the other side.

"They must be mad," grumbled the man next to Robert. "That's the whole bloody British army over there."

"Come along, lad," the veteran who had been addressed said as he picked up his musket. "Just follow old Hawk. He'll get us through."

The artillery guns were firing heavily when the First Virginia, following the tall figure of their general, prepared to enter the river. Robert felt clear-headed and calm. His early-morning nerves had quite disappeared.

"Back!" he heard someone calling. "Fall back! Get to your original positions!"

"What the hell?" the man next to him said.

"Wish to God they'd make up their minds at headquarters," someone else grumbled, but they all fell back in good order and Robert found himself once again in position behind the artillery.

At four-thirty in the afternoon word came to Washington confirming the report that had caused his indecision earlier. A column of ten thousand British had crossed the Brandywine some three miles upriver and were falling on his badly outnumbered right wing. Washington sent word that Greene's division was to march to the rescue.

Alan moved his Virginians out immediately. They were tough campaigners and they covered the four miles to their new position in forty-five astonishing minutes. Robert kept up because he was young and healthy. When they finally reached their destination it was to find the American line in chaos. Sullivan's right wing had been charged successively by columns of British guards, grenadiers, and light infantry and had been fighting now for an hour and a half. Many of the Americans had fired their last cartridges. General Sullivan ordered Alan to strengthen his quickly disintegrating line.

To Robert it all seemed like madness. As half of the American army retreated in disorder, Alan's men stayed solidly together, retreating slowly from wood to wood, fighting stubbornly the whole time. Robert simply stuck with his company and followed, as they all did, the figure of his brother—still on horseback, dangerously visible, seemingly ever-present.

"Where the hell is the rest of Greene's division, General?" one man had shouted to Alan earlier and Alan had grinned and replied, "I reckon they can't move as fast as Virginians, Sergeant." But now, as they fled from the last copse of wood, they stumbled upon the rest of their division. Arriving too late to restore the disintegrating battle line, Greene had taken up a position that would enable him to resist the British advance and cover the American retreat. As the First Virginia tumbled out of the woods, the ranks of their fellows opened to let them through.

"Thank God," Robert panted to the boy next to

him. Then they both heard Alan calling, "Fall in!" and Robert stopped, turned around, and raised his musket once again.

A few minutes later a flood of British grenadiers came tearing through the trees and the scrub, flushed with victory and with no idea that the Americans could be capable at this point of producing anything like an organized resistance. They were stopped by a round of murderous fire.

Not long after, the British General Lord Cornwallis arrived on the scene and as the twilight deepened, the British and the Americans shot it out at fifty paces. It seemed to Robert that Alan was everywhere at once on their line, galloping fearlessly up and down amid the hail of fire, encouraging and directing his men.

Behind this steady defense the routed remainder of the American army regrouped and made its retreat to Chester, fifteen miles to the rear. When darkness fell, Greene withdrew his brigade in good order and they too fell back on Chester.

There was no British pursuit.

It was after midnight when Alan sought out his brother.

"How are things with you, Robert?" he asked.

Robert had been preparing to throw himself down exhaustedly to sleep on the ground but now he got to his feet. "I'm fine," he said, and looked up into his brother's face.

The dim light of the campfire threw shadows across Alan's cheekbones and the line of his jaw. "You look tired," Robert said.

"It was a long day."

"Yes." Robert looked around him at the camp, which was settling itself to rest. "It's a funny thing, Alan. We lost and yet no one seems discouraged. 'We'll do better next time.' That's what they're all saying."

Alan clapped his brother on the shoulder. "We lost, but we held together and we weren't routed. We did very well, lad. Next time we will do better." A very faint smile crinkled the corners of his eyes. "*You* did very well, Robert. I was proud of you."

In the darkness Robert's cheeks flushed with pleasure. "It was a bit confusing. I just followed the other men."

"That's the sort of army we are, I'm afraid. No training—we learn by experience. All of us." Alan's voice was half-humorous, half-rueful.

Robert frowned a little. "What happened, Alan? Why were the British able to sneak up on us like that?"

"The local farmers assured his excellency that the Brandywine couldn't be forded upriver," came the reply. "Damn Tories."

Robert stared at his brother. He swallowed. "You were splendid," he said after a minute.

Alan grinned and suddenly seemed quite human again. "Get some sleep, Robert. Thank God you're all right."

Twenty

The sound of artillery could be heard all day long in the city of Philadelphia. Never had Barbara felt so alone. It was as if her isolation were a tangible thing, a space of cold air around her through which filtered only one sound: the noise of the guns.

She was alone in the house. Mr. Pemberton, along with nineteen other well-known Tories, had been sent to Virginia a few days earlier by order of the Pennsylvania Executive Council. Mrs. Pemberton had chosen to accompany her husband, and in their absence, she had let the entire house to Barbara.

The day seemed to drag on forever. Alan had

been in battle before, many times, but Barbara had not known of it until after. Somehow, during these years, she had never really thought that Alan might die. He was so alive, so strong and competent; he had seemed to her invulnerable. But now, with the sound of the guns ringing in her ears, the reality of his war came home to her for the first time.

Silence came with the dark, but still there was no word as to the outcome. No word about casualties.

It was not until early afternoon of the following day that she knew her husband was safe.

Two days after the Battle of Brandywine Alan got leave to come into Philadelphia to see his wife. She was at breakfast with Ian when she heard the sound of his booted feet on the stairs. She knew who it was even before he pushed open the door.

"Alan," she said in a low, throbbing voice, and ran straight into his arms. He held her tightly.

"I was so afraid," she repeated over and over into his shoulder. "So afraid. Thank God you are all right."

"I'm fine, sweetheart." He took her slender face between his two big hands and looked down at her. Their eyes locked together, intent and deadly serious.

"Papa!" Ian had now come over and he tugged on his father's sleeve to gain their attention. "How many Redcoats did you shoot?" the little boy asked eagerly.

Alan looked at his son and drew a deep, steadying breath. "A few," he replied at last.

Barbara made an effort to recover herself. "You must be hungry, darling," she said. "Sit down and I'll ring for some breakfast for you."

They all sat down at the breakfast table and Alan answered his son's questions and ate the huge breakfast the maid Tillie served him. Barbara said scarcely anything, only moved her chair very close to her husband's, and when, once, he reached out to cover her hand with his, her lashes lifted and she gave a quick revealing glance at his face.

"When do you have to leave?" she asked finally.

"This afternoon. We're moving to the other side of the city today and I got permission to come in early to see you. I have to rejoin my brigade later."

This afternoon. Barbara stared at him blindly. Then, "Is there going to be another battle?" she whispered.

"I'm afraid so, sweetheart." He looked very grave.

Ian bounced on his chair with excitement. "Another battle! You'll beat them this time, Papa. I know you will."

At this moment Tillie came into the room. "Tillie, I want you to take Ian out for a few hours," Alan said authoritatively. "Take him shopping and buy him something."

Ian thrust out his lower lip. "I don't want to go." He looked at his mother, who usually could be counted on to accommodate his wishes. "Mama, I want to stay here with you."

Barbara was unmoved. "Do as your father says, Ian."

"Mama!" Ian's blue eyes opened wide in astonishment. He raised his voice. "I don't want to go out."

"Tillie will buy you a new toy, darling."

"I don't *want* a new toy."

"Ian." Alan's voice was very quiet. "You will go downstairs with Tillie. Now."

Blue eyes met brown and Ian pushed back his chair.

"Come along now, Master Ian," Tillie said comfortingly. "Your mama and papa have things to talk about. You and me, we'll have a good time together." Ian did not look as if he were planning to have a good time, but he left the room without further protest. As soon as the door closed behind him, Barbara turned and threw herself into her husband's arms.

Never before had she experienced the wild abandon she felt when he took her to bed that morning. It was as though the grim shadow of battle and death hung over her, urging her to heights and depths of sexual passion she had never before reached. She wanted to pour everything she had out for him, be to him everything she could be, do for him everything she could do. This might be the last time ever she held him in her arms.

Later, when Ian had returned and they were dressed once again and seated in the parlor, she tried to maintain a semblance of normality. "Perhaps you should remove from Philadelphia, Barbara," he said. "The British may very well take the city."

"What if they do?" Barbara asked. "Will that be the end of the war?"

He smiled wryly. "It will be a blow, of course, but it will not mean the end of the war. In fact, I'm of the opinion that it might not be a bad thing for us to lose Philadelphia. It will keep Howe tied up here and he won't be able to go to the assistance of Burgoyne in the north."

"Oh. Well, I'm not ready to go home yet," Barbara said. "Not while there's still a chance of our seeing each other."

"I'm surely not going to argue with you about that." Their eyes met and locked together. "You might think about removing to York or Lancaster, though," he went on. "That's where Congress will go in the event of an occupation."

"Then I can imagine what it will be like trying to find housing there. No, for the moment at least, I'll remain in Philadelphia."

"Well, you'll be all right, I reckon, even if the British do occupy the city. Lady Abingdon's daughter." He raised a sardonic eyebrow.

"Mama is old friends with Sir William Howe," Barbara replied. She looked at her husband with concern. That friendship might prove very useful, she thought, if Alan should ever be captured. Or wounded. . . .

"Will there be another parade today, Papa?" Ian asked.

"No parade, son. Today we just want to get from one side of the city to the other as quickly as possible." He looked at his wife. "I must go, sweetheart."

Barbara's lips were pale. "All right." She rose when he did and they stood close together in the middle of the parlor. Barbara felt as if her heart were bleeding inside of her. This was even worse than the last time.

He held her close against him for one brief moment and then turned, stooped, and picked Ian up to kiss him.

"God keep you," Barbara managed to say, and at the door, he turned to give her a quick careless grin. Then he was gone.

In the days that followed Alan's departure, while the two armies maneuvered for position within twenty miles of Philadelphia, the city began to empty in anticipation of a British occupation. The town was scoured to remove any supplies that might fall into enemy hands. Even the city's bells were taken down and sent to safety in order to prevent their being melted down for cannon. Thousands of people moved out into the country or across the Delaware into New Jersey.

Late in the evening on the night of September 19, Barbara was disturbed by the clamor of horses' hooves in the street. She went first to the front door and then out onto the sidewalk to investigate. The street was filled with carriages.

"What is happening?" she asked the Quaker gentleman who occupied the adjacent house and who was, like her, outdoors in the night.

"Congress is leaving the city, Lady Barbara," came the reply. "The rumor is that Lord Cornwallis will enter Philadelphia tomorrow."

"Tomorrow?" Barbara's hopes rose. Perhaps Washington was not going to risk another battle after all.

It was six more days, however, before part of the British Army under Lord Cornwallis finally marched into Philadelphia. There had as yet been no battle, but Washington's army was still in the vicinity.

Barbara and Ian went to see the British entry, just as they had once watched the Continental Army parade proudly through its capital city. Ian's small dark face was sober as they watched the light horse come down Chestnut Street, guided by local Tories. As a band marched by, Barbara looked around her at the crowd lining the street. There were very few men present; the crowd of thousands consisted mainly of women and children like herself and Ian.

After the band there came another line of horse, and then, finally, riding at the head of the troops, there appeared the splendid figure of Major General Charles Lord Cornwallis. Shouts of joy rang all around Barbara as the crowd recognized him. Ian glowered. Riding next to Cornwallis was a group of leading Tory citizens. The British were cleverly making their entry in the guise of liberators, not conquerors.

It seemed to Barbara that the contrast between the ragged American Army and this highly polished instrument must be painfully clear to anyone who had watched both parades. The British soldiers marched in unison. They were clothed in full uniform and immaculately shod. They looked, quite simply, invincible.

As the parade broke up, a few of the tall grenadiers came among the crowd, shaking hands with the children. The atmosphere was friendly—euphoric, almost. But as a red-coated officer bent to Ian, hand outstretched, Barbara's son set his face and, quite deliberately, put his own hands behind his back. Amused, the tall officer looked over at Barbara. As he met her eyes, his face underwent an astonishing change.

"Lady Barbara!" he said. "By Jove, is it really you?"

"Yes. Lieutenant Bradford, I believe?" Barbara replied calmly.

"Captain now, actually." The young man shook

his head. "Fancy meeting you like this. I thought you had gone to Virginia."

"My home is in Virginia but I have been in Philadelphia these last few weeks to meet my husband. He is with the American Army, you see."

The young man brushed that aside. "Did you know Harry was here?"

A blue spark flamed briefly in Barbara's eyes. "No, is he really? I confess I was watching for him during the parade, but I did not see him."

"He's with General Howe. Cornwallis only brought the grenadiers and the Hessians into Philadelphia. The main part of the army is encamped at Germantown."

"I see. How is Harry?"

"He's fine—a major now, don't you know."

"No, I didn't know. Good for him."

"I'll tell him you're here. Do you have a direction?"

Barbara gave the captain her address and after a few more pleasantries she began to move Ian out of the crowd and toward home.

"You knew that Redcoat!" Ian said accusingly as he walked along beside her.

"Yes. I expect I shall know quite a few of the British officers, Ian. You forget—I am English. I used to dance with Captain Bradford in London."

Ian looked puzzled. "But, Mama, the Redcoats are our enemy."

"They are not *my* enemy, Ian," Barbara said

clearly. "I grew up in England. My mother and father and brothers still live there. My father—your grandpapa—is a member of the British government."

"But Papa is shooting Redcoats, Mama."

"I know," Barbara replied grimly. "Isn't it stupid, Ian? No wonder you can't find the sense in it. I confess, it doesn't make any sense to me either."

"Aunt Libby says King George is a ty . . . ty . . . a ty-something-or-other."

"A tyrant. Yes, I know." Barbara looked down into her small son's puzzled face. "You see, Ian," she tried to explain, "Mama doesn't like war. I'm like the Quakers, I suppose. I don't believe in fighting."

"But what if someone hit you, Mama? Wouldn't you hit back?"

"Well, I should try to find out why that person hit me and see if we could come to some understanding."

"But if he *still* hit you?"

Barbara was beginning to get a headache. "I don't know, Ian, but it seems to me there must always be something one can do besides fighting." Ian looked unconvinced and Barbara took his hand. "Come along," she said peremptorily. "We're late for dinner."

Twenty-one

The British moved quickly to secure their hold on the city of Philadelphia. Of the 5,470 houses in the city and immediately surrounding area, 587 had been vacated by fleeing patriots. The British moved into these and made themselves comfortable.

The first thing Lord Cornwallis did to secure his position was to seize all the boats on the Schuylkill. Then the army began to build batteries along the Delaware. In order to speed up the construction, Cornwallis offered the unheard-of price of eight shillings a day to any man willing to work. Of the 21,767 people who remained in the city, however, 17,285 were women and children. The

British were able to attract very little American labor to their cause.

As Captain Bradford had told Barbara, the remainder of Howe's army had pitched their tents at Germantown, and a few days after the British occupation, Major Harry Wharton called on his cousin.

At first Barbara was uncomplicatedly glad to see him. Harry was as dear to her as her brothers and as closely associated with childhood and home.

"Harry!" she cried delightedly when he came into the parlor, and she raised herself on tiptoe to kiss his cheek. "Let me look at you," she went on, stepping back a little so she could look up into her cousin's face. He was still holding her hands in a tight clasp.

"You look older," she said. "More authoritative. As well you should, *Major* Wharton. Congratulations."

"Thank you," he replied automatically. His eyes had never left her face. "You are as beautiful as ever."

That was what Alan had said when first they met again. . . . Barbara disengaged her hands and gestured to the sofa. "Sit down, Harry. You must tell me all about yourself."

He took the seat she had indicated. "I couldn't believe my luck when Bradford told me you were in Philadelphia."

She looked at him gravely. "I came last month

to see Alan. He hasn't been home since the war began."

Harry's blue eyes darkened infinitesimally. "He's been with Washington the whole time, then?"

"Yes." Barbara turned her head to look at the door. "Tea, please, Tillie." She turned back to Harry with a challenge in her eyes. "It's Dutch," she informed him.

He smiled a little crookedly. "I won't complain."

"What do you hear from home?" Barbara asked, moving the subject to the safety of neutral ground.

They chatted comfortably for half an hour, catching up on old friends and reminiscing about old times.

"Aunt Elizabeth used her influence with Sir William Howe to get me posted to major," Harry said at one point. "I've been very lucky. I would never have made it to major in a peacetime army."

Barbara felt herself go rigid. "I'm glad the war has been useful to you," she replied coldly. "We in America have not found it so pleasant."

"I didn't mean that the way it sounded, Barb," Harry said hastily. "Of course I'm not happy that we are at war with America. But I am a professional soldier, you know. And the job of a professional soldier is to fight wars."

Barbara could almost feel the ice coming into her veins. "Unfortunately, we are not professional soldiers," she said. "We are only poor civilians who have been forced to take up arms for the protection of our homes."

Harry stared at his cousin out of astonished blue eyes. "Barbara," he said, "surely you haven't turned into a rebel?"

"I did not approve of this war," she replied, "but now that we are in it, of course I desire America to win." The look of stunned amazement on Harry's face was almost ludicrous. "Good God, Harry," she said impatiently, "how should you expect me to feel? My husband and my home are here."

"But *you* are English!"

"I am English, yes." There was real bitterness in her voice now. "But so were the Americans until your 'professional' army drove them into rebellion."

"We didn't start this," Harry said reasonably.

Barbara's blue eyes were hard as diamonds. "And we did not send our armies to invade your shores— just because we would not pay a bloody tax on tea!"

Harry did not know if he were more shocked by her ideas or by her language. He had never seen his cousin like this before. Barbara was always so serene, so invincibly gracious.

There was the sound of someone in the hall and in a minute a small boy appeared at the parlor door.

"I'm back, Mama," he said.

"Come in, darling, and meet your cousin," Barbara said. Her face had recovered its usual tranquillity. "Harry, this is my son, Ian. Ian, your cousin, Major Harry Wharton."

Harry held out his hand and after a brief but noticeable pause Ian stuck out his own grubby hand. Harry looked down at Barbara's son.

He looked five, not three. The slender boy's body appeared strong and sturdy and the eyes that looked out of his dark, Maxwell face were as blue as his mother's. He was an extraordinarily striking child. It was quite obvious he did not like the idea of shaking hands with a Redcoat.

Ian turned immediately to his mother. "Mrs. Bledsoe said we're all going to starve, Mama," he announced. "Is that true?"

"Of course not. Whatever did she mean, Ian?"

"She said the Redcoat navy couldn't get up the river, and there wasn't enough food in Philadelphia, and we would all starve." Ian seemed pleased by the prospect.

"Good heavens." Barbara looked at her cousin. "Is that true, Harry?"

"It's true that the rebels have blocked the river," Harry returned easily. "There are chevaux-de-frise at Billingsport and at Red Bank, and two forts at Red Bank as well. But we shall soon take care of those."

"We are not rebels!" Ian said fiercely, and glared at his mother's cousin.

Barbara put a hand on her son's shoulder. "What are chevaux-de-frise?" she asked quietly.

Harry's grim face relaxed slightly. "Arrangements of transverse beams bolted together and pointed with iron stakes. They rise to the level of the river's surface. The ships can't get up the Delaware until they are got rid of."

Barbara raised a winged eyebrow. "They sound formidable. What will happen if Admiral Howe can't get the supply ships up the river after all?"

"Then we will live on the surrounding country."

The blue eyes regarding him were inscrutable. "You may find it more difficult than you anticipate, Harry, to live off the country. The American Army is in the vicinity."

"We will deal with the American Army," Harry said confidently.

"You haven't yet." Barbara's hands tightened warningly on Ian's shoulder.

There was a pause. Harry stared at his cousin. "No," he said finally, "we haven't, have we?"

Ian narrowed his eyes and stared at Harry's uniform. "*My* papa is a general," he said loudly.

Harry looked startled. "A general? I did not know that."

"My papa is a friend of General Washington."

"Ian, love," Barbara spoke softly into her son's ear, "go wash up and change, please."

"Yes, Mama." Ian shot his English cousin a distinctly unpleasant look and obediently left the room.

After the sound of his steps on the stairs had

died away, Harry said to Barbara, "Well, there's no doubt where *he* stands, is there?"

"It is hardly surprising," Barbara returned. "He is, after all, the third generation of his family to be born in this country."

There was a long pause. Then, "You have surprised me," Harry said candidly. "I had thought you would be a Tory."

Barbara looked down and then slowly up. It had always been a seductive gesture, the slow lifting of those long lashes, the sudden revelation of those astonishing eyes. It was entirely unconscious on her part; Harry remembered the gesture from her childhood. But now it produced a profoundly disturbing effect, even more so than he remembered.

"I told Ian a few weeks ago that I stood with the Quakers," she replied slowly and carefully. "And I thought I did . . . then."

"But you don't now?" His voice was harsh with suppressed feeling.

"I don't know anymore how I feel." She looked at him, at his immaculate uniform and shining boots. "I have hated seeing British soldiers swarming all over Philadelphia," she said honestly. "I never thought I would hate it as much as I do."

"Well, I hope that doesn't mean you hate *me*," Harry said with difficulty.

She looked up into his fair, handsome, well-remembered face and her eyes were suddenly wet. "Oh, Harry," she said, and impulsively reached out to him. "Of course not! How could I ever regard *you* as an enemy?"

He put his arms around her and held her against him. She rested her cheek for a brief moment against his shoulder. Harry closed his eyes. Unseen by Barbara, there was a line of pain about his mouth. When, after a moment, she pulled away from him, he forced himself to smile at her. "There can be no different sides where we are concerned. There's only us."

"Yes." She smiled back. "Just Harry and Barbara, the way we were as children."

His eyes flickered. "I must be going," he said then. "I'm due back at headquarters."

She smiled at him a little mistily. "I will be here in Philadelphia for another month at least. Come and see me again."

"Of course I will." He drew a deep, difficult breath. It took all the self-control he possessed to walk out the parlor door and leave her.

Harry passed a disturbed night filled with thoughts of Barbara. It had been a mistake to see her, he thought as he tossed restlessly on his hard and narrow bed. He had tried so hard to put her out of his mind, and now, just this one meeting, and it was starting all over again.

What if Maxwell were killed? She would be a widow then, and free to marry . . . He mustn't think that way, he told himself sternly. But his thoughts, it seemed, were not his to control. He did not fall into a deep sleep until just before dawn.

He was awakened after less than an hour by the sound of guns. As a member of General Howe's staff, he was sharing Sir William's quarters, a comfortable farmhouse just behind the British lines. He felt someone shaking his shoulder and groggily he sat up in bed.

"What is it?" he mumbled to Captain Archer, a fellow aide and old school friend who was bending over him.

"Don't know. We'd better find out," came the terse reply, and in a very short while General Howe and his staff were in their saddles and heading toward the front.

The morning was extremely foggy and as Harry galloped on, the noise grew louder and more intense. Then disordered parties of light infantry began to stream past them.

General Howe began to circle around on his horse. "For shame, Light Infantry!" he shouted to the men who were passing him in the opposite direction. "I never saw you retreat before. Form! Form! It's only a scouting party."

"It's more than a scouting party, General!" shouted one of the men, and as if to back him up, a salvo of grape roared in front of them. Looking ahead, Harry saw a column of Americans loom out of the mist. With absolute incredulity, he realized that Washington had attacked.

The next few minutes were utter chaos. A rattle of small-arms fire from the left told Harry that the Hessians were fighting for the heights above the Wissahickon. From the farther end of the village street came the crackle of musketry punctuated by the thud of cannon shots. Immediately in front of him, to the right and left of the market square, the British lines were barely holding their ground against the fury of an American bayonet charge.

Christ! thought Harry. After a split second's hesitation, he shouted to General Howe, "Shall I go down to the village, sir?"

"Yes!" General Howe roared back. "Rally the men, Wharton! Make them hold!"

"Yes, sir," and Harry was gone through the mist. The fog thickened. Down in the village he managed to rally a company of men and they held on grimly, fighting for every doorway, garden wall, and orchard close. Out in the fields, the British set fire to the unmown hay and the smoke added to the lack of visibility caused by the fog.

Then luck turned in the British direction. In the American lines one regiment mistook another for British and, in the ghastly visibility, began firing on their own men. Confusion began to reign among the attacking ranks, although still they pressed on.

Alan was with Greene's division on the left. They had made a long, flanking march and, due to the ineptitude of their guide, were late in making contact with the rest of the army. As they finally came up in the confusion of the fog, they were hit by three thousand grenadiers and hessians just arrived from Philadelphia under Lord Cornwallis. The Philadelphia troops were fresh and Alan's men had been marching all night. The fighting soon became hand-to-hand and vicious.

The arrival of the troops from Philadelphia put fresh heart into General Howe's men and they ceased to retire and began to press the fight forward. Alan, struggling to get his men clear from the surrounding enemy, had his horse shot out from under him in the melee. One of his men pulled him clear of a deadly British bayonet thrust, and regaining his feet, Alan began to shout to rally his men.

In the terrible confusion, the American rear guard formed in line. As the infantry fell back in good order, streaming past their disappointed commander in chief, they raised their empty cartridge pouches to show the reason for their retreat.

Alan's men, though deathly tired, held on tenaciously. In fact, the entire American rear guard stood so firmly that the British, although they kept up the pursuit for five miles, declined to press an attack. By nine o'clock that night the Americans were once again in their old camp by Pennypacker's Mill.

In the last twenty-six hours they had marched forty-five miles and fought from daybreak until noon. They had lost the battle, but the defeat was due to fog, confusion, and lack of ammunition rather than to the superiority of the enemy troops. They had withstood three British bayonet charges and retired in good order. As they fell into exhausted slumber, the Continental Army, from general down to private, was well pleased with itself.

Barbara learned about the battle from her cousin Harry two days later. She had already been informed, by Dr. Foulke, an American army surgeon whom Washington had dispatched at General Howe's request to help with the American wounded left on the field, that both Alan and Robert were safe.

Harry arrived at Barbara's house on Chestnut Street with Captain Archer, who remembered Barbara from London.

"We were never introduced, Lady Barbara," he said with a shy grin when Harry presented him, "but I remember seeing you at the opera and driving in the park."

Barbara smiled graciously and held out her hand.

"I believe your husband is unhurt," Harry said when they were all seated in the parlor.

"Yes, I know," Barbara replied tranquilly. "Dr. Foulke was kind enough to send me word. But I have been unable to discover precisely what happened." And she looked inquiringly at the two young men.

"Washington attacked us." Captain Archer's faintly freckled face looked absolutely astonished. "He collected that ragamuffin army and actually attacked. Amazing."

"We beat them, though." It was Harry speaking now.

"You beat them all the time." Barbara raised a winged brow. "It doesn't appear to stop them, however."

"They're getting better, too," said Captain Archer. Harry's mouth thinned and set. "If it hadn't been for the fog," Captain Archer went on, "God knows what the outcome might have been."

Tea was brought in and Barbara poured. When everyone had a cup, Barbara asked the question that had been on her mind for the last two days. "What will happen now, Harry? Is there going to be another battle?"

"I don't know about another battle, Barb. For a moment, General Howe is pulling back into Philadelphia. The biggest problem we face at present is one of supply. We've got to open the Delaware for the navy. That's the little project next on Sir William's agenda."

Barbara nodded tranquilly and sipped her tea. The entire British Army was being drawn back into Philadelphia. Evidently the Battle of Germantown had been a close-run thing indeed.

Twenty-two

The British Army poured into Philadelphia and began to build field fortifications. Every available house was occupied—some, in fact, were used as stables. With the military added to the civilian population, recently augmented by an influx of Tories, General Howe was faced with a great many mouths that needed to be fed.

On October 25 came the news that the British general Burgoyne had surrendered his entire army to the American Horatio Gates on October 17 at Saratoga, New York.

Barbara kept delaying her departure for Virginia.

"I want to see Alan one more time before I leave," she said to her cousin the afternoon after the news of Saratoga had been received in Philadelphia. "Do you think you could possibly arrange for me to leave Philadelphia, Harry, so I could ride out to meet the American Army?"

"Don't be insane, Barbara," he responded angrily. Harry was not in a cheerful mood. "It's impossible. I can guarantee you safety from British attack, but parties of rebels are everywhere in the countryside. You know the difficulty we are having just trying to get in food. Good God, when headquarters sends dispatches to England, it takes a whole regiment to escort the messenger to his ship!"

They were seated in Barbara's parlor. Soldiers had been quartered on most of the residents of Philadelphia, but Barbara, in a brief meeting with General Sir William Howe, had managed to get him to allow her the sole occupancy of the house on Chestnut Street. Barbara rose now and went to the window to look out. Harry regarded her slender back in silence.

"I received a letter today from my sister-in-law in Virginia," she said at last, turning to face him. "She says her husband is leaving to join the Continental Army. I must go home shortly. I cannot leave Libby to carry on alone."

"You cannot leave Philadelphia now, Barbara. Not to join your husband and not to return to Virginia. It is impossible to pass through New Jersey at the moment, rebel forces are so active. We can't spare the number of men we would need to cross the Delaware. That's why food is so scarce."

"I shall be perfectly safe from the Americans, Harry. After all, my husband is one of Washington's generals."

"They shoot first and ask questions later," Harry said grimly.

Barbara's face in the light from the window was strained and pale. "I should have gone to York when the Congress left Philadelphia. I didn't want to cope with the discomforts of another move, and look where I've landed us. Stuck in a city under siege."

"We are not under siege." Temper flared in Harry's blue eyes.

Barbara looked at him steadily and after a moment he turned away from her and looked out the window.

Barbara took a long, slow breath. "Is there any way I can get a letter to Alan?"

"Certainly," he said over his shoulder. "Just find one of Washington's spies. They come in with every wagonload of food, damn them."

Barbara stared at her cousin's rigid back. "How do you know?"

"Because he bloody well knows about every foray we're going to make, that's how," Harry returned furiously. "And there's precious little we can do to stop it. We need the wagonloads of food too badly."

Barbara's face was thoughtful. "I see."

Harry turned to face her. "We will get the river open soon enough, Barb. That will change the picture here altogether."

"Will it?" Barbara smiled ruefully. "Much as I dislike being in a city under siege, Harry, I'm afraid I cannot find it in me to wish you success."

"No. I suppose not. Well, I must go, Barb."

Barbara accompanied him to her front door and gave him an absentminded kiss on the cheek before she went to her desk to compose a letter to her husband.

Alan's mail delivery was scarcely regular, so it came as a distinct surprise to him to receive two letters on the same day. He recognized his wife's elegant slanting script and opened her missive immediately:

> It seems I am trapped here in Philadelphia, darling. Harry says the countryside is too dangerous for me to think of trying to reach your camp, and I must say that from what I can see, he is right. If you can arrange somehow to get me safely out of the city, Alan, do let me know, but I won't do anything unless I hear from you.
>
> Things are very difficult here just now. There is not enough food and I understand from Captain Archer that ammunition is also low. General Howe is determined to reduce the forts on the Delaware so that he can supply the city from the ships.
>
> Ian and I are very well. We have plenty of food—

General Howe has been most thoughtful. I understand from Mama's last letter that they are not happy with him at home. I don't think he wishes to alienate her sympathy—Papa, after all, is in the government.

I have heard from Libby that Mr. Dwight plans to leave Virginia to join the Continental Army. I wrote to her immediately that I did not think I would be home until the spring. The letter went with General Howe's dispatches, so I hope it will be delivered before Mr. Dwight leaves. I hate to think of her all alone at Newland.

Darling, I miss you so. I feel so cut off from you, so isolated. It was better in Virginia, when I did not know what was happening until a month after it was all over. I should have gone to York as you suggested. Perhaps then we would have been able to meet.

Please do try to get a letter to me. You are always in my thoughts and in my prayers.

Your loving wife,
Barbara

Alan read the letter through again and then folded it carefully and put it into his pocket. He had written to her a week ago, but apparently the letter had never reached its destination. He would write again immediately and tell her to stay where she was. At least that damn cousin of hers had the sense to keep her from doing anything foolish.

He was frowning slightly, his mind preoccupied with the situation of his wife, when he picked up the other letter to read. He went very still when he saw who it was from.

Lucy Thornton was in York and she wanted to see him. The sense of urgency conveyed by her letter was unmistakable. He would have to go. It was with a distinct feeling of doom hanging over his head that Alan went to see his commander in chief about a leave.

York was serving as the temporary capital of the United States during the occupation of Philadelphia, and the small town was filled to capacity with congressional delegates. Alan found Lucy at a small tavern on the outskirts of the town. The fact that she had come so far to see him, and come alone, was the lever that had got him to York so quickly.

The landlady went upstairs to inform Lucy that he had arrived and Lucy did not keep him waiting for long. "Let's go outside," she said to him in a low voice after they had exchanged a rather constrained greeting. "There's a walk I know where we can be private."

Privacy was something Alan profoundly desired. He did not want to take the chance of one of the Virginia delegation seeing him here with Lucy. He was more than happy to leave the busy tavern and head for the quiet tree-lined path Lucy had suggested.

She walked beside him in silence for a few minutes and he made no attempt to introduce speech of his own. She looked very much as he remembered. Gladness had flared in her eyes when first she saw him, but there had been no answering gladness in him; only a growing dread. When finally she began to speak, he was braced for the worst.

"I guess you think I was presumptuous, asking you to come here like this, but I have something to tell you that I just couldn't put into a letter." She stopped and looked up into his hard-set face. "Alan . . ." She faltered a little bit at that bleak look, but then went resolutely on, "I'm going to have a baby."

He had been afraid of this ever since he got her letter. Damn! he thought viciously. The only time in the whole bloody war he'd been unfaithful to Barbara, and this had to happen. What bloody rotten luck he had.

"I'm sorry," she said in a small voice, and for the first time since his arrival in York he really looked at her. Her big dark eyes looked frightened and lost. What a swine he was, thinking only of himself. This situation was much more disastrous for her than it was for him. "It's just . . . I don't know what to do."

He felt absolutely wretched in the face of her distress. "I can't marry you, Lucy," he said helplessly. "You know that."

"Yes, I know. I always knew you were married, you never made any secret of that. But I never thought this would happen, Alan. *I* was married too—for five years—and there was never any hint of a child. I thought I was safe."

"So did I," he returned grimly. He drew a deep, steadying breath. "When?" he asked.

"March."

March. He calculated rapidly. She was about three months gone then. "I don't suppose there is anyone else you might marry?" he asked tentatively.

She shook her head and stared straight ahead.

"Well then, as I see it, we have two choices. You can go away, to New York perhaps, or Boston. You can say your husband was killed at Germantown; say the baby is posthumous. There is little likelihood of the truth ever coming out. But it will mean your uprooting yourself, Lucy. I can give you the money to settle yourself comfortably, but I'm afraid it will be lonely for you, my dear."

Her face did not change its expression. "And the other choice?" she asked.

He sighed. "Go to New York and have the baby and I'll find someone to take it. That way you can go home and no one will be the wiser."

She gave him a wide-eyed look. "Who would take the child?"

"My sister Helen in England would, if I asked her."

She looked down at her feet. "Or I could go home, face the scandal, and have my baby there."

A thrill of horror ran down his spine. He didn't want her to do that. Everyone would know who the father was. . . . There was a white line around his mouth as he replied grimly, "Or you can go home." He stopped walking and turned to look at her. "I will provide for you and for the baby, Lucy, but I'm afraid there is little else I can do." She looked so young to him, and so frightened. "Oh, my dear," he said, and his voice now was soft and gentle, "I am so sorry to have brought this sorrow on you."

She took a step toward him and he put his arms around her and held her in a strong, comforting embrace. It was the first time he had touched her since they met. "I know there's nothing you can do," she said in a voice muffled by his shoulder. "And it's as much my fault as it is yours."

"No. The fault is mine." He had little doubt of that. He had taken advantage of her loneliness and his position as guest in her household. And now that she had come to him in her distress, all he could think of was how to keep the news from Barbara. What a bloody rotten swine he was. He patted Lucy's back gently. "Tell me what you want to do," he said, "and I'll do everything in my power to assist you."

She pressed her cheek into his shoulder. "I'll go to New York," she said, "and start a new life." He was ashamed of the relief that flooded through him at her words.

Twenty-three

On November 15 the American defense at Fort Mifflin, conducted with incredible bravery under impossible enemy fire, was finally forced to give up. The Delaware River, despite Washington's best efforts, now lay open for the British fleet.

However, the long, drawn-out process of gaining control of the Delaware left the British in Philadelphia feeling less than perfectly secure. To ward off another attack by Washington, General Howe had erected a chain of fortifications between the Delaware and the Schuylkill on the heights just north of Callowhill Street.

The defenses were necessary. American scouts and cavalry were annoying the British pickets and outposts and harrying the traffic on the main roads into the city. Some traffic did manage to get through, however, and one of the wagons coming into Philadelphia on the morning of December 2 was driven by a very tall, dark farmer whose shabby clothes looked as if they had seen many winters of wear.

The day was cold and bleak and promised rain or sleet before evening. Barbara was sitting in front of the fire in the parlor of the house on Chestnut Street when a note was delivered to her door. She took the message from Tillie with her gracious smile and opened it as the maid left the room.

The bold black handwriting almost leapt off the page at her. "Sweetheart," she read with a pounding heart, "expect me tonight at eight."

That was all.

Barbara read the letter again and again; then, with none-too-steady hands, she leaned forward and cast it into the fire.

He was in Philadelphia.

She would see him tonight.

Alan.

She got Ian into bed at seven and by seven-thirty had dismissed the servants to their own quarters. Then she sat in the parlor with her hands clasped tensely in her lap, her whole being alert for any unusual noise.

At ten after eight there came the faintest of taps on the front door. Barbara flew to open it.

"Come in," she said breathlessly, "before anyone sees you." She closed the door behind her husband and turned to look up at him. His arms came around her in a strong, vigorous hug.

"Alan," Barbara said in his ear, "come upstairs to the bedroom." Her feet were off the ground.

"Certainly," he drawled in reply, and at that deep, familiar accent, tears stung behind Barbara's eyes.

The fire was burning brightly in her bedroom and she lit the candles before turning once more to look at him.

"Good God," she said faintly, "wherever did you get those clothes?"

He smiled in reply, but it was not his usual carefree grin. "I couldn't very well wear my uniform into Philadelphia, sweetheart."

Barbara was still staring at the shabby breeches and slightly torn coat that were adorning her husband. Then she raised her eyes to his face. It had been almost two months since last she saw him. "I suppose not," she replied softly. Then, "You look .too thin."

"You're the only person who ever tells me I'm thin," he said. He held out a hand. "Come here."

She walked over to stand before him at the fire and he cupped her face in both his hands and gazed down at her. Then he touched her cheekbone with his finger. "How is Ian?" he asked.

"Fine. He misses Newland, though."

"You should go home, sweetheart. Once we go into winter quarters, the military situation will quiet down. You can get through to Virginia. I'll give you a letter just in case you get stopped."

She smiled up at him. "So you want to get rid of me?"

"Get rid of you?" At that he pulled her against him, hard. "Don't be stupid." Over her head his voice sounded rough and harsh.

Barbara pressed against him. Oh, the wonderful feel of that big strong body against hers. "I miss you so much, Alan," she whispered. "I miss you so much."

He put his cheek against her hair. "You smell so sweet."

She raised herself on her toes and kissed the line of his jaw. "Come to bed, darling," she said huskily. "Come to bed and I'll show you how sweet I can be."

It was after midnight when Barbara, a warm robe over her nakedness, went down to the kitchen to fetch Alan some food. He had made the fire up again by the time she returned and she set a table in front of its warmth and sat down to watch him eat.

"How are things in the city now that the river is open?" he asked while he was eating the cheese and bread and apples she had got for him.

"Easier," she replied. "The army is back on full

rations. I think General Howe is nervous after Germantown, however. He's been building defenses all around the city."

"Yes," said Alan. "I know." His mouth was smiling but his eyes were shadowed by his lashes and Barbara could not see their expression. She pushed her loose hair back.

"You could have been recognized, darling, even without your uniform. There are a number of officers in Philadelphia who would know you from London." Barbara looked worriedly at her husband's face. "You aren't the sort one forgets very easily."

Alan's lashes lifted. "Who is here that *you* know?"

"Well, Harry is here, of course. He's a major now, on General Howe's staff. Did I tell you that?"

Alan chewed his food and watched her thoughtfully. The firelight illuminated his dark, unshaven face and rumpled hair. Barbara could not read his expression. "So Cousin Harry is on General Howe's staff?" he said at last.

"Yes. Harry, of course, would never betray you, but there are several others who very well might. So do please be careful, darling. Under British law you are a traitor; and you know what the sentence is for a traitor." Her eyes were wide and fightened-looking.

He patted her head soothingly. "They won't hang me, sweetheart. If they catch me they'll just throw me into the Walnut Street prison with all the other poor bastards who are freezing and starving in there.''

Barbara frowned. "I did not realize there were many American prisoners.''

"The wounded, mostly, captured on Brandywine and Germantown. The British won't execute them outright—we have too many of their men in our hands for them to risk reprisals. But they're killing them by neglect. His excellency has protested their treatment ceaselessly.''

"I did not realize," Barbara repeated.

Alan took another bite of an apple. "Who are these other officers who are likely to recognize me?" he asked.

"Well, there's Captain Archer.''

"Is he on General Howe's staff as well?''

"Yes. And Captain Bradford. He's in the grenadiers. I'm sure there are others as well, but as I have not joined in the social round, I haven't met them.''

"Perhaps you should join in the social round," Alan suggested.

Barbara stared at him. "What?''

He chewed slowly, reflectively. "I would find the gossip from General Howe's aides extremely interesting," he said.

His dark eyes were steady on hers. He looked perfectly serious. "Are you asking me to *spy* for you, Alan?" she asked incredulously.

"Not spy, sweetheart. Just listen.''

"Well, if I listen and then tell you what I've heard, that's spying," she returned tartly.

He didn't reply, just continued to look at her out of those intent dark eyes.

"You know how I've felt about this war, Alan," she said shakily. "I don't think it should ever have been started."

"Well, it has started, Barbara. It is no longer possible to play the neutral."

"The Quakers are neutral," Barbara said stubbornly. "They are against all fighting."

"Quakers." There was such contempt in his voice that she winced. "Damn Tories is what they are. They've done nothing but kiss British asses since Howe landed."

"That's not true. Or at least it's true for only a few of them."

"Barbara." He stood up and came around to her side of the table. He took her hands in his and drew her to her feet. "Sweetheart, I'm not asking very much." His voice was softly coaxing. "If I thought there was any danger involved for you, I would never ask it. Just listen to the military gossip and let me know what is said. That's not so very difficult, is it?" His dark eyes were mesmerizing.

"I thought you wanted me to go home."

He put his hands on her shoulders. "Do you want to go home?"

Wordlessly she shook her head. His hands on her shoulders felt so warm. He was right: it was no longer possible to be neutral. His way had to be her way too. She wet her lips with her tongue. "I won't put anything in writing," she said.

He smiled down at her faintly. "Then I reckon I'll just have to come to Philadelphia to see you," he said.

"Well," Barbara's voice sounded breathless to her own ears, "if it will help to end this war. I'd do almost anything to help end this war."

His eyes began to blaze. He had never really expected this concession from her. "God, sweetheart," he said, "how I love you." He was holding her so tightly that he hurt her, but she didn't mind, hardly noticed. She dug her nails into the hard muscles of his shoulders and closed her eyes. She would do anything for him, she thought. She loved him so much. That night, as the fire crackled and glowed against the dark night outside, he got her with child.

He left before either Ian or the servants were up the following morning. "If you have anything of importance to tell me, just send a message that you want to see me," he said.

"All right." These partings were like a small death to her. She looked up at him anxiously and said, "Please be careful, Alan. Pull your hat down over you face."

He complied, pulling it down almost to his nose. "Like this?" He grinned.

Barbara thought her heart would break. She

reached up and put her arms around his neck. "I wish we were at home," she whispered. "I wish I never had to say good-bye to you again."

"I know." His voice was deep and gentle. Carefully he removed her arms from around his neck and looked for a moment into her face, as if he were memorizing it. Then he turned to go. Barbara dug her nails into her palms to keep from reaching after him.

"Oh." He turned at the door. "I never told you, Charles Dwight arrived in camp a few days ago."

"Charles? But didn't Libby get my letter?"

"Apparently not."

"Oh dear. That means poor Libby is all by herself at Newland."

" 'Fraid so, sweetheart." He took a short, hard breath. "Give my love to Ian," he said, and was gone down the front steps.

Two days later General Howe marched out of Philadelphia with horse, foot, and guns in what was supposed to be a surprise maneuver. Washington, however, had been expecting the move and the Americans were prepared. For three days General Howe probed Washington's lines around Whitemarsh, looking for a place vulnerable enough to attack. But the heights bristled with abatis and guns, behind which the American infantry were lined up, muskets at the ready.

Sir William Howe had led the British attack on

Bunker Hill at the beginning of the war, and the specter of that painful victory was always with him. He had lost one thousand out of thirty-five hundred men he had under him at Bunker Hill, and if he attacked Washington now he was afraid of similar results. So instead of attacking, he turned his troops, marched back to Philadelphia, and declared the army in winter quarters until spring.

On December 17 General Washington issued general orders to the Continental Army stating that they too would be going into winter quarters. The place he had chosen was some twenty-two miles northwest of Philadelphia and so situated that it would allow the army to protect the huge number of patriot refugees who had fled from Philadelphia and also to prevent the enemy from drawing supplies from the rich farm country nearby.

The name of the place which Washington had chosen was Valley Forge.

As soon as the British Army was back in Philadelphia, Barbara made Harry take her to the Walnut Street prison. He resisted her at first and it was only when she threatened to go on her own that he gave in and made the arrangements.

The Walnut Street prison had been built to house the city's lawbreakers; now it contained the American prisoners of war captured at Brandywine and Germantown. It was grossly overcrowded. It was filthy. Barbara, walking with Harry along one of the corridors, prayed she would not disgrace herself and retch. The smell of unwashed men was unspeakable.

The men, of course, did not know who she was. All they knew was that she was escorted by an English officer, and Barbara could feel their hostile stares as she walked down the aisle. Most of the prisoners were virtually naked and the prison was damp and freezing.

Barbara stopped abruptly in the middle of the corridor and took a long, careful breath. "Is there an officer present among the prisoners?" she asked very carefully.

"Barb!" Harry stared at her nervously. Two other British officers stood at the end of the corridor, impassive.

There was a moment's silence and then a nasal New England voice said, "I'm Colonel Wheeler, ma'am." A gaunt, bearded shape made its way to the iron bars that caged about twenty men.

Barbara ignored Harry and walked over to the American. "What are your most pressing needs, Colonel?" she asked simply. "I will do what I can to help you."

There was a low murmur of surprise and excitement. "Quiet!" the colonel snapped, and silence fell. Barbara felt the weight of hundreds of eyes upon her.

"We need food, ma'am," the colonel said. "They

only allow us meat once a week. And clothing. And blankets."

"Very well." The man's eyes were a clear hazel. "I will try to procure you supplies, Colonel." She looked around her and could not suppress a shudder. "I will try."

"Thank you, ma'am." The hazel eyes looked directly into hers. "Who are you, ma'am?" he asked curiously.

"I am General Maxwell's wife," she replied.

"Old Hawk's wife?" the New Englander said incredulously.

Barbara smiled faintly. "Yes."

"Well, anything you can do for us will be greatly appreciated, ma'am. Men are dying here from hunger and cold."

"I will do my best, Colonel," Barbara said firmly, and, turning, she walked quickly down the aisle. She did not look at Harry until they were standing outside in the cold winter sunshine. Then she said, "I want to walk home. I need to clear my nostrils."

Harry fell in beside her. "I tried to tell you, but you wouldn't listen."

She stared straight ahead. "The treatment of those men is nothing short of barbarous," she said fiercely.

Harry cleared his throat. He had been shaken too. "Cunningham is in charge of them and Cunningham is a swine." Then, trying to justify the scene he had just beheld to himself as well as to her, "You know, though, Barb, that by rights the Americans shouldn't be prisoners at all. They should all be hanged for treason."

"The reason they are being held prisoners is that there are hundreds of British officers and men in American hands," Barbara said, quoting her husband's words to her. "The government simply does not want to risk reprisals."

"Yes," said Harry after a minute, "there is that."

"But, my God, Harry, for a civilized nation to treat its prisoners like that!"

Harry looked bleak. "You promised that fellow you would help. What do you have in mind to do, Barb?"

"I am going to call together a few of my Quaker neighbors and see if I can interest them in helping to collect supplies for the prison."

"Do you think they'll do it?"

"Yes."

"You'll have to get General Howe's permission," he said.

"I'll get it."

He had no doubt that she would. The look on her beautiful face was absolutely implacable. "If you do, I'll help get the supplies delivered," he heard himself offering.

She smiled at him, a radiant, glowing smile he had never had from her before. "Thank you, Harry. I'll take care of contacting the Quakers. Your task is to get me invited to dine with General Howe."

"That will be no problem at all," he replied promptly. "General Howe is very fond of beautiful women."

"So I understand," Barbara replied dryly, and after a minute, Harry laughed.

General Howe was a tall dark man with the marks of self-indulgence written on his face and his increasingly bulky figure. He was connected to the royal family through his mother and he and his brother, Admiral Howe, had risen high in their respective services. But his reputation was presently in eclipse in England. The newspapers were demanding to know why he had not swept away Mr. Washington's puny army, and questions had been raised in Parliament as to his leadership. According to Lady Abington, the joke in London social circles was that Sir William ought to be raised to the peerage with the title of Lord Delay-ware.

Barbara was not certain what the relationship between her mother and General Howe had been. She was never certain about her mother's friendships. But whether or not they had been lovers, Sir William clearly considered Lady Abingdon to be one of his supporters and he was delighted to have her daughter dine with him at his headquarters, the former home of Richard Penn.

Barbara took care with her dress that evening. She had not had a new dress since the war began, and she was certain her London gown was sadly out of fashion, but, she reasoned, General Howe had been out of England for too long himself to notice. She wore a dark blue silk that complemented her eyes, and around her neck she hung the string of pearls Alan had given her when Ian was born. They were scarcely less luminous than her skin.

Sir William's hostess was his longtime American mistress, Mrs. Loring. Mrs. Loring was known in the army by the nickname "the Sultana," and Barbara quickly understood how she had earned that title. She was a flashy blond and she condescended to Barbara with almost comical majesty. Or she tried to condescend. No one, thought Harry, who was present and watching the scene appreciatively, had ever successfully condescended to Lady Barbara Carr.

Barbara looked down first and then slowly up. She smiled graciously—that invincible graciousness, Harry thought, with a mixture of amusement and respect, and spoke softly. "Mrs. Loring," she said. And looked back at General Howe. Harry saw Mrs. Loring's face and suppressed a smile.

Dinner was equally amusing. Barbara and the general talked about London, about people and places the American blond knew nothing of. The Sultana was reduced to queening it over the two Tory ladies and their escorts and Harry.

They were halfway through dinner when Barbara introduced the subject of the American prisoners of war. "They are crowded unmercifully into that huge prison on Walnut Street, General Howe," she said gently. "There is not enough ventilation. And the blankets and the food are inadequate as well."

"I keep hearing from Mr. Washington on this very subject, Lady Barbara," General Howe replied to her in his indolent way, "and I can assure you, as I have assured him, that the prisoners are under the supervision of a British officer and that their rations are the same as those issued to British troops when on board ship."

"Perhaps that is what you are being told, Sir William," Barbara replied quietly, "but I can assure you it is not so. I have been to the prison. The men are starving."

General Howe frowned. "In fact, Lady Barbara, his majesty's government is being most magnanimous in its treatment of rebel prisoners. By the law of the land they are all guilty of treason and destined to be hanged. We were not so generous with Jacobite rebels as we have been with the Americans. They are fortunate to be alive."

There was not a scintilla of change in Barbara's serene expression. "The British government has been most lenient," she agreed, and did not mention the British prisoners in American hands. "However, since the men are being kept prisoner, they ought to be provided for. I was wondering, Sir William," and here she smiled at him, "should you object if the Quakers donated food and clothing and blankets to the prison? They have kindly offered to do so."

"Of course I won't object, Lady Barbara." The general put his hand over Barbara's on the table. At the far end of the table, Mrs. Loring frowned direly.

"Thank you, Sir William," Barbara said softly, and slowly lowered her lashes.

"This is not an easy situation for you, I understand that." He patted her hand. Harry tried not to grin at the expression on the Sultana's face. "It is most unfortunate that your husband chose to follow Mr. Washington."

Barbara gently withdrew her hand from under the general's. "Yes," she said. "Did I tell you what my mother wrote to me recently about Lord Sandwich?"

General Howe's eyes snapped to attention. "No," he said.

"Well . . ." And Barbara went on to regale him with one of Lady Abingdon's political analyses.

The ladies retired to the parlor after dinner and Barbara sat and returned gracious replies to Mrs. Loring's barbed comments. When the men came into the parlor after only a brief time spent over brandy, Colonel Maher moved directly to Barbara's side.

"I knew your brother George in London," he said. "We were at school together."

Barbara smiled and returned yet another polite reply. They spoke for a few moments of London and mutual friends; then he said, "I understand your husband is with Washington at Valley Forge."

"Yes," Barbara returned tranquilly.

He looked at her with curiosity. "Our reports are that the American Army at Valley Forge is virtually starving, you know. We razed all the farms in the area last month."

Barbara's narrow nostrils were white. "Did you? Then they will have to look farther afield for food."

He shook his head. "The German farmers have no love for the Continental Army—or for Continental currency either. They are bringing their food into Philadelphia for good British gold."

With a great effort, Barbara kept her face expressionless. She would not give him the satisfaction of seeing how distressed she was. "Well," she said sweetly, "perhaps you will be successful in starving General Washington into submission. You certainly have not been able to drive him from the field by force of arms."

The colonel did not like that at all, Barbara was happy to see. She smiled pleasantly and let her eyes wander to Harry, who promptly joined her.

"I rather think I'd like to go home, Harry," Barbara murmured. "I'm a trifle fatigued."

She had spoken the truth about being tired, but Barbara found she did not sleep very well that night. Colonel Maher's words about Valley Forge lay heavy on her heart.

Twenty-four

The British were enjoying Philadelphia. The best homes in town were open to wellborn young officers and local girls were teased that they had caught "scarlet fever." All winter long there were drums and routs and dances. There was skating on the Delaware and races on the commons. Captain John André and Captain Oliver Delancy opened the South Street Playhouse and the theater soon became so popular that people had to send servants at four o'clock in the afternoon to hold places for them, although the curtain did not rise until seven.

For the wilder young officers there were club dinners at the Indian Queen and rowdy suppers at the Bunch of Grapes. There were cockfights in Moore's alley and a faro bank where one could lose one's pay. Many officers openly kept mistresses. Of army discipline there was little to be seen.

On the bare hillsides of Valley Forge there were not enough shoes or clothing or breeches. Cries of "No Meat!" resounded along the Spartan dirt-floored huts which housed most of the men.

The commander in chief wrote to Congress: "Without arrogance or the smallest deviation from truth it may be said that no history now extant can furnish an instance of an army's suffering such uncommon hardships as ours have done, and bearing them with the same patience and fortitude. To see men without clothes to cover their nakedness, without blankets to lie on, without shoes—by which their marches might be traced by blood from their feet—and almost as often without provisions as with, marching through frost and snow, and at Christmas taking up their quarters within a day's march of the enemy, without a house or hut to cover them till they could be built . . . in my opinion can scarce be paralleled."

Barbara was finding it very difficult to obey Alan's injunction to join the Philadelphia social round. The thought of Valley Forge weighed on her spirit like a leaden blanket. She couldn't put a log on the fire without thinking of it. She couldn't put a morsel of food in her mouth or a warm cloak around her body without thinking of it. Deserters from the American camp had come into Philadelphia throughout the winter and the tale they told was horrifying. And yet the number of those deserters was amazingly small. The main bulk of Washington's army stayed, and endured.

Barbara's biggest comfort during this time was the work she did for the prison. The Quakers had responded generously to her requests for aid and many men's lives were saved by their donations of warm clothing, blankets, and food. Barbara also spent time visiting the men and sending messages from them to their families.

She sent letters to Alan periodically through the clandestine courier service he had arranged, and heard from him via the same route, but he had not been to Philadelphia since the army had settled at Valley Forge.

One chill damp day in late January Harry came to the house on Chestnut Street to escort Barbara to the prison. He was a little early and he found her writing a letter in the parlor. She asked him to sit down by the fire to warm himself.

"It's such a dreary day," she remarked, resuming her seat at the secretary, and turned to face him. She smiled a little ruefully. "Very English-looking."

Harry stared moodily into the fire. "This winter seems to be going on forever. I'm sick to death of inaction."

Barbara lifted a winged eyebrow. "Most of the other officers appear to be enjoying themselves."

A distinctly disgusted expression crossed Harry's features. "Some army we are. We drink and whore and drink some more, and there is Washington, as vulnerable as he'll ever be, and we do *nothing!*"

"I understand Valley Forge is very well-fortified," Barbara said quickly.

"Perhaps, but they're sick and hungry out there. We could take them if we tried. But we won't try, dammit. General Howe has applied to be relieved of his command. He's just waiting out his time until spring."

"I see," said Barbara thoughtfully.

Harry's lip curled. "Have you heard what your Dr. Franklin was reported to have said in Paris when they told him General Howe had taken Philadelphia?"

"No. What did he say?"

"He said, 'I beg your pardon, sir. Philadelphia has taken General Howe.' And he's right, damn him. He's bloody well right."

Barbara smiled at her cousin sympathetically. "Should you mind waiting one more minute while I finish writing this letter to my sister-in-law?"

"Of course not," he replied more courteously. "I'll look through the newspaper."

Barbara turned back to her desk, and when she heard the crackle of Harry's paper, she picked up a pen and began to write. Her letter, however, was not to Libby but to her husband. His courier would pick it up today, from Mr. Alving's shop as usual. The letter had been almost finished when Harry arrived, and now she added only a request that Alan come to see her as soon as possible. For the first time she thought she had some information for him: the news of General Howe's resignation.

Barbara sealed her letter, gave it to Tillie to deliver to Mr. Alving's shop, and went out to her carriage with Harry to deliver supplies to the prison.

There was nothing to tell her that this prison visit would be any different from the dozens of others she had made before. She delivered the food she had collected and made a list of the things that Colonel Wheeler said they needed. She collected a large number of letters she promised to post and distributed a bundle of letters that had come to the house on Chestnut Street for various prisoners. Then, as they were leaving, Harry excused himself for a moment to talk to one of the guards. Barbara was left alone in the small hall just outside the cell area. The prisoners did not see her; they thought she had gone.

"She's a saint from heaven, is Mrs. Maxwell," she heard a voice say distinctly.

"That she is," came another, rougher voice. "And a beauty. Old Hawk sure can pick 'em, can't he?"

"Yeah. I thought that little widow lady he had at

Morristown was pretty, but she don't hold a candle to his wife."

Barbara froze. Then, after a brief, breathless moment, she turned on her heel and went down the stairs to the street to wait for Harry.

"What's wrong?" he asked as soon as he joined her. "You look pale."

"I felt a little faint," she replied quietly. "I think I would like to go home, Harry."

He helped her into the carriage and lectured her all the way home about how it was not necessary for her to visit the prison personally. She sat and let his words flow over her and did not hear a thing he said.

That little widow lady he had at Morristown. The words reverberated around and around inside her skull all the while she smiled at Harry and assured him that she was all right. Once home, she forced herself to play a card game with Ian and to have a semblance of dinner with him. It was not until Ian was finally in bed that she went into her own room, closed the door, and let herself consciously think about what she had heard.

That little widow lady he had at Morristown. Alan had stayed in the farmhouse of a widow, she remembered. He had written her that information when he asked her to join him. She hadn't joined him. In her absence, had he turned to the comforting arms of the widow?

Bitterness began to rise in her heart. She had not

joined him because there had been an influenza epidemic at Newland. While she had been nursing the sick, *he* had . . .

It may not be true, she told herself. It was hardly fair to convict him on the word of an anonymous soldier. But they had all seemed to know about it. "Old Hawk sure can pick 'em," the other man had said.

She thought of the miserable journey she had made to Philadelphia so she could see him. She thought of the anguish she had endured worrying about his safety; the passionate abandon she had shown in his arms.

Bitter, bitter gall filled her heart. If it were true, she thought, she would never forgive him. And she had allowed him to give her another child—she was almost sure of it.

She had asked him to come to see her. She would find out the truth from him soon enough.

He came five days after she sent her letter. As before, she received a message in the late afternoon that he would be there that night, and she waited up for him downstairs in the parlor.

It was a wretched night, sleeting, not snowing, and Barbara took him quickly upstairs to her bedroom, where the fire was burning brightly. Alan went to its warmth immediately, and Barbara, at the foot of the bed, watched him out of veiled eyes. The sleet was drumming against the window and there was the chill whisper of a draft along the floor. Somewhere a shutter banged in the wind. Alan turned and gave her a weary smile. "It's good to be here, sweetheart," he said.

He looked gaunt and shabby and very, very tired. "Was it difficult to come into the city?" she asked.

"Not really. The bloody German farmers send enough wagons in that we can slip one of our own among them easily enough."

"Then why haven't you come before?"

His head lifted a little, like an animal scenting danger. It was as if for the first time he realized the trace of hostility in her manner. "I couldn't." He rubbed a hand along his unshaven jaw in a gesture of tiredness. "I don't know how to tell you this, sweetheart, but Charles Dwight is dead. It was typhoid."

Barbara was visibly jolted. "Oh, Alan! No!" She came across the room to him at last.

"I kept him at camp." She could hear by his voice how hard this was for him. "I didn't send him to one of those death-hole hospitals. I tried, Barbara. My God, I tried. But we couldn't save him."

Barbara's lips were white. "When?" she asked.

"Two days ago. I wrote to Libby yesterday."

"I heard from her only last week," Barbara said. "She is having a baby."

"I know." His face was unutterably bleak. The sleet hissed against the window and he reached out and drew her to him. "That's why I haven't been to see you," he murmured into her hair.

Barbara could not relax against him. She felt chilled to her very soul. Charles Dwight—dead.

"I'm getting you all wet," Alan said and, stepping back, took off his overcoat and draped it over a chair. He held out a hand to her. "Come sit with me."

She allowed him to pull her down into his lap in the big chair in front of the fire. How happy she would have been with him, she thought, if only she had never overheard those words at the prison. But she had overheard, and they were burned on her soul, corrosive as acid. She put her head against his chest and listened to the beat of his heart. "Alan," she said, "did you have an affair with the widow you stayed with at Morristown?"

She felt all the muscles in his body tense. So, she thought bleakly, it was true.

There was a long silence. "So someone did see us at York," Alan said heavily. It was too late to deny it, he knew. She had been too close for him to disguise his reaction.

York! So he had met her in York too, while she, Barbara, was caught here in Philadelphia. Barbara scrambled off his lap and went to stand at the far side of the fire, her back to him. "I didn't know about York," she said in a low, trembling voice. "Just Morristown."

Oh Christ, he thought. He had only made matters worse. If only he weren't so tired. . . . He got to his feet. "Sweetheart," he said. "It wasn't important, believe me. And I only went to York because she wrote me she needed to see me urgently. Nothing happened between us at York, I swear it."

"But something happened between you at Morristown?" She swung around to look at him.

"Yes." God knows how she had found out, but it was out now and he wasn't going to deny it. "Try to understand, Barbara," he went on carefully. "It had been one and a half years since we parted. And then you weren't coming to Morristown."

"I was nursing *your* sick slaves," Barbara put in bitterly.

"I know. I'm not trying to excuse myself, but you could try to understand."

"Understand! I understand well enough." Barbara's eyes were hard as diamonds. "You had a convenient widow at hand."

And of course that was exactly the way it had been. Alan's mouth hardened. He drew a deep breath and went over to the window as if he were seeking air. "Yes," he said over his shoulder. "I had a convenient widow at hand."

"Get away from the window, Alan!" Barbara said sharply. "Someone might see you."

He didn't move. "The curtains are drawn."

"Yes, but you can see through them when the

candles are lit. And you are an American officer out of uniform. *Get away from that window!*"

He stepped into the shadow of the wall and turned to face her. Drawing a long breath, he tried again to explain. "What I did with Lucy had nothing to do with you, Barbara. She was not important to me. In that way, I did her a greater wrong than I did you."

"Any woman who goes to bed with another woman's husband deserves what she gets," Barbara said implacably.

He thought of what poor Lucy had got and felt his own temper begin to rise. Barbara was making a mountain out of a molehill.

"Christ, what does it matter if I slept in another woman's bed a few times, Barbara?" he asked impatiently. "I wouldn't have done it if you had been there. I didn't love her—I love you. I won't do it again. So can't we forget it?"

"Forget it!" She stared at him incredulously. "My God, but you take infidelity lightly."

"Compared to what I see every day at Valley Forge—yes. If a little infidelity was the worst thing that happened in war, we could all count ourselves fortunate."

Barbara was incensed. "You beast," she said. "And to think I let you give me another child."

His dark eyes opened wide with shock. "Oh no," he said involuntarily.

Barbara recoiled as if he had hit her. When

finally she spoke, her voice was shaking. "Never for as long as I live will I forget those were your words to me at this moment."

"I didn't mean it the way it sounded," he protested. He came across the room and tried to take her in his arms. "You surprised me, sweetheart, that was all."

"Don't touch me."

He stared down into her cold, set face. "Are you really going to let this stupid affair come between us now?"

"It already has come between us. As far as I am concerned, it will always lie between us."

He was in the wrong, he knew, but he felt she was being unreasonable. He was so weary, so sick at heart over Charles. He needed comfort from her, not reproaches. There were greater tragedies in the world than his going to bed with another woman. "You said you had something to tell me," he said, and his voice now was as cold as hers.

"I would't tell you the time of day, Alan Maxwell," Barbara said furiously. She had never been so angry in all her life. That he should stand there so calmly! "Get out. Get out of my sight, you . . . you *womanizer*."

"You sound ridiculous," he said coldly. "Write to me at camp when you come to your senses."

"I shall never come to my senses about this." The words came from between clenched teeth.

Alan shrugged, walked to the door, and unlocked it. For a moment he paused, his back to her, but she said nothing. Then with his fist he struck the door open and went out. A moment later she heard his steps on the stairs and the front door opening. Had she bothered to look out the window she would have seen him walk off down the street, his bare head intermittently illuminated by the streetlamps along the way.

Twenty-five

Barbara was aflame with anger against Alan. Never, never would she forgive him, she vowed. His infidelity had been bad enough, but then to be so callous about it! She decided early the following morning, after a miserable, sleepless night, that she would go home to Virginia.

She sent a note to Harry to inform him of her decision. She was in the midst of packing when he arrived that evening to see her.

"But what happened, Barb?" he asked in bewilderment when she joined him in the parlor.

"I received word yesterday that my sister-in-law's husband died at Valley Forge," Barbara replied. "I

cannot leave her alone at Newland, Harry. I must
go home.''

"The roads will be abominable," he said automatically.

"I suppose, but it can't be helped." She gave
him a shadowy smile; she was so weary. "Would
you like tea?"

"No." He was standing in front of the fire. "So
you're going," he said in an odd voice.

"Yes, I'm going. Do sit down, Harry." She moved
toward the settee and gestured him to a chair. He
didn't change position.

"It will be dreadful in Philadelphia without you,"
he said.

Barbara sat down. "I haven't been precisely merry
company for you, Harry. You won't miss me very
much.''

"Not miss you!" The words were almost a cry of
anguish and Barbara's eyes opened wide. "God,
Barb, have you entirely forgotten what was between us?"

She had. Her life had so centered itself on Alan
that all other ties had receded and faded. Alan. Her
heart hardened. He was not worth any woman's
love.

"Oh, Harry," she said. "That was all so long
ago.''

"*I* haven't forgotten." He came to kneel in front
of her. "I haven't forgotten that you would have

married me and not him if circumstances hadn't been against us."

Barbara looked into Harry's blue eyes. He loved her still, she realized with a shock of surprise. Even after all this time. . . . A very grave look came slowly over her face. "What are you thinking of, Barb?" he asked softly.

She had been thinking of her mother. When Lady Abingdon had discovered her husband's infidelity, she had paid him back in his own coin. It would serve Alan right, Barbara thought now righteously. She wondered if he would take infidelity so lightly if the shoe were on the other foot. She smiled at Harry tenderly. "I was remembering too," she said.

"Barbara." His voice sounded hoarse. He took her hands into his and held them tightly. "I love you. I have always loved you. You know that. This last month has been hell, pretending we were just cousins, pretending there was nothing more between us than that. But now that you are leaving . . ." He raised her hands to his mouth.

Barbara looked at the shining fair head of her cousin bent over her hands. She had not had to pretend anything; she had indeed forgotten that once there was more between them and she had assumed Harry felt the same. "I love you so much," he muttered into her hands.

"Harry . . ."

"Be kind to me," he said. "Barbara." Then he

was beside her on the settee and had taken her into his arms.

She let him kiss her. She thought of Alan and how this would pay him back and she put her arms around Harry's neck.

The quality of his kiss changed, became harder, more demanding. The buttons of his uniform were scoring into her flesh.

Quite suddenly, Barbara panicked. She couldn't do this. She couldn't let him touch her, do to her the things that Alan did ... The very thought frightened and revolted her. She tried to push him away.

"No! Harry, stop! I don't want ..." But he seemed to be beyond hearing her. His weight was over her and he had her pushed back hard into the settee. Abruptly Barbara's fear changed into anger. She took her hand away from his shoulder and, getting a good grip on his queue, she pulled. Hard. The pain from his pulled hair brought him to his senses and he sat up. Barbara was across the room in a flash. She didn't say anything, just watched him out of wide and wary eyes.

Very slowly he got to his feet. He looked terrible, Barbara thought. Sad and shaken and ashamed. Abruptly *she* was ashamed. This was all her fault. She had been using Harry to get back at Alan and had given no thought at all to poor Harry's feelings. "Oh, Harry," she said contritely, "I feel like such a wretch. Do forgive me."

He stared at her. "*I* am the one who should be apologizing," he said.

"No." She shook her head. "It was my fault." She came across the room to him again and, reaching up, planted a gentle kiss on his cheek. "I do love you, you know. But as a cousin."

He was very white. "I think I had better go," he said in a choked sort of voice. He could not bear the pity in her eyes.

"Yes, you had better," she replied. "Good-bye, my dear. Godspeed."

After he had left, Barbara sat for a long time staring into the fire. She felt thoroughly ashamed of herself. She also felt that the whole embarrassing and painful episode had been Alan's fault.

Barbara went home to Virginia. In February Baron von Steuben arrived at Valley Forge and began to drill the American troops into the discipline of a real army. In March Alan heard from Lucy Thornton in New York City that she had borne a son and named him Christopher.

In June Sir Henry Clinton, who had taken over command of the British Army from Sir William Howe, marched his troops out of Philadelphia and headed them toward New York. On June 28 the newly disciplined American Army attacked the British at Monmouth Courthouse, New Jersey, and drove them from the field. General Clinton hurried his beaten troops to the safety of Manhattan Island and refused to be lured out again.

By August Alan was back in Morristown, where he wrote to Barbara for the first time since their parting in January. The thought of her pregnancy had been a growing concern to him. He did not even know when the baby was due. He received a brief, cool note in return that let him know in no uncertain terms that he was not forgiven.

He heard again in November that Barbara had had another son two months before. He was still at Morristown, where he settled in for yet another winter. Conditions at Morristown this year were scarcely better than they had been at Valley Forge the previous winter. Alan spent most of his time and energy trying to feed and clothe his increasingly hungry and tattered men.

In March Alan received word from a woman calling herself a friend of Mrs. Thornton's. Lucy had died of pneumonia and had named Alan guardian of her child.

It was a very grim Alan who sent his brother, Robert, dressed in civilian clothes, into New York to collect the baby and bring it to Virginia.

"Tell Barbara and Libby to send him to Helen in England," Alan said. "She will take care of him for me."

Robert had protested at being made a nurse-maid, and he did not think it was a good idea to let Barbara know about Christopher's existence.

"Maybe not," Alan had agreed, "but there is no one else I can entrust with the baby's welfare but Barbara and Libby. And in this case, the baby's welfare must come first. I owe that much, at least, to poor Lucy."

Alan had looked unutterably bleak and Robert felt an unaccustomed pang of pity. Poor bastard, he thought, what a bloody situation for him.

"Remember," Alan was going on, "you're Lucy's cousin from New Jersey. I have some papers for you to carry. I don't think there's any danger for you in this, Robert. Your face isn't known to any of the British."

"Unlike yours." Robert gave his brother a sardonic look. It was a good imitation of one of Alan's most typical expressions. All of his officers had cultivated it.

"Unlike mine." Alan's sardonic look was the genuine article. "I'll give you a letter for Barbara."

Robert cast his eyes upward. "I'm glad I'm not in your shoes," he said piously.

"Thanks," Alan muttered. "At least you'll be able to see Virginia again."

Robert was gone for almost a month, and when he returned it was with the news that Barbara herself had taken Christopher to raise at Newland.

"She is an angel from heaven," Robert rhapsodized to his brother. "What other woman would be so kind, so forgiving?"

Alan said nothing to his brother, but he was not

pleased to hear that Christopher was to remain at Newland. Nor did he have Robert's illusions as to Barbara's motivation. She was keeping Christopher in order to punish her husband; the child was to be a constant, living reminder of his infidelity.

Well, let her sit at Newland and nurse her grudges, he thought hardly. He had more important things to do.

IV

The Yorktown Campaign

1780–1781

Twenty-six

It was Christmas Eve, 1780, and the moon was sailing high over Newland plantation. Barbara stood at her bedroom window and looked out. The moon shone over the boxwood gardens and made the river glitter like glass. It was cold at the window but Barbara made no move to return to the fire or to get into her big bed. Instead she crossed her arms upon her breast and stared out at the familiar scene, so beautifully and eerily transfigured by the moonlight.

Another Christmas, and still the war went on. This past year had been particularly difficult; for the first time since the war began, there was fighting in Virginia. The British had sent General Leslie into the state in the spring to raid and burn at will. As most of Virginia's fighting men were in the north with Washington or in the Carolinas with Greene, Virginia had been virtually helpless to defend itself. The British had not got as far up the river as Newland, but Barbara knew it was just a matter of time.

The draft from the window was chilling her and she turned to go check on the children before she herself got into bed.

Ian shared a room with Libby's son, Charlie, and Barbara went in to them first. Her eldest, born shortly before the war started, was now six. Barbara looked at the boy's face, sleeping so peacefully on its pillow. His cheeks had lost their childish roundness; he had his father's cheekbones, Barbara thought, and his father's mouth and chin. She pulled the cover up over his shoulder and then did the same for Charlie, who looked very small in the big bed next to Ian. Her nephew was a particularly sweet-natured child, and Barbara was very fond of him. He was quiet and thoughtful, unlike her own brood, who were noisy, athletic, and, in their mother's opinion, sorely lacking in discipline.

Her two youngest sons shared the adjacent bedroom and Barbara went in there next. Christopher was sound asleep with a toy soldier clutched firmly in his hand. He would be three in March, this child of Alan's whom she had taken to raise as her own. And of all his sons, this was the one who had inherited Alan's charm. Barbara bent to drop a kiss on his forehead. Christopher had belonged to her since he was an infant and it had been a very long time since she regarded him as anything but her own child. She loved him as she loved all her children: deeply, fiercely, primitively.

William stirred and opened his eyes. "Mama," he said sleepily.

"Ssh, darling," Barbara whispered. "I just came in to say good night. Go back to sleep now."

His eyes closed and Barbara waited for a minute, to be certain he had really gone off. How lovely it was to have William quiet, she thought ruefully as she watched the small sleeping face. Of all the boys, he—the youngest—was the most headstrong and difficult.

When he didn't stir again, Barbara went back to her own room and crawled into the big bed. Where was Alan this Christmas Eve? she wondered. The last she had heard, he was still at West Point, where he had been put in charge after Benedict Arnold's treason last September.

That treason had rocked the country. For an American general to have plotted to turn over General Washington to the British! Alan's comment in his letter to Barbara pretty well summed up the general feeling about Arnold: "May he rot in hell," Alan had written, "the treacherous bastard."

Barbara and Alan were once again corresponding, but the breach between them was not healed.

Barbara thought of him all the time. She thought of him when she did the accounts and made decisions that would affect the plantation, she thought of him when her children were happy and joyful, and she thought of him when they were stubborn and disobedient. Everything she did, she did with him in her mind. But she had not forgiven him.

Usually it was not in her to store up anger, to harbor resentment. When others had wronged her—her mother, her father—she had always been able to forgive and forget. But with Alan she could do neither. His infidelity was like a wound in her soul that went on smarting and bleeding and swelling and throbbing. She could not forget. She loved Christopher as if he were her own son, but she could not forgive his father.

The new year came in and with it came a new threat to Virginia. General Clinton had sent the traitor Benedict Arnold, with two thousand British regulars, to raid in the state. For the inhabitants of Newland, Arnold posed a danger they had not yet encountered during the course of the war, for Arnold was coming up the James.

"What shall we do, Barbara?" Libby asked her sister-in-law when the news of Arnold's direction reached them. "Should we evacuate the children and go inland?"

"No." Barbara's face was pale and set. They were seated in the office, she and Libby and Gavin, and Barbara looked around now at the room where she had spent so much time these last five years, had worked so hard. "No," she said again. "If we evacuate, they may burn Newland to the ground. I will not let that happen."

"What shall we do, then?" Gavin asked reasonably. "Give them food? We have crops in the storehouses. I reckon we could fob them off with some supplies."

Libby stared with horror at her cousin's face. Gavin was dark, like all the Maxwells, but his features were cast in a weaker mold. "Feed them!" she said. "Are you mad, Gavin? Alan would never forgive us."

"Well . . ." said Gavin. "Then what are we to do?" And both pairs of brown eyes swung to Barbara.

It did not seem strange to either of them that they should look to Barbara for a decision. She had been making decisions for so long now that they all automatically assumed hers would be the final word.

"No, we won't feed them," she said now crisply. "The more underfed they are, the faster Virginia will be rid of them. I will speak to Arnold when they arrive." She spoke the name Arnold as if it left a bad taste in her mouth.

"Good God, Barbara," Libby said forcefully, "what can you possibly say to Arnold that will make any difference in how he treats us?"

Barbara raised her chin. "You forget, Libby dear, that I am not just an ordinary American citizen. I think it might matter a great deal to Benedict Arnold that I am the daughter of the Earl and Countess of Abingdon."

They stared at her in silence for a minute. Barbara was dressed in a plain blue homespun gown and her hair was drawn back neatly into a smoothly coiled chignon on her neck. There were ink stains on her fingers. Yet, sitting there at her busy desk, she looked every inch an English aristocrat. Libby grinned. "What will you say?"

"I knew his wife in Philadelphia," Barbara replied. "Peggy Shippen she was then. A bourgeois little snob." Barbara looked more aristocratic with every word. "Depend upon it, she will be very anxious to cut a figure in London after the war. I'll tell him I'll have Mama blackball her from society if he doesn't leave us alone."

"And you think Arnold will back off just because you threaten his wife with social ostracism?" Gavin asked in astonishment.

Barbara raised her eyebrows. "Of course he will, Gavin," she replied regally. "You see Mr. Arnold is a bourgeois snob as well."

On January 4 Benedict Arnold burned the contents of Berkeley, the Harrison plantation, a few miles downriver from Newland, and took off forty slaves. Ben Harrison, a signer of the Declaration of

Independence and thus a prime target for the vengeful traitor, had evacuated his family from the plantation earlier. The following day the British were at Newland.

Barbara made her preparations with calm authority. In fact, she seemed so calm and self-assured that the children, who had been frightened at first, began to think the whole thing was a great lark. Gavin was sent out to the storehouses and the boys persuaded Libby to take them into the Blue Parlor where they could look through the window and see what was happening. It was shortly after nine when the long scarlet column of the enemy was first seen marching up the winding pine-shaded drive of Newland plantation.

Libby opened the window in the Blue Parlor so she could hear what was being said. She and the children watched tensely as two figures dismounted and walked up the path to the house. The boys were very quiet. The reality of all those soldiers was more daunting than they had expected. One of the approaching officers was short, dark, and walked with an obvious limp. He wore the uniform of a general. "That's Arnold," Libby said in a low voice to Ian. She stared at him with inimical eyes.

But Ian was staring at the tall blond major who was accompanying the traitor. "I know him," he said to Libby. Then they all heard Barbara's startled voice say clearly, "Harry! What are you doing here?"

"Good heavens," said Libby. "It must be Barbara's cousin."

The two men had disappeared under the portico of the house, but the light male English voice was very audible to the listening Libby and Ian. "I was ordered to accompany General Arnold, Barb. By Jove, but it's good to see you. I thought Newland was along this road somewhere."

"Well, you have found me." Barbara's voice now was quiet and noncommittal. "What may I do for you, Harry?"

"We need provisions," came the voice of Harry's companion. "I understand this is a prosperous plantation, Lady Barbara. I need food for my men."

"Barbara, may I present General Benedict Arnold," Harry said hastily. "General, Lady Barbara Maxwell."

Barbara did not deign to acknowledge the introduction. "I have no food for you," she said.

"I understand differently," the traitor replied. "I understand this is the most productive plantation in the Tidewater. Surely you can spare some food to your fellow-countrymen, Lady Barbara."

Barbara's voice was cold as ice. "I have no food for British troops," she said.

There was a long, pregnant pause. "Barbara," Harry began to say at last in a reasonable voice, but Arnold cut in.

"If you don't give it freely, Lady Barbara, then we will be forced to take it."

The traitor had dropped his pleasant manner. In his voice now there was an undisguised threat. Barbara's reply was soft and gentle. "Do you know, General Arnold, I really do not think that would be wise of you?"

In the Blue Parlor William said loudly, "I can't see, Aunt Libby. Where is Mama?"

"Ssh, William," Libby said hastily. "Mama is under the portico. Be quiet and you can hear her."

Arnold was speaking now, his voice heavily sarcastic. "And why is that, Lady Barbara?"

Barbara's voice kept its gentle intonation. "After the war I presume you and your wife will make your home in England. My father is the Earl of Abingdon and a minister in his majesty's government. My mother is one of the most influential women in London society."

"What she says is quite true, sir," put in Harry. "Very high up in the world, the Abingdons."

"They would not be good enemies to acquire, General," Barbara's cool, well-bred voice went on. "And they would most certainly be enemies if they learned you had burned their daughter's home."

"I said nothing about burning, Lady Barbara."

"I have given my factor orders to burn our storehouses if your men attempt to come near them."

"Then it will be you, not I, who have done the burning."

"I doubt the nuances will make much difference to Lord Abingdon, General Arnold."

There was a long moment of tense silence. Christopher, sensing the uneasiness, asked, "What is happening, Aunt Libby?"

"Hush, Christopher," Libby answered in a low voice. She took his hand. "Listen."

"We are not asking you to empty your storehouses, Barbara." Harry's voice was reasonable. "We just need a few nights' rations."

"I will see you in hell before I give you a crust of bread from my table," Barbara replied with perfect calm.

"Barbara!" Harry sounded both startled and appalled.

"We will pay you, Lady Barbara. In gold, not in worthless Continental currency."

"You can't buy Americans, General Arnold. But then, that's something you wouldn't understand, would you?"

The contempt in Barbara's voice was clear and Libby held Christopher's hand more tightly. "Careful, Barbara," she breathed. "Please be careful."

Evidently Barbara's words had made Harry anxious as well. "There's no need to be insulting, Barb," he said hastily. "And since when did you consider yourself an American?"

"Since an army of mercenaries came pillaging and burning its way through my land and the land of my friends," she replied bitterly.

"Mercenaries!" Harry sounded indignant. "We have no Hessians with us, I'll have you know."

Barbara's voice was tense with concentrated fury. "You are all mercenaries, Harry, every last one of you. What are you fighting for? King and Country? No. You are fighting for promotion, my dear cousin, and your men are fighting for pay. Is it we who are fighting for our homes. You turned thirteen colonies of Englishmen into Americans the minute you landed an army on our soil." She drew a deep, shaken breath. "I repeat, try to approach our storehouses and they will be set on fire."

There was a catastrophic silence. Then, "Quite an eloquent speech, Lady Barbara," said the heavily ironic voice of Benedict Arnold.

"I knew your wife in Philadelphia," Barbara said. "She is wellborn and beautiful. She may possibly be able to swim in the London sea—but not if she has enemies."

"You threaten me."

"Yes," Barbara replied. Her voice sounded almost pleasant. "Yes, that is precisely what I am doing."

There was a long, tense pause. Then, "Your husband is Alan Maxwell, is he not?"

"Yes."

There came the sound of spurs and the clanking of a sword. "Come, Major Wharton," said the voice of Benedict Arnold. "As officers of the king we would not wish to disturb the home of a good British subject like Lady Barbara."

"Of course not, sir." Harry's voice sounded muffled.

"Good morning, gentlemen," Barbara said firmly.

Libby and Ian stared out the window and saw two scarlet-clad figures walking down the path to their horses. The entire interview had been conducted on the front steps of Newland. Barbara had never even let them into the house.

There was the sound of the front door closing and then silence. "Mama!" Ian cried, and ran out of the parlor, followed by the rest of the children and Libby.

They found Barbara leaning against the front door looking very pale. Ian ran up to her and threw his arms around her waist. "You were wonderful, Mama!"

Barbara's face softened as she bent and kissed the shining black head of her oldest son. He was very conscious of his superior age these days and rarely offered her such a public caress. She looked up at Libby. "I told you he was a parvenu," she said.

Libby laughed. "Was that really your cousin?"

"Yes." Ian had let her go and now Christopher and William crowded around her skirts, asking questions. "Hush, boys," Barbara said. "Come into the parlor. Ian, go tell Solomon to send Matthew out to Gavin at the storehouses."

As they all moved toward the parlor, Barbara

346

said to Libby with a rueful smile, "Poor Harry. I'm afraid I was rather hard on him."

"Well, he's been rather hard on *us*," Libby returned tartly. "They're probably heading straight for Richmond now. I only hope they don't burn the city down."

"They will," Barbara replied. "After all, who is there to stop them? Governor Jefferson?"

"He wouldn't think it was constitutional." Libby's voice was heavily sarcastic. Thomas Jefferson's refusal to countenance a standing militia in Virginia had made him an extremely unpopular figure in his native state. "The situation here is unpardonable," Libby went on. "General Washington must send us some assistance! Barbara, haven't you written to Alan about it?"

"Of course I have written to Alan. Many times. All he says is that the situation in the Carolinas is more critical." Her mouth set. "But if the British burn Richmond . . . I'll write again. You're right, Libby. *Something* must be done."

Twenty-seven

Alan was all too aware of the vulnerable state of Virginia, as was General Washington, but the precarious state of affairs in the North and in the Carolinas was of greatest military priority. The fall of Charleston the previous year had been succeeded by the disastrous defeat of Gates by Lord Cornwallis at Camden. Washington had sent one of his best generals, Nathanael Greene, south to relieve the inept Horatio Gates, but he was not expecting miracles even from Greene. As he wrote to Congress: "I think I am giving you a general. But what can a general do, without men, without arms, without stores, without provisions?"

Robert had ridden south with Greene while Alan

remained at West Point. Despite the drastic situation in the South, Washington could not afford to leave the North open to the arms of Sir Henry Clinton.

At the outset of the war a threat to Virginia would have been of paramount importance to Alan. Virginia was his home, and he was rooted there as deeply as one of the great oaks that shaded his sprawling lawn. But he was a Virginia planter no longer. After six years he was a soldier, a commander who continually struggled against increasingly difficult odds to feed and clothe and keep his troops. No other army in the history of the world, he thought, would have endured what these men had endured. His first loyalty was to them and to the country for which they struggled. Painful as the thought was, Virginia would just have to wait.

Richmond burned, but on January 17 the tide began to turn in the South: Nathanael Greene defeated Lord Cornwallis at the Battle of Cowpens in South Carolina. By February Washington felt it was at last possible for him to send some assistance to Virginia.

He asked Alan to accompany the Marquis de Lafayette and twelve hundred of Washington's best soldiers, the light infantry, on an expedition to Virginia. Alan received his commander in chief's request while he was still at West Point, and the letter from Washington was most cautiously worded. As Washington was clearly aware, Alan had every right to object to placing himself under Lafayette's command. True, Lafayette was a full major general while Alan was only a brigadier, but the Virginian had seen far more active service than the enthusiastic young Frenchman. However, Lafayette was a potent symbol of the French alliance so vital to American interests. "The marquis is young and ardent and brave," Washington wrote to his fellow Virginian, "but he knows little of Virginia. An experienced, knowledgeable soldier such as yourself would be an invaluable asset to his command."

Alan thought not at all of what others might take as a slight upon his rank. "I shall be very happy to place myself under the marquis's orders," he wrote to his commander, and made preparations to join Lafayette's force as it started south. At last, after six long years, Alan would see home again.

It was April before the Continental forces under Lafayette finally reached Virginia. In that period of time Nathanael Greene's Southern Army had fought the battle of Guilford Courthouse in North Carolina, a battle that left the British technically holding the field but badly damaged. After the fight Lord Cornwallis returned to the coast, leaving Greene virtually master of the Carolinas. As Charles Fox in England said wryly, "Another such victory would ruin the British Army."

General William Philips was placed in charge of his majesty's troops in Virginia and he was no less rough than his predecessor, the traitor Arnold. The Virginia militia had begun to try to organize, but they were completely untrained. The most unpopular man in the state was its governor, Thomas Jefferson.

Lafayette and Alan arrived in Richmond on April 29 and only a few hours later Philips and his British troops appeared on the opposite bank of the river. The presence of the Americans prevented the British from their goal of once more burning the capital, but they managed to destroy warehouses and twelve hundred hogsheads of tobacco that were stored on the south bank of the James. Then the British fell back down the river toward Jamestown. The Americans made camp on the outskirts of Richmond to await developments. The following day Alan left Richmond and rode south along the winding river road toward his plantation of Newland and his wife.

It looked exactly the same. It did not seem possible, after all this time, that nothing had changed here at home. The pastures were lushly green, the house looked as gracious and as prosperous as always. It was evident that the British had not burned Newland.

Alan halted his horse at the top of the drive and stared at his home with mixed feelings. He was so glad to see it again, this talisman of normal life and happiness, and to see it whole and untouched, its red brick mellow in the late-afternoon sun.

But . . . Barbara must have bought off the English. The surrounding plantations had all been plundered and here was Newland dreaming quietly in the afternoon sun. She must have bought them off.

A small, sturdy little boy came around the side of the house, stopped, and stared at the stranger on the big gray horse. Then he began to come across the lawn. Alan dismounted and for the first time looked upon his son.

"I don't know you," William announced when he was within ten feet of his father.

Alan looked at the toddler's shining brown hair and direct gray eyes. The little boy's skin was tanned to a light gold by the spring sun. "Who are you?" he asked gently.

"William Maxwell. I'm two and a half years old. Who are you?"

Alan squatted on his heels and held out a hand. "I'm your father, William."

William looked bewildered. "My father? Papa?"

"Yes. Papa."

William's eyes flew open wide, and without another word he turned and began to run toward the back of the house. "Mama!" Alan heard him shouting. "Mama! Papa is here! Papa is here!"

Slowly Alan straightened up and began to walk after William around the side of the house to the back patio. He had reached the corner when there came the sound of running footsteps and more children appeared, a tall black-haired boy in the lead. Ian stopped when he saw the big man in uniform. "Papa?" he asked.

"Good God, Ian," Alan said incredulously, "can this be you? You've gotten so big!"

"Papa!" Ian shouted joyfully, and ran right into his father's arms. Then there was a whole troop of little boys clinging to his legs and shouting "Papa, Papa!" in faithful imitation of their leader. Alan looked over the children's heads and met the eyes of his wife.

The children were shouting and jumping up and down.

"He's not *your* Papa, Charlie," Ian was saying to a slender, green-eyed little boy. "He's your uncle. Isn't that right, Mama?"

Barbara came forward, saying composedly, "Yes. This is your Uncle Alan, Charlie. And William and Christopher, this is your Papa."

Alan heard the children shout again, but his eyes never left his wife. She came up to him and raised her face. "How are you, Alan? It's been a long time."

Her lips were cool under his. "Yes. I don't think I even need ask how you are doing. Everything looks just the same."

"We have worked hard," she replied.

"Alan!" He turned to see his sister coming out

the front door of the house. "Alan!" she shrieked again and, running, flung herself into his arms. "Oh, it's so *good* to see you," Libby said, raising a glowing face to his. "We thought you'd never get here!"

"There were all sort of delays."

"Where are your soldiers?" Christopher asked, looking behind Alan as if he expected to see the whole American Army coming up the drive.

"I left them in Richmond," Alan replied, and looked gravely down at this son of his who had caused so much discord between him and his wife. Christopher was dark-skinned and black-haired like all the Maxwells, but he had Lucy's large brown eyes. He looked confidingly back at his father and said, "I'll show you *my* soldiers if you like. I got them for my birthday. I'm three." He looked exceedingly proud of himself for having attained this advanced age.

"When's *my* birthday?" William demanded immediately of his mother.

Ian cut in, speaking across his small brother's head, "Did you fight General Philips, Papa? Are you going to chase the English out of Virginia?"

"We'll do what we can, Ian, but we haven't many men."

Barbara finished her explanation to William, an explanation he clearly wasn't satisfied with, and said to Libby, "Let's go inside."

"Yes, let's," Libby replied. "Alan, I reckon you're longing to see the house. It's been a long time."

"Yes, it has," he replied slowly.

A small hand was slipped into his. "Come along, Papa!" Christopher said gaily. "I want to show you my soldiers."

The whole party began to move slowly toward the terrace door.

Alan walked around the house, touching things here and there and saying over and over, "Everything is just the same."

"Will you be staying for the night?" Barbara asked him. His dark eyes locked with hers for a minute and she felt her stomach muscles tighten.

"Yes," he said after an infinitesimal pause. "I told the marquis I would be gone for two days. If he needs me, he knows where I am."

"I see." She was relieved to hear that her voice sounded somewhat normal. "Dinner will be in half an hour," she said, "if you want to tidy up upstairs first."

He went up to her bedroom—their bedroom—and when he came down they went in to dinner. Libby and she had taken to having all the children at the dinner table with them and Barbara felt it would be cruel to banish them because of their father's presence. She and Alan faced each other at opposite ends of the table, with the four boys and Libby between them. The only member of the household who was missing was Gavin; he was in Williamsburg on business.

Everything was just the same, Alan thought again as he looked around the sunny dining room. He found himself unwilling to ask how that could be so. If Barbara had bought off the British, he didn't want to know about it.

"Did you get my letter telling you about Arnold's visit?" Libby asked him directly.

"No." Alan looked at his sister and avoided looking at his wife. He didn't want to hear about Arnold's visit, didn't want to know anything else that would come between him and Barbara. "The mail, as usual, is wretched," he replied. "You seem to have survived it, however." He smiled at Libby and tried to change the subject. "*You* are looking very well indeed."

"Mama wouldn't give Arnold anything," Ian's proud voice said on Alan's other side. "She made him go away. She made them all go away."

Alan's head lifted and he stared at his wife. Her lovely face was perfectly serene. All of a sudden he found he did want to hear this story. "What happened, Barbara?" he asked. "You never wrote me anything about this."

Barbara looked at her youngest son. "William," she said gently, "sit still and don't kick Charlie."

William gave his cousin another kick under the table. "He kicked me first, Mama."

"William, you will sit still or you will leave the

table," Alan said. William stared wide-eyed at his father for a minute, then looked at his plate. Alan turned back to his wife. "Tell me about Arnold's visit," he said.

Barbara was gazing at William, who was now quietly eating his dinner. Then she looked back at her husband. Her voice when she spoke was pleasant but cool. She might have been addressing a total stranger. "Oh, Arnold marched up here right after he left Berkeley. He was looking for food and supplies. Harry was with him," she added.

"Was he, by God?"

"Yes." She looked away from him and moved Christopher's glass away from his elbow. "I told them I would burn the storehouses if they attempted to come near them. Then they went away."

"They went away," he echoed in astonishment.

"It wasn't quite as simple as that, Alan," Libby put in.

"Mama told them she wouldn't give them a crust of bread from her table," Ian informed his father eagerly. "Then when Arnold said he would pay her in gold, she said you couldn't buy Americans."

Alan's eyes began to blaze. "Did you really say that, sweetheart?"

She stared back at him and didn't answer. "She also said," put in Libby, "that that was something Arnold would scarcely understand."

Alan grinned, and at the sight of that familiar expression something inside of Barbara turned over.

"Good for you, Barbara!" he said. "Christ, but I would have loved to see his face when you said that."

Barbara tore her eyes away from Alan and frowned at William, who was once more kicking Charlie under the table.

"But I still don't understand how you avoided being burned to the ground, particularly if you insulted him like that," Alan was saying.

Barbara drew a long, annoyingly unsteady breath. "I reminded General Arnold that after the war he would have to make his home in England and that my father was the Earl of Abingdon," she replied.

There was a brief startled pause and then Alan threw back his head and began to laugh.

God, but it was good to be home. It was so sweet to be called "Papa" and to hear the sounds of happy noisy children. His sons were all such beautiful boys—even Christopher. He had not looked forward to meeting Christopher, but it was soon perfectly clear to him that Barbara genuinely loved the child. There was no distinction between the way she treated him and the way she treated her own sons. And Christopher was obviously so happy, so secure in his place in the family.

His wife was a woman in a million, Alan thought as he watched her giving orders to one of the housemaids. Imagine her standing up to that bastard Arnold like that. "You can't buy Americans."

He grinned and Christopher asked, "What's so funny, Papa?"

He gave the little boy some sort of an answer and glanced at the clock on the mantel. Surely it was time to put the children to bed. It was with deep pleasure that he heard his sister say, "Bedtime, Charlie. You can play with Uncle Alan in the morning."

Alan took each of the children up to bed on his shoulders and waited with well-concealed impatience as the little band of brothers was settled for the night.

It was ten o'clock before he finally closed his own bedroom door behind him. Down the hall he heard Libby's door closing gently too. The children were asleep. At last they were alone together.

Barbara crossed to her dressing table and picked up her hairbrush. Her back was to him but she felt him there as clearly as if she had been looking right at him. One forgot, she thought confusedly, how overwhelming Alan's presence could be. He just stood there inside the door and his vibration filled the entire room.

"I wasn't happy to hear you had taken Christopher," he said. "I thought you had done it to punish me. I'm sorry. I should have known you better."

Barbara turned, brush in hand, to face him. It was exactly why she had taken Christopher. Her narrow nostrils quivered. "It isn't Christopher's fault his father is a philanderer," she said. "I love him for himself. He is a darling little boy."

"Barbara," he said, and began to cross the room toward her, "surely you aren't still holding that episode against me?"

He stopped before her and she forced herself to look up into his face. She felt as if someone were squeezing all the air out of her lungs. "It was only once," he said tenderly. "Only once in all these years. It's you I love. You know that."

"Do I?" She tried to keep her voice from trembling but was not entirely successful. This was not how she had planned their meeting at all. She had intended to be cold and distant and to send him to sleep in the office. She had not reckoned with the irresistible attraction he always had for her.

"Sweetheart," he said, and his drawling voice was as physically potent as a caress. Barbara felt a stab of desire shoot through her body.

"Alan," she said sharply, trying to pull herself together, but he was drawing her toward him.

"Let's start again," he murmured. "Let's forget the past and start again." He kissed her and there was passion in his kiss, and pleading, and love.

Barbara made one last effort to hold onto her anger, but it was as if her body belonged to someone else, and all the resentment she had so zealously harbored was helpless before the leaping response of her flesh to his. His big hands were on her narrow back almost enveloping it as he pulled her against him.

Her mouth answered to his and the last remnants of resistance drained out of her. He felt the surrender in her mouth and body. "Barbara," he said. "Almighty God, how I have wanted you."

Her eyes were wide open and he looked down into their dark, dark blue. "Come to bed, sweetheart," he said. "Come to bed with me."

She stopped thinking. His hands and his mouth and the muscles of his splendid body were all she knew. She shivered and arched up against him, seeking the triumphant release his lovemaking always brought her. When he came into her she whimpered and her nails scored into his back.

"I love you," he was saying. "Barbara. My angel, my love, my star."

Her body was taut as a strung bow, aching, aching, wanting, wanting. He was poised over her. "Love me," he said clearly. "Tell me that you love me."

"I love you," she whispered. "Alan. Oh, Alan." And he took her over the edge and into a wild, shuddering explosive climax that left her brimming with sensory fulfillment.

His body was still half covering hers, his face was buried in her throat. She ran her hand down his smoothly muscled back, misted now with sweat. He was so strong. The thought that he had lain like this with another woman filled her heart with anguish.

"What would you do if you learned I had slept with another man?" she asked him in a low voice.

"Kill him." He kissed her throat and her shoulder and then rolled away from her and onto his side. He did not even bother to pretend to take her seriously. He knew there was no one else. "You are the only woman for me, sweetheart," he said now. "After you, no one else can matter."

"So you say now."

"Ever since the day I first saw you standing halfway up the staircase of a London town house, there has been no one else who matters. I swear it." He drew close and she did not resist. "God," he said, "but it's good to be in my own bed." In two minutes he was asleep.

After a while Barbara arose, careful not to disturb him, piled her discarded clothes neatly on a chair, and put on a nightgown. She got back into bed and lay awake, her eyes wide open in the dark.

She had never meant this to happen. After all her plans and all her anger, he had only to appear in her bedroom and she dropped into his hand like a ripe peach. She was furious with herself and even more furious with him. So he thought it was all over, did he? Buried in the past. She should have gone to bed with Harry that time. She wondered if he'd be able to bury her infidelity so casually. And damn him, he had known exactly why she took Christopher. Libby and Robert had thought she was so noble; Alan hadn't been fooled.

It was late when Barbara finally fell asleep, only to be wakened half an hour later by a small voice saying next to her ear, "Mama, I had a bad dream. I'm scared."

William was already climbing into bed with her. "What's Papa doing here?" he asked in astonishment.

"This is where Papa sleeps when he's home," Barbara whispered. "Shh, darling. What frightened you?"

"A bear was chasing me." William snuggled down in the bed next to his mother. "This is better," he announced, and promptly fell asleep.

Barbara, sandwiched between her husband and her son, scarcely slept for the rest of the night. William was a restless sleeper and had soon spread himself over most of her side of the bed. Alan scarcely moved, sleeping the sleep of deep exhaustion. Barbara finally dozed off about five, to be awakened an hour later by Alan's voice saying, "Good God, what is he doing here?"

William was still asleep, his little rump stuck straight up in the air. "He had a bad dream," Barbara murmured, pushing the hair back out of her eyes.

"Do you realize I haven't a stitch of clothing on?" he said. He looked at her appraisingly. "You put your nightgown on."

To her great annoyance, Barbara could feel the

color flush into her cheeks. "Yes. With a houseful of small children, I take care to sleep in a night-gown."

The ghost of a smile touched his mouth. "You've been too long without a husband, sweetheart."

"Well, that isn't my fault," she replied tartly.

He laughed softly, low in his throat, stretched himself, and yawned. He got out of bed, went over to the wardrobe that held his clothes from before the war, and began to dress. Barbara sat up against her pillows and watched him.

"How much extra food do you have available, Barbara?" he asked. "The army, as always, is poorly supplied. I told the marquis I would try to send provisions."

"Is that why you came home, then?" Barbara asked coldly. "To collect supplies for your men?"

He put his shirt down on the chair and turned slowly to look at her. He was bare from the waist up, No wonder that other woman had wanted him, Barbara thought fleetingly. But this morning, with her son sleeping beside her, she could harden her heart. It had all been too easy for him.

"No," he replied softly, "that is not why I came home. I came to see you."

Next to her William began to stir. "We have supplies in the storehouses," Barbara said. "I'll give Gavin a list of the things we can spare you. He should be back this afternoon from Williamsburg."

A lock of black hair had fallen over his forehead.

His face looked younger this morning, relaxed and rested. He grinned at her. "You must be the only plantation in Virginia, sweetheart, with extra supplies."

"They are not extra," Barbara replied coldly. "We will have to do without here at home. But I will spare you what I can for the army."

The good humor slowly faded from his face as he assessed her mood. "I do not want to deprive you," he said slowly.

Barbara shrugged. "I shall manage. I have learned very well how to manage—alone."

Alan stood in a shaft of sunlight from the window, looked at his wife, and understood that, after all, he was not forgiven.

Twenty-eight

A lan spent the early morning roughhousing with the boys. The children loved it and came down to breakfast with eyes like stars. After breakfast Alan proposed to ride around the plantation.

"I'm afraid I can't accompany you, Alan," Barbara said. "I am needed in the smokehouse this morning."

Libby shot her sister-in-law a brief startled glance. Then Ian said quickly, "May I go with you, Papa?"

"You are supposed to work with your tutor in the mornings, Ian," said his mother.

"I think he can have a holiday today," Alan overruled her easily.

"Me too," William announced.

"No, William," Barbara said. "It's too long a ride."

"Ride with Papa."

"No, darling," Barbara began.

William's face began to get very red. "Yes!" he shouted.

"That is quite enough, William," Alan said quietly. "I do not ever want to hear you speak to your mother in that tone of voice. Tell her you're sorry."

William glared at his father. "Won't!"

"Then you may go up to your room."

William got even redder. He was setting himself up for a major temper tantrum. "Won't," he said, and slammed his small fist on the table. His father got up from his seat.

"Alan . . ." Barbara said nervously.

He ignored her and, plucking an astonished William from his chair, bore him from the room. William's loud protests could be heard all the way up the stairs.

There was dead silence at the table until Alan returned to the dining room. He sat back down and addressed himself to Barbara. "He is to stay in his room until I return from my ride."

"You'll be gone for hours," Barbara protested.

"It will give him time to think," her husband replied imperturbably. He turned to the other two small boys, who were watching him out of big eyes. "When Ian and I get back, I'll take you sailing on the river."

Charlie's and Christopher's faces lit up. "*Thank* you, Unca Alan," said Charlie.

"Alan, they don't know how to swim." Barbara's voice was low and urgent.

"I'll take them one at a time," her husband replied. "Now, Ian, are you ready?"

"Yes, sir!"

As Alan and his eldest son left the dining room, Libby looked at Barbara's face and, prudently, decided to say nothing.

When Alan returned to the house he went upstairs and brought William down to his mother "I'm sorry, Mama," William said sweetly.

"That's all right, darling."

William turned and grabbed his father's hand. "We go sailing, Papa?" he asked eagerly.

"After dinner, William."

"Now."

Alan looked at his small son. "After dinner."

William looked back and, as if by magic, the threatening cloud lifted from his face. "After dinner," he said sunnily, and swung happily on his father's hand.

Alan took the boys sailing one at a time, as he had promised. Barbara sat in the summerhouse and watched, her heart in her throat, but the boat never once tipped over.

While Alan was putting the boat away, Barbara went into the office and made a list of the items he could have for the army. When Gavin returned from Williamsburg she gave him the list and told him to arrange for the transport. Alan went along with his cousin to help oversee the arrangements. The army was as usual desperate for food.

"Are the supplies what you needed?" Barbara asked when next she saw Alan. He was on his way down to the paddocks to look at the horses. Ian was at his heels.

"Yes." His smile was not a smile of good humor. "We need every morsel we can find. Notwithstanding your fine words to that bastard Arnold, too many Americans *can* be bought. There are plenty of farmers who would rather sell to the British for gold than to us for worthless Continental currency." There was a pause and his face softened. "I'm going down to the paddocks. Would you like to come along?"

"Do you need horses too?"

"*I* need a new horse. The gray has come up lame several times lately."

"Oh, take what you need," she said in an impatient voice. "I won't even ask for your Continental currency. Just leave me enough horses to do the fieldwork, please."

Alan didn't reply but turned on his heel. "Come along, Ian," he said. Barbara watched her son trotting eagerly next to his father, trying to keep up with that long stride. The children were all so thrilled to see him, Barbara thought crossly. They couldn't wait to leave her and follow in the magic wake of Papa. She supposed she should be glad her sons were pleased to see their father, but somehow she was not. She had done all the work of rearing them and all Alan had to do was arrive, snap his fingers, and they all came flocking to him. Even she, last night—had she not done the same?

Her mind veered away from what it did not want to contemplate. He should not have taken the boys out on that boat, she thought. It hadn't been used since the war began. She had been terrified that it would sink.

She said as much to Alan when they were once again alone in their bedroom. It was the only time they had been alone all day.

"It needs work, but it was safe," he said. "I checked it."

"To take all those little boys . . ."

"Sweetheart"—he came over to put his hands on her shoulders—"the boys are growing up. You can't keep them tied to your skirts forever."

"Yes," she returned bitterly. "You're home for one day in six years and you know all about rearing children."

His hands on her shoulders tightened a little.

"I'm not saying that." He was so obviously trying to be patient that he only made her angrier. "But I was a boy once, and you weren't." He smiled down at her, consciously trying to charm her out of her bad mood. "What you need," he said caressingly, "is another baby."

Barbara's narrow nostrils quivered. His closeness, his hands on her shoulders, were causing her heartbeat to accelerate and she was furious with herself for this reaction. She flung up her head and stared into the hawklike face above her. "Yes, you're very good at that, aren't you? You give me a child and then go away for a few years until it's time to have another."

She had made him angry. She saw that in the suddenly hard lines of his face. She tried to back away from him, but the hands on her shoulders tightened with sudden violence.

"And all of this just because once, *once* in six years, I went to bed with another woman! Christ, Barbara, you couldn't carry on more if you had come from a family where the word 'infidelity' was never heard of. Compared to your family, I'm a model of morality."

She was incensed. "Don't you dare say one word against my family," she hissed. "You come back here and you think we're all going to dance to your tune—"

"You were happy enough to see me last night," he said in a goaded undertone, and pulled her into his arms.

Barbara tried to push him away, but she was helpless before his superior strength. His mouth was on hers and her feet were off the ground. He began to walk toward the bed.

"You've had a sour face on you all day," he muttered between his teeth. "Well, since nothing I do can please you, I might as well please myself."

Barbara tried to kick him in the shins. "You bully. Take your hands off me."

He laughed and, scooping her up, slung her onto the bed. She tried to scramble off, but with a quick movement he was beside her. Then he rolled and, his body pinning her down, began to kiss her again.

She struggled against him but she was caught. Lying there, with his mouth on hers, he began to caress her breast. Even through the fabric of her dress he could feel the nipple stand up taut. He moved his mouth to the hollow of her throat.

"Don't be so hard on me, sweetheart," he whispered. "Love me." Then he kissed her again and this time her mouth gave him a response. He moved a little away from her and, still with his mouth on hers, began to unhook her bodice. Her breasts when finally he freed them were so perfect, fuller than they had been when first they married, he thought, but still firm and white. He bent to take her nipple in his mouth and she gasped and, burying her hands in his hair, held him to her. Then she helped him to finish undressing her and lay there quivering while he took off his own clothes.

She adored him. There was no disguising that

fact. He had only to lay a hand on her and all her anger evaporated into longing. Barbara looked at him as he lay asleep next to her in the bed and very gently she smoothed the hair back from his face. His hand was still on her breast. She didn't move for fear of wakening him.

She should be happy, but lying there in the darkness beside her husband she felt as if her heart was broken in her breast and bled and bled and bled.

He left early the following day, taking supplies to the army in Richmond. She had risen before him and was in with the children when he appeared, dressed in uniform, booted, and spurred. They breakfasted together as a family and then he left. Ian rode down the drive with his father to the main road.

Alan was back a few days later with the Marquis de Lafayette for dinner. They brought news for the household at Newland: General Cornwallis and the whole Southern Army were moving into Virginia from North Carolina.

"Well, then, is General Greene going to follow?" Gavin asked.

"No," replied the young Frenchman, who commanded the Continental Army in Virginia. "General Greene is moving back to South Carolina and retaking British-held posts in that state."

"The British seem to have this mad notion that if

they once march through a country they have conquered it," Alan drawled.

"Does this mean they will now march through Virginia?" Libby asked anxiously. She was looking at her brother but he raised an eyebrow at Lafayette and the young marquis answered the question. "I am afraid so, Mrs. Dwight."

They were sitting in the Green Parlor waiting for dinner to be announced and Barbara looked appraisingly at the young French nobleman who had so heroically volunteered his services to the new American republic. Lafayette was red-haired, not noticeably good-looking, and next to her husband's splendid physique he seemed chubby and awkward. He was twenty-three years old, and due to his exalted connections, a major general. Alan seemed genuinely to like him.

"Do you have enough men to stop Cornwallis?" Gavin asked. His face, a weaker, thinner version of Alan's, looked worried.

Lafayette looked at his second in command. "General Maxwell thinks no."

"We don't have enough men even to get beat," Alan said bluntly. "All we can do is play a game of cat and mouse until we get reinforcements."

"Are reinforcements coming?" Barbara asked quietly.

"General Wayne, he is coming south with the Pennsylvania line," Lafayette said enthusiastically. "I hear from General Washington yesterday."

"Well, that is good news," said Libby.

Barbara looked up and saw Solomon standing in the doorway. "Dinner is served," she said graciously, and rising, put her hand on the arm of America's foremost French patriot.

Lafayette and Alan spent the night at Newland, but Alan was very late coming to bed. Barbara lay still when he came in, and pretended to be asleep. He undressed quietly and got in bed beside her. He made no move to touch or awaken her and in a short time his slow, even breathing told her he had gone to sleep.

She had been furious when he forced himself on her his last visit. She was even more furious now at his neglect.

In the morning the two generals left once again for Richmond.

Cornwallis crossed into Virginia leading an army of forty-five hundred men, all regular soldiers veterans of Camden and Guilford Courthouse. The American Continentals could only elude the British forces and move north and west, hoping to meet up with Anthony Wayne and his Pennsylvanians.

All through late May and early June the two armies crossed a succession of Virginia's great rivers, moving toward the center of the state, away from the Tidewater and toward the mountains. On June 4 a detachment of British just missed capturing the state's governor, Thomas Jefferson, as he sat down to breakfast at his home of Monticello. Several Virginia assemblymen were captured in Charlottesville and the rest of the Assembly fled to the mountains, where they finally reconstituted themselves in the Shenandoah Valley town of Staunton.

To no one's regret, Thomas Jefferson resigned as governor and Thomas Nelson Jr. was elected by the Assembly to replace him.

On June 10 Anthony Wayne and his one thousand veteran Pennsylvanians finally joined up with Lafayette, and the reinforced Continental Army began to move back toward Richmond.

For a month the two armies, American and British, moved slowly through the state, the Americans keeping always slightly behind the British. Cornwallis finally settled at Williamsburg and Lafayette encamped at New Kent Courthouse about twenty miles away. On July 5 Lafayette's spies brought him word that Cornwallis was going to cross the James River and move to Portsmouth. The Frenchman, forgetting all the caution he had so laboriously exercised since entering Virginia, determined to try to inflict a damaging stroke upon the British while they were crossing the river. The significant factor in this decision was the absence of Brigadier General Alan Maxwell, who was away trying to commandeer supplies.

Alan learned of the marquis's decision when he and his detachment returned to camp on the morning of July 6 to find it deserted save for a few militiamen who had been left with a message for him. Alan read it and cursed.

"The bloody fool," he said, and changed to the fresh horse his commander had so thoughtfully left for him. "That's just what Cornwallis will expect him to do." He put spurs to the horse and was off, leaving his men to follow as best they could.

At five in the afternoon Alan found the Continental Army in the vicinity of Green Spring plantation, just outside of Jamestown. Lafayette greeted him joyfully and explained that the entire British force with the exception of the rear guard had crossed the river. The Continentals were in position, waiting to fall upon the rear and teach them an unpleasant lesson. In order to accomplish this, the marquis had General Anthony Wayne and five hundred men positioned in a small wood close to where the rear guard was thought to be stationed.

Alan looked at the marquis's dispositions and took a long, deep breath. "Marquis," he said calmly, "are you *very* sure Lord Cornwallis has crossed the main part of his army?"

"Mon Dieu, but yes. We have been skirmishing for hours and they have fallen back."

"Have you looked closely across the river?"

There was a pause. "No."

"Then I suggest we do so immediately," Alan said grimly.

"I did not wish to leave my command," the young general explained as they rode toward a tongue of land at the river's bank. From this vantage point they could see a number of British troops on the other side of the James.

"*Christ*," said Alan. "He's only got a few hundred men over there."

"It looks like more," Lafayette said doubtfully.

"It's supposed to look like more." Alan wrenched his horse's head around. "Come on!" he commanded. "We have left Anthony Wayne with just five hundred men to stand off the entire British Army."

They arrived back at the field in time to see two columns of British regulars marching upon Wayne. It could not have taken the American general long to realize that his opposition was not just the rear guard. With scarcely a moment's hesitation, he charged.

"Mon Dieu!" said Lafayette.

Alan grinned. "He's a lion. Let's go, Marquis, and help get those poor bastards out of there."

Wayne's men advanced to within seventy yards of the enemy and the exchange of fire was heavy and destructive. Alan galloped his horse along the front lines, ordering a retreat and attempting to hold the men together as they fell back. His horse was shot down under him and, regaining his feet, he shouted again. There were dead or dying horses all over the field and men were falling as well. Alan felt the heavy thud of the ball that hit his shoulder but it took a moment before he felt the pain. He managed to stay on his feet until they reached the reserve line at Green Spring. By the time he lost consciousness, he was covered in blood.

Twenty-nine

Word came to Barbara at Newland midway through the morning of July 7 that Alan had been hurt. She went white as a ghost. "Badly?"

"Pretty badly, ma'am," the young soldier who had brought her the news replied. "General Lafayette thought you should come."

"Do you wish me to accompany you, Barbara?" Gavin asked later as she made ready to leave for Chickahominy Church, where the American Army was encamped with its wounded.

"No, Gavin." She sounded very calm although her face was still extremely pale and strained-looking. "I shall do fine, thank you."

"You don't want to wait until tomorrow morning

to leave? Then you will not have to stop on the road."

"I don't intend to stop on the road. I'll ride right through."

"The coach can't possibly make that trip before dark!"

"Ready, Matthew?" Barbara asked someone over Gavin's head, and Gavin turned to see a young black man dressed in riding clothes. "Ready, ma'am," he replied.

Barbara looked back at Gavin. "I am not taking the coach. I am riding."

"What!" Her husband's cousin looked horrified. "You can't do it, Barbara. You'll be exhausted."

She didn't even deign to reply. "Libby will pack the coach with my necessaries and send it off in the morning." She was pulling on her gloves as she spoke. She had already said good-bye to the children. They were upstairs now, with Libby, and as Barbara rode down the drive she turned once in her saddle to wave at the window where she knew they were.

He was hurt. The words of the soldier had shaken her to her core. After so many years, she had almost begun to think him invulnerable. "Pretty badly." What if he should die?

Her mind shied away from that terrible thought. No. It could not happen. She could not live without Alan.

The July heat was burning, but not as burning as the pain in her heart. He was hurt and she had sent him away in anger. How could she have done that? How could she have been so hard, so unforgiving?

She could not understand herself as she rode south along the dusty, hot river road that day. She had never really doubted that he loved her. She knew that he had turned to that other woman only because she had not been there. Then why had she held that lapse so against him, and for so many years?

He had said to her that her background should have enabled her to be more understanding but she thought now that her background had had quite the opposite effect. It was precisely because she had seen so much infidelity that she valued constancy so much.

And Alan was hers. She did not want to share him, not even for a moment, with any other woman on earth. It was because she loved him so much that she was so hard on him. With others she had learned to be understanding and patient and forgiving, but not with him. When it came to Alan she was still a girl, wild and passionate, striking out at both him and at herself. Stupid. How could she be so stupid?

He was the core, the center, the very heart of her. If ever she lost him . . . She wouldn't. She *couldn't*.

Save him for me, God, she prayed as she rode along in the brilliant sunshine. Please, please save him for me, and I'll be so good, so wise, so forgiving. . . .

Alan, my love.

It was a long, exhausting ride in the summer heat but Barbara slowed the pace only in order to rest the horses.

When they arrived in camp a soldier took her directly to Lafayette and he in turn escorted her to the tent where Alan lay wounded.

The tent was dark after the late-afternoon sun and it took Barbara's eyes a few moments to adjust. Then she saw him lying on a cot in the middle of the tent. Lafayette tactfully stayed outside while Barbara went to her husband's side.

His eyes were closed. The bandage on his arm and shoulder looked very white against the darkness of his bare skin. It was stained over the shoulder with blood. His face under its tan was pale.

"Alan?" Barbara said softly. "Darling."

Slowly his lashes lifted. His eyes were heavy with pain and fever. They looked at her for a long moment. Then, "Sweetheart," he said. "What are you doing here?"

Barbara dropped to her knees beside the low cot. "The marquis sent to tell me you were hurt. Oh, Alan." Tears were pouring unregarded down her face. "Oh, Alan," she said again and, picking up his hand, held it to her cheek.

His hand was wet with her tears. "I'll be all right, Barbara," he said. He gave her the ghost of his old cocky grin. "You won't get rid of me that easily."

She buried her head in his sound shoulder. His skin was hot against her face. "I love you," she said fiercely. "I love you. And I am staying right here with you until you are better."

His hand came up to caress the silky softness of her hair "Barbara," he said. Absolute relief sounded in his voice. "Barbara. God, but it's good to have you back."

Alan ran a high fever for three days and Barbara scarcely left his side. She changed bandages and bathed him with cool water and tried to quiet him when he became restless. Then, on the fourth day, the fever subsided and he looked at her and knew her once again.

He slept for a long time, a peaceful, restful sleep this time, and when he wakened it was dark. Lafayette had had a cot moved into the tent for Barbara and she was lying down, but as soon as he tried to sit up, she was by his side, her hand on his chest gently pushing him back.

"I feel much better," he protested. "And I'm sick of the horizontal."

"All right, darling, just be patient," she replied softly, and deftly propped him up with some pillows behind his back. "There. Does that feel better?"

"Yes." He took her hand in his. "Were you asleep, sweetheart? I didn't mean to wake you. You must be exhausted."

"No. I was only resting, not sleeping." She had left a single candle burning and in its dim light she studied his face. He was unshaven and haggard-looking, but his eyes were clear. She smiled. "You are looking better."

His hand on hers tightened. "You make a first-rate nurse."

"I had a personal stake in this particular recovery."

There was a long pause, then he said slowly, "I've been such a rotten husband to you, Barbara."

"That's not true!"

He smiled a little crookedly. "Oh, yes it is. I've been thinking and thinking about what you said to me . . ." His voice trailed off.

"What did I say?"

"That I was very good at giving you babies and then leaving you to rear them by yourself. Do you remember that?"

"Yes," she said in a low voice.

"Well, it was perfectly true. I didn't like hearing it and I behaved . . ." His mouth tightened. "Well, you know how I behaved."

"Oh, Alan." She smiled at him. "My children are a blessing to me, every one of them, including Christopher." She ran a gentle finger along his cheekbone. His beard pricked her skin. "Was that why you stayed away from me the next time you came home?"

"Yes. I felt like such a bastard."

Barbara looked at him gravely. "*I* am the one whose behavior was unpardonable," she said. "I never thought I was the sort of person who stored up resentment, but that's what I did with you." She bit her lip. "You were perfectly right about Christopher, you know. I did take him to punish you. But then I came to love him as much as my own."

The candlelight caught a flicker of expression in his eyes, but he said nothing.

"When I was a little girl," she went on slowly, "I had one particular doll that I loved. I never minded sharing my other things, but that doll was mine and no one else could touch it. Then one day my brother George took the doll—just to tease me—and hid it. I can still remember how angry I was. I wanted to *kill* him."

Alan was looking at her with a very faint smile in his eyes. "And now I am the doll?" he asked.

Barbara smiled ruefully back. "Something like that."

He ran his fingers up and down her hand. "When first I married you I wondered if you'd be able to cope with life in America. You seemed so fragile to me, a delicate English rose." He looked into her eyes. "I didn't know what I was getting."

"Are you disappointed?" she asked softly.

He shook his head slowly, his eyes still on hers. Barbara felt a tremor stir deep within her. There was the sound of a sentry changing outside in the camp and then silence fell once more. They didn't need words any longer. In that quiet, dark tent, with only their hands clasped, they were closer together than they had ever been before. Finally Alan said, as if he were closing a conversation, "Get some rest, love. You're tired."

She nodded. "Yes. I am." She rose. "Good night, darling." He didn't answer, but she smiled as if he had and went over to her cot and went to sleep.

Lafayette moved his army to Malvern Hill and Barbara took Alan to their house in Williamsburg to recuperate. She could have taken him home to Newland, but the journey was much shorter to Williamsburg, and besides, she wanted him to herself. The children and the plantation had been her life for six long years; now there was only Alan.

It was the first time since their voyage to America that they had been alone for any extended period of time. At first Alan was very weak and Barbara tried to keep him in bed. He was up and about, however, more quickly than she thought wise, and he ended by opening his wound once again.

"See," she told him sternly as she put him back to bed again, "that's what you get for not listening to me. I *told* you not to lift that wood."

He moved his head restlessly on the pillow. "I know. I know," he grumbled. "I just hate feeling so useless."

"You deserve a rest." Her voice was very firm. "Are you so anxious to leave my company?"

His lashes lifted and he looked at her. "You know that's not the reason."

"Then behave yourself."

He grinned. "Yes, ma'am."

They talked. They had six years of filling in to do and during the long summer afternoons they shared a chaise longue in the garden and they talked. They talked about the war and they talked about what they would do after the war was over. Alan was certain the end was in sight. "Now that France has come in, it's more than just a rebellion," he told Barbara. "It's an international conflict, and England will not be able to sustain the burden of garrisoning America for much longer—not when she has France menacing her from across the Channel."

"I never ever thought I would be wishing France well in a fight against England," Barbara said wonderingly.

"I never did either," he replied humorously. "When I think of the way you nearly took my head off when I first started drilling militia . . ."

"I still say it was a stupid reason to fight a war," she returned. Her head was pillowed against his good shoulder and her body was relaxed against his on the chaise. "However, the major stupidity was England's. And there are plenty of good Englishmen who would agree with me. Charles Fox and Mr. Pitt and Mr. Burke have been against this war all along."

"I know. But if it had not been the tax on tea, it would have been something else, sweetheart."

She sighed. "I suppose."

Letters came that afternoon from Lafayette and Alan insisted upon writing a reply almost immediately. That night he also insisted on sitting at the dining-room table instead of eating off the usual supper tray in his room. Barbara eyed him with concern as he got up from the table and went to stand by the window. It seemed to her he was leaning on the wall for support.

"You're tired, darling," she said. "Don't you think you ought to go to bed?"

He surprised her by agreeing without an argument. As he stepped away from the wall, he seemed to stagger slightly and she quickly went to put a supporting arm around his waist. He had been much more active today than she had previously allowed.

He leaned a little of his weight on her as they went into the downstairs bedroom. She walked him over to the bed, but as she went to move away from him, his own arm tightened and he pulled her down with him. He looked into her face.

"I like it when you take care of me," he murmured. She was lying next to him, her body stretched along the length of his. "Kiss me," he whispered.

It was a long, slow, leisurely kiss, not at all the quick, placating caress she had planned. Lying there, with his mouth on hers, his body against her body, Barbara began to feel a familiar sweet, melting languor. She had refused to sleep with him since his injury, she had been so afraid he would reopen the wound in his shoulder. They had been so close she had not even felt the lack. But now . . . He ran his hand over her breast and down to her hip, where it rested, undemanding yet headily potent.

"Lie with me," he murmured against her mouth.

"Your shoulder . . ." she whispered back.

The hand on her hip moved caressingly. "Please," he said.

She couldn't breathe. He insisted on undressing himself. Her own hands were trembling as she unhooked her dress and let it fall to the floor. He watched her out of such intent dark eyes. The last of her undergarments dropped and she came back to the bed again, lying down next to him and stretching out her body for him to touch.

During the last weeks their togetherness had been of the mind and the spirit. Now, as he filled her full and she arched her back in ecstasy, it was as if there were no empty places left in her at all; every part of her being was filled with Alan and his love.

*   *   *

At the end of August the Marquis de Lafayette arrived in person to consult with Alan. Barbara tactfully left the two men in the parlor and went outside to sit in the shade of the garden.

Lafayette would not stay for dinner and after he had left Alan related his news to Barbara. "Washington is marching south with Rochambeau's French troops and the entire Northern Army," he said. His dark eyes were brilliant. "Cornwallis is at Yorktown. And Admiral de Grasse is sailing for the Chesapeake with a large French fleet."

He had come out to the garden to find her, and Barbara gestured him to the chaise longue. He sat down, but on the edge of the footrest, and faced her lawn chair. "Well, that is certainly good news," she said composedly. He was taut with excitement. "What will happen next?" She tried to keep her voice steady. "Another battle?"

"Not a battle, sweetheart, a siege. The key is de Grasse. If he can wrest control of the sea for just long enough, then we can take Cornwallis and his entire army at Yorktown."

Barbara felt the iron bands around her chest begin to relax. "How?" she asked.

"Cornwallis is counting on Clinton being able to reinforce him by sea; that's why he's positioned himself directly on the York. But the river can be either a relief or a trap—it depends upon who controls the sea. If de Grasse can prevent the English fleet from sailing to Virginia, Cornwallis is caught as neatly as a rat in a hole."

"He will have to surrender? Without a battle?"

"He will have to surrender without a battle."

She began to breathe normally again. "But won't General Clinton come to Cornwallis' aid as soon as he realizes Washington is moving south?"

Alan grinned at her "He didn't know Washington was moving south. That's the whole beauty of the plan. The army was already at Trenton before Clinton realized it was moving to Virginia. Washington disguised the whole maneuver into New Jersey as an attempt upon Clinton in New York. He even waited to write to Lafayette until he reached Trenton, for fear the communication be intercepted."

Barbara's eyes were very blue. "How very clever."

"Yes." He stood up and began to pace. "And for once it looks as if everything will go smoothly," he said as he walked restlessly up and down. "If only the French fleet gets here in time!"

She watched him for a moment in silence and then said, "Did Lafayette come only to tell you this? He doesn't want you to rejoin the army?"

He came and put a hand on her shoulder. "The army is joining us, sweetheart. Lafayette will shortly be coming to Williamsburg."

"I see."

His hand on her shoulder tightened. "Cornwallis must not learn of Washington's movements. He must be kept at Yorktown!"

She rested her cheek against his hand. "It sounds as if Washington is being very discreet, darling."

"Mm." His voice over her head was abstracted. "Wayne ought to pretend he is getting ready to march to joine Greene in South Carolina. That would help throw Cornwallis off the scent. I'll send a message to that effect to the marquis tomorrow."

He wasn't thinking of her at all. Their idyll was over, Barbara realized. The war was their reality once more.

Thirty

On September 4 Lafayette's Americans marched into Williamsburg. Also encamping in the small town were three regiments of French troops under General Saint-Simon. The French, originally stationed in the West Indies, had been landed by Admiral de Grasse's fleet off Jamestown. De Grasse had then put out once more to sea.

Lafayette promptly fell ill of a fever. Anthony Wayne was accidentally shot in the leg by an American sentry whose challenge he didn't hear. Alan, whose shoulder was healing well, was consequently the healthiest of the senior officers and he assumed command.

The food supply was, as always, dire and Barbara sent to Newland to tell Libby to strip the plantation of all but the barest necessities for the army. The hot Virginia weather was hard on the soldiers and a large number came down with fever. The College of William and Mary was turned into a hospital and Barbara spent a great part of her day here nursing.

The face Alan showed to his officers and his men was unruffled and good-humored. He exuded confidence and, consequently, the atmosphere in the camp was amazingly cheerful under the circumstances.

At home Alan was not so confident. "I wish to God I knew what was going on at sea," he said to Barbara about every other sentence. "The whole fate of this campaign hangs on de Grasse. He *must* gain control of the Chesapeake."

There had been a report that the British fleet had engaged de Grasse in action on September 5, but then both fleets had disappeared out to sea and no further word had been forthcoming.

On September 14 Barbara was leaving the hospital when she noticed the French troops encamped on the grounds hurriedly adjusting their dress equipment and forming into lines. She looked toward the west and saw a small group of horsemen coming at a hard gallop through the dusty afternoon sunshine.

Barbara shaded her eyes with her hand and tried to see who was causing the stir. She could see the bright French uniforms quite clearly but it was the figure riding in front who caught and held her attention. He was a big man dressed in a uniform of blue and buff. Washington had arrived.

There was a formal military dinner that night which Alan attended along with the American senior officers and the French commanders. Barbara was in bed but not asleep when he returned home at eleven.

She pushed herself up on her pillow and yawned. "How did it go, darling?"

"Oh, very convivial. Saint-Simon's cooks managed to produce a first-rate meal. The French band played a tune from Grétry's opera *Lucille*—you know, the one that indicates the joy of a family at the arrival of its father. All very complimentary and jovial."

He was undressing as he spoke and now he sat down to take off his boots. Barbara watched him without speaking. Finally, when he had the boots off, she said softly, "No word from de Grasse?"

"No word from de Grasse." He came over to the bed, his face grim. "If the English Navy gets through, Barbara, it's all over for us. The country is so weary of war; it can't take another inconclusive engagement. And the French court will be disheartened as well. They may recall their troops."

She had never seen him so discouraged. He got into bed next to her and she turned to put her arms around him. Under her hands his muscles felt tense with stress. "We've got the best army right now that we've ever had," he said over her head into the dark. "Not our usual untrained militia, but professional soldiers." A note of irony crept into his voice. "The armies of Rochambeau and Saint-Simon; French, not American." Barbara began to rub his back. "And the outcome of this whole campaign," he went on, "depends upon what has happened at sea between the French and the British navies. You know, Barbara, there isn't a single American present on any of those ships?"

She was silent for a minute as she massaged the knotted muscles in his back. Then, replying to the tone of his voice as much as to the words, she said, "The reason there is a French army and a French fleet in Virginia today is that for six long years there has been an *American* army in the field. No one thought you could do it, but you did. What was it Nathanael Greene said recently: 'We fight, get beat, rise, and fight again'?"

"Um." Some of the tenseness was beginning to drain out of him.

"The American Army simply doesn't know the meaning of the word 'defeat.' And it's because of *that*, that Rochambeau and de Grasse are here today. The French came into this war, darling, because they knew they had a winner."

She saw his teeth gleam in the darkness. "This surely is a reversal of roles for us, sweetheart, isn't it? You reassuring me."

"I reckon it is," she replied, imitating his drawl.

He laughed deep in his throat and drew her closer. "It's just that everything has gone so perfectly so far. I'm not used to such success, I reckon. It makes me nervous as a cat."

She put her cheek against his chest. The beat of his heart was so steady, so . . . indomitable. "No English ships have appeared in the Chesapeake, Alan. And Cornwallis is still at Yorktown. I would say that things look very hopeful."

"Mmm." She could feel the change in his thoughts in his body, and she smiled faintly in the dark. Good. Let him concentrate on her for a little. That would do more than anything else to take his mind off his troubles.

Her lips opened under the pressure of his and a heavy languor crept across her body. They knew each other so well and they knew it was not a bonfire of passion they needed tonight. It was her sweetness and his strength coming together in reassurance and comfort and love; a promise that, no matter what happened, they would never be alone.

The following day they heard from Admiral de Grasse. The French fleet was back in the Chesapeake and the English fleet under Admiral Graves was returning to New York. De Grasse had taken control of the sea.

Washington was almost as jubilant at de Grasse's second piece of information. Admiral de Barras and his fleet had arrived in Virginia from Rhode Island with siege artillery and salted meat for the armies.

The noose around Cornwallis' neck was in place. Now all that was required was to tighten it.

On September 28 the combined French and American armies moved out of Williamsburg along the sandy, wooded roads that led to Yorktown. It was still hot in Virginia and the flat land of the peninsula shimmered in the steamy weather. The allied army marched past thickets of bayberry cat-brier, and holly; past pine and hardwood forests; past sluggish tidal creeks and war-ravaged fields of tobacco, cotton, and corn, and at three o'clock in the afternoon they were in sight of Yorktown.

The following day the allied engineers began to lay out positions for the artillery. The siege of Yorktown had formally begun.

On the American side it was a question of moving their guns ever closer to the town. Trenches were dug and earthworks thrown up. Then more trenches were dug in front of those already existing. The British were able to do nothing but try to return fire and to endure.

On the night of October 14 the two British redoubts in front of their defense line were taken by the allies and a new trench was dug.

On October 16 Lord Cornwallis, desperate by now, attempted to evacuate at least part of his army by small boats across the York. The plan was to cross the river at night to Gloucester, destroy the boats on the north shore, and be many miles away before Washington realized what the British were doing.

Major Harry Wharton was one of the officers who pressed for the attempted escape. As he wrote in his diary several hours before taking boat, "A retreat by Gloucester is the only expedient to avert the mortification of a surrender."

Harry was among the one thousand soldiers who went across the river in the first wave. They landed about midnight and sent the boats back to the south shore to collect more troops. The boats were scarcely launched when a vicious rainstorm swept down the river, scattering the craft and unmercifully pelting the shelterless British on shore.

The rainstorm went on all night. British guns fired in the wet darkness but there was no response from the French and American lines. Harry, shivering and cursing on the far side of the river, wondered what the hell was going on.

In the morning the rain let up and with the daylight Harry and the rest of his companions were able to see what they had not seen from Yorktown: there were trenches around the entire Gloucester garrison, and behind the trenches was a cordon of French hussars.

"We will not get out by way of Gloucester, my lord," Harry reported to Lord Cornwallis when he and his fellows had been returned to Yorktown by boat later in the day. Then, because he was curious, "Why were the American and French guns so silent last night?"

Cornwallis looked bleak. "Toward morning they brought a trench and a strong battery of fourteen guns so close to our hornwork, Major, that one could throw stones into it."

Harry watched his commander in chief walk away and thought: That's it, then. That's the end of the British Army.

On October 17 the American batteries perceived a British drummer boy high upon one of the parapets. He could not be heard because of the noise, but as one by one the batteries fell silent, the steady roll of the call to parley could be heard. Then an English officer came out, holding a white handkerchief over his head.

Alan sent word to Barbara the night of the seventeenth that Cornwallis had asked for terms. All during the following day the two commanders negotiated through intermediaries. By the morning of September 19 Cornwallis had declared his army prisoners of war. The formal surrender was made that afternoon, with the entire British Army filing between two columns of Americans and French to throw down their arms. As soon as the official ceremony was over, Alan got leave and rode back to Williamsburg to visit his wife.

It was dark when he pulled up in front of his house on Duke of Gloucester Street. He put his horse in the stable, and as he was walking up the path to the house, the door opened and Barbara was there, a candle in her hand. "Alan!" she said. "Is it all over, then?"

"Yes." He entered the house and shut the door behind him. "This afternoon."

"This afternoon," she repeated. "Cornwallis surrendered?"

"Cornwallis surrendered. The British Southern Army is no more."

"Oh, Alan." She put her candle down and threw her arms around his neck. His cheek against hers was very cold. "Come to the fire," she said breathlessly. "I want to hear all about it."

He followed her to the two chairs that were positioned to get the heat from the fire. They sat down together. "What happened?" she asked, looking at him expectantly. "Did Lord Cornwallis surrender his sword to General Washington?"

Alan looked sardonic. "Cornwallis didn't have the stomach to make the surrender himself. He said he was sick and he sent his second in command, General O'Hara. O'Hara tried to give Cornwallis' sword to Rochambeau."

"Not to Washington?"

"I reckon he wanted it to look like he was surrendering to the French, not to us. But Rochambeau pointed to his excellency and said, 'We are subordinate to the Americans. General Washington will give you your orders.' "

Barbara smiled. "And did he?"

Alan grinned. "Washington made O'Hara surrender to *his* second in command, Lincoln."

"My, my. Such protocol."

"They hated it," Alan said. "My God, how they hated it. We were all lined up on either side of the road, the French on one side and the Americans on the other, and after they threw down their arms they had to march between the allied lines back to Yorktown.

"The French looked splendid. The English didn't mind so much surrendering to the French. But to us—a parcel of farmers and shopkeepers who didn't even have uniforms! The German officers were crying."

"They never believed it could happen," Barbara said.

"You know, Barbara, I could hardly believe it myself." The house was very quiet. The only sound was the crackling of the fire in the chimney. "What are we, after all? Washington is a farmer, Greene is an ironmonger, and Knox a bookseller. We are all civilians. We have perhaps half a million men of fighting age in the whole country. Christ, when this war started we weren't even a country, just thirteen separate colonies on the fringe of civilization. And here we were, with the army of the greatest military power in the world surrendering to us. To *us*." He shook his head. The candles from the candelabrum threw a flickering shadow across his face. "I know I kept saying this would happen—and I even believed that it would happen but when it did, I was . . . overwhelmed."

Barbara got up and came around to stand behind his chair. She put her hands on his shoulders and bent to kiss his black hair. He leaned his head back against her breast.

"Ever since you left for Yorktown I have been thinking of something that Libby wrote to me right after she sent Charles off to Valley Forge," she said softly. She was gently massaging his shoulders and his eyes closed with pleasure.

"What was that?"

"She said that I would never be able to understand the importance to a man like Charles of what this country stood for. 'That all men are created equal.' Isn't that what Jefferson wrote?"

"Um. The despised Jefferson."

She put her cheek briefly against his hair. "Let him stick to the pen." He chuckled and she went on "But that's why you have triumphed, Alan, you farmers and ironmongers and shopkeepers. You weren't just fighting for a country. You were fighting for an idea."

She realized that his eyes were open and looking up at her. "I never expected you to see that," he said.

"I see it when I look at Christopher," she replied. "I look at this shining, happy little boy, with so many talents, and I know that in England he would never have the chance to stand beside Ian and William. But here . . . here, all men are created equal." She drew a long slow breath. "I know I am only a woman—" she said, but he cut her off by getting to his feet.

"Enough of this 'only-a-woman' speech. I don't believe a word of it anymore. You've been doing my job for six years now and under far more difficult circumstances than I ever faced. Will you send me to the cookhouse when I get home?"

"Oh, darling." She put her arms about his waist and her head on his shoulder. "I will be so *glad* to have you home. You can do anything you want to do."

"Can I?" He put his mouth against her hair. "Well, I think I'd like to relandscape the gardens," he murmured, and felt her stiffen slightly in his arms.

"Not the boxwood gardens, Alan, surely? They are so lovely as they are."

"And then there is the matter of our sons," he went on, ignoring her interruption. "They are sadly in need of a father's discipline."

Barbara pulled away from him. "They are very good children, Alan," she was beginning defensively when she saw him start to grin. "You're teasing me," she accused.

"Only a little, sweetheart, only a little."

She stared up into his hawklike face. He had commanded men for the last six years and he looked it. The general. But *she* had commanded Newland. "We probably will have some adjustments," she said candidly.

He laughed. "Adjustments, hell. We'll have fights."

She shook her head determinedly "No. I've promised myself never to fight with you again."

He was looking at her with amusement in his eyes. "And you probably think you mean it."

"Of course I mean it." Her voice was sharp. "Don't be so smug, Alan." Then, as the amusement in his eyes only deepened: "Why are you the only person in the world who can irritate me like this?"

He reached out and pulled her close. "Because you love me," he said in her ear.

She put her arms around his neck. "I suppose so."

"I saw your cousin at the surrender," he said after a minute.

Her eyes widened and she pulled back to look up at him. "Did he see you?"

Alan grinned. "Sweetheart, I'm pretty hard to miss."

Barbara stared for a minute into the face she loved and felt a stir of pity for Harry. "How did he look?" she asked.

"Impassive."

"Oh dear. Alan, what is going to happen to the English?"

"We're going to ship them home. Cornwallis
signed an agreement promising that none of the
captured soldiers would ever fight in America again."
Then, as Barbara just continued to look at him:
"Don't worry, sweetheart. There will be plenty of
work for your cousin in Europe against the French."

"Poor Harry." Barbara, however, was not thinking of the war. She was thinking of her last meeting
with him in Philadelphia. She had no intention,
however, of ever telling Alan about that particular
encounter.

"I'm starving," her husband said. "Is there anything to eat in this house?"

Harry was banished from her mind as thoroughly
as if he had never existed. "Of course, darling.
Come along with me and I'll get you something."

She fed him and listened to him as he told her
about the siege. This is happiness, she thought as
she nodded her head at something he said. Just to
sit with him in their own dining room, with the fire
crackling and the house silent all around them. To
have him eat the food she had prepared and to
watch the play of expression on his face. She didn't
need anything or anyone else. Only Alan.

"Can it really be over?" she asked wonderingly
when he had finished talking.

"Well, Clinton still has an army in New York.
But England isn't going to send him reinforcements; she can't, not with the French threat across
the Channel. It may take a while before they come

to the treaty table, but I think the fighting is over sweetheart.''

She closed her eyes and when she opened them again it was to find him beside her. "Are you all right?" he asked in concern.

"I'm fine." She drew a shaky breath and gave him a radiant smile. "Oh, Alan," she said, "to have you home again!"

He drew her out of her chair and into his arms. "Peace is coming, Barbara," he said, his cheek against her hair. His arms tightened. "Have patience. This time, peace is almost here."

Epilogue
Newland, October 1788

Helen Brandon walked slowly up the path that led from the river through the boxwood gardens to the house. She paused at the top of the path and, turning to look around her, drew a long, deep satisfied breath.

It was so good to be home. After thirteen years of living in England, it was so good to be home. Edmund felt the same way, although he was less vocal than she. After all, it had been his decision to leave Virginia before the start of the war. She didn't blame him. Under the circumstances, there had been nothing else to do. It would have been impossible to remain in Virginia and remain loyal to the king. But the war was over, the treaty granting America her independence signed, and a new constitution ratified. When Alan had written to ask Edmund to return, he had not required much persuasion.

The sound of dogs yelping came floating through the clear autumn air and Helen followed the noise around to the front of the house. Her brother, sister-in-law, and three oldest nephews were just riding in from a morning's hunt. Helen smiled at the picture they made; the Maxwells were an extraordinarily good-looking family.

"We had a few splendid runs," Barbara called to her sister-in-law. "You should have come, Helen."

"Papa jumped a six-foot fence!" Christopher said excitedly.

"Five feet, Chris," Alan murmured. "And you are not to attempt it, William."

William looked at his father innocently. "Me, Papa?"

"I could do it, Papa. I know I could," said Ian.

"Well, we'll see. Perhaps with a little practice . . ."

"Alan! That fence was *enormous.*"

"It's getting bigger by the minute," Alan replied humorously. "Ian, hold your mother's horse for her, please."

The tall, slim fourteen-year-old slid down from his own horse and went to stand at the head of his mother's. Alan dismounted and went to lift his wife down. When she was on her feet next to him he turned to Christopher. "You and Ian take the horses to the stable, Chris, and see they get a good rubdown."

"Yes, sir." Christopher dismounted and came to take his father's reins.

"William." Alan's voice was perfectly pleasant but William stopped lounging on his horse and sat up straight. "Yes, sir?"

"You may do your own horse but then I want you right back here. You have mathematics to finish."

"Yes, sir." William looked resigned. At age ten he was as wide through the shoulders as Ian. William was going to have his father's size, Helen thought.

Barbara shook the dust from her midnight-blue riding skirt and came over to stand beside her sister-in-law. "I hope you didn't mind us deserting you this morning, Helen. You should have come."

Helen shook her head. "I couldn't possibly keep up with you all. Galloping frantically across country has never been my favorite activity."

Barbara's eyes, as deeply blue as her riding habit, smiled. "We love it."

Helen laughed. "You're every bit as mad as your sons, my dear."

"She's worse," said Alan's deep, slow voice as he joined them. His own eyes glinted as he looked at his wife. "The only reason she didn't take that famous fence was that she didn't want to set a bad example for the boys."

"They get quite enough encouragement to break their necks from their father," Barbara replied smoothly, and Alan grinned.

"Where is Edmund?" Barbara asked as they walked toward the house.

"At Stanley. He's anxious for us to move in before the winter, and there's still so much to do. He feels the work will progress more quickly if he is there to supervise."

"He's right," said Alan laconically.

Barbara linked her arm through her sister-in-law's. "But there is no rush, Helen. You're welcome to stay at Newland for as long as you like." She turned her beautiful face to her husband. "Isn't that so, Alan?"

"Of course. But I reckon I know how Edmund feels. A man wants his own roof over his head."

There was a brief flash of something between husband and wife that Helen felt rather than saw. In the three weeks that she had been staying at Newland, Helen had caught it before—that quick sense of two people communicating quite beyond the words that were being spoken—and it made her feel left out. She didn't think that Barbara and Alan realized this, however, and Barbara was certainly smiling at her now as if there had been no interruption in the conversation. As, Helen supposed, there hadn't been.

The entire family gathered around the dining-room table for dinner at three o'clock and Edmund returned from Stanley to join them. Helen looked at the shining boyish heads surrounding her and repressed a sigh. "I wonder how James is faring at Eton?" she asked her husband.

"I thought he was my age, Aunt Helen," Christopher said. "Isn't he too young to be sent away to school?"

"In England, Christopher, boys go away to school at eight."

Christopher's long-lashed brown eyes enlarged. "Eight!" he said. "I wouldn't like that at all."

"Neither would I," William put in with feeling. He looked at his aunt. "Will Charlie have to go away to school, Aunt Helen? I reckon he's English now that Aunt Libby has married Captain Archer."

"Charlie went to school with James this year," Helen said.

Christopher and William exchanged a look of mutual commiseration. "Poor Charlie," Christopher said.

"I'm sure Charlie will enjoy school very much," Barbara said firmly. She turned to her sister-in-law. "Isn't it odd, Helen, that of all of us, Libby should be the one to live in England? She was such a fierce rebel, while you and I wanted only peace."

Helen smiled. "It is odd. But she's very happy with Philip Archer, particularly since he sold out of the army. And your mother has been most kind about introducing Libby to London society."

"You didn't know what you were doing when you invited Captain Archer to come to Newland on parole after Yorktown," Edmund said genially.

"Well, we didn't precisely invite *him*," Barbara replied. "It was my cousin Harry who was my chief concern. He asked if he could bring Captain Archer along." Her attention was distracted by her youngest son, two-year-old Luke, who was seated next to her at the table. Luke had begun to bang his fork against his dish. Barbara removed the utensil from his small fist and started to feed him his lamb.

"How is the work coming along, Edmund?" Alan asked, and as the two men talked and Barbara fed Luke, Helen surreptitiously studied her brother.

Physically he had changed very little in the past thirteen years. His shoulders were as wide as she remembered, his stomach as flat, his hips as slim. The only sign he gave of his forty-one years was the gray that was just beginning to show in his thick black hair.

Yet he had changed, a change that was immediately recognizable although hard to define. It was in the look of his face, the quality of his presence. The authority was so deeply ingrained in him that he had to do nothing more than raise an eyebrow to draw one's instant attention.

He was formidable. Helen felt that, even though she was perfectly comfortable in his presence. He was charming as well; that disarming grin of his would put anyone at ease. But no matter how ood-humored and genial he seemed, he was not he Alan she remembered. She liked him. She njoyed his company. But she didn't feel she knew im very well.

He was a very important figure in Virginia. Helen ad been home for only three weeks but already hat was clear. Newland was one of the political enters of the state. Today's dinner was a rarity, in act, in that there was no visitor present other than hemselves. And still, for all his vast circle of friends, Helen thought that there was probably only one erson to whom Alan really opened his mind.

Her sister-in-law was calmly wiping Luke's chin vith a napkin. Serene and beautiful, surrounded y her handsome, well-mannered sons, she pre-ided over her table like a duchess, Helen thought.

Alan and her husband were talking absorbedly bout the new herd of dairy cattle Alan had put in t Newland. Helen watched Ian listening intently to he men and thought how much nicer was this merican custom of having children at the dinner able than was the English way of banishing them o the schoolroom to eat. It made the whole family o much closer. . . . The second-youngest Maxwell, ve-year-old George Washington, suddenly made choking noise over his food. Alan was on his feet stantly and behind the child's chair.

George was coughing and tears streamed down is face. "Alan!" Barbara said sharply.

"He's all right, Barbara. He's taking in air." Then,

as the coughing lessened a little, "Here, George, take a drink of water." The little boy drank the water, coughed a little more, drank some more water, and then subsided.

"Sorry, Papa," he said.

"Cut your meat into smaller portions and be sure to chew," his father recommended as he returned to his place at the head of the table.

"Perhaps you ought to cut the meat for him, Alan," said Barbara.

"Not at all. George is a big boy now."

"I can do it, Mama," said George stoutly and frowning with concentration, he began to cut his meat.

Helen couldn't help saying, "Five is rather young for such manual dexterity, Alan."

"I could cut my own meat when I was four," Christopher announced proudly.

"It's not nice to brag, darling," Barbara murmured. "And George is doing very well."

William kicked Christopher under the table. Barbara didn't notice and Helen pretended not to notice as Christopher deftly kicked him back and then moved his leg away. Christopher's big guileless brown eyes met Helen's and she tried not to laugh.

"I hope you're going to take Harrison's advice and run for the Senate," Edmund said to Alan.

"I don't know about that," Alan replied comfortably.

"You're the most qualified man in the state,"
dmund said categorically. "You'd be elected al-
ost unanimously. And we need good men in
overnment if this new constitution is to succeed,
lan."

Helen was conscious of Barbara's sudden still-
ess. She turned to look at her sister-in-law and
aw that all the warmth had left her eyes.

"What's the Senate, Papa?" Ian asked.

"It's one of the two houses of the new federal
gislature, son. Each state will send two senators
represent them in making the laws for the whole
ountry."

"Will it be in Richmond, like the Virginia legis-
ature?"

"No." Alan's eyes moved from his son's face to
is wife's. "The federal government will sit in New
ork City."

"And you have a plantation to run in Virginia,"
arbara said tightly.

"And I have a plantation to run in Virginia,"
Ian agreed good-humoredly. "I reckon Richmond
far enough away for me to go these days,
dmund."

"Nonsense. It's not as if you'd be away for the
ntire year. This is important, Alan. It's essential
at Virginia have the right representation."

"There are plenty of men to represent Virginia,
dmund," Barbara said tartly. "Alan has more than

done his fair share of duty. Let someone else tak
a turn."

Helen glanced quickly at Alan to see how h
would react to this statement and caught such
look of tenderness in his eyes as he watched hi
wife that she felt a shock run through her. Then th
expression was gone, replaced by a look of fain
amusement.

"There *is* no one more qualified than Alan,'
Edmund said to Barbara.

Alan spoke firmly. "There is only one indispens
able man in this country, Edmund, and he is goin
to be our president. Poor beggar, he's been s
happy at Mount Vernon these last years." Ala
grinned at his wife. "Let Tom Jefferson go to Ne
York as Virginia's senator."

"Jefferson," she replied with withering contempt
and her husband chuckled.

The day clouded up during the afternoon and b
the time Alan and Barbara retired it had begun t
rain. Alan was in bed, arms behind his head, whe
Barbara came back from checking on the sleepin
children.

"Counted all your gold?" he asked softly, an
she smiled at him.

"All counted. All safe." She went to the windo
and looked out at the rain. Alan watched her bac
in silence. Finally she turned to look at him. "Ho

420

many people have approached you about running
or the Senate?"

"A few," he answered peacefully.

She walked toward the bed, untying the belt of
er robe as she came. With her loosened hair and
lim arms and throat, she looked scarcely older
han she had when he married her, he thought.
"You never told me," she said.

"I didn't want to upset you. I knew you wouldn't
vant me to run. And I'm not *going* to run, sweet-
eart, so there's an end to it."

She laid her robe neatly across a chair and came
ver to his side of the bed. "Because I don't want
ou to?" she asked, looking down into his relaxed
lark face.

"Because you don't want me to," he agreed
asily, and reached up a lazy arm to pull her down
ext to him.

Barbara lay against him quietly. After all these
ears, she still rejoiced at the feel of that big strong
ody next to hers in bed. If she awoke during the
ight she would still put her hand out to touch him,
o make sure he was really there. She did not want
im to go away again.

"New York is too far," she said.

"I know, sweetheart. I'm not going to desert you
gain."

They lay quietly together and listened to the
ound of the rain against the window glass. Alan
awned. "I have an idea for enlarging the stable,"

he said, and began to tell her about it. This wa
their time together, away from the children, th
time they discussed everything from their most pri
vate feelings to the repair of the garden shed
Tonight, however, Barbara wasn't listening to him
Her mind was on this question of Alan's runnin;
for the Senate.

She didn't want him to do it and he had said h
wouldn't. She believed him; that wasn't the ques
tion. The question was, was she wrong to stand i
his way?

He was the best man for the job. Of that she ha
no doubt at all. Barbara had been bred in an aristoc
racy which considered government service as pai
of its hereditary duty and now that she had wo
such easy acquiescence from Alan she was gettin;
twinges of conscience. If she had had to fight him
she would have dug her heels in and refused to l
him go. But she had not had to fight him. . . . "Ar
you certain you don't want to run for the Senate?'
she asked right in the middle of his description c
the new stalls he was planning.

There was a brief startled pause and then h
said, "Of course I'm sure."

"Who else besides Edmund and Ben Harriso
asked you to run?"

"Oh . . . Pendleton, Burwell, Randolph."

"You *would* be the best man," Barbara said in
small voice.

He leaned up on an elbow so he could see her ce. "Do you want me to run?" he asked.

Barbara looked up at him. He was such a splen- d man. After Washington himself, he was proba- y the most respected, the most loved man in all rginia. Was it fair of her to want to confine him to small plantation when he could be helping to ide and mold a nation? She reached a hand up touch his cheek. "If you really want to run, it will all right with me," she whispered.

His dark eyes studied her speculatively. "Sweet- art, I would have sworn on a stack of Bibles that u would move heaven and earth to keep me m running for the federal government."

She moved her hand along the hard plane of his eek. "I tried to stand between you and your duty ce," she said. "I don't want to do that again."

"Ah." He bent his head to kiss her throat; then lay back again and looked up at the canopy er them. "This isn't the same thing at all."

Barbara turned on her stomach and propped her in on her hands. "Isn't it? Why not?"

His face was perfectly tranquil. "Before, we were war, sweetheart. Everyone had a duty to serve. is is something that requires only a few."

"But if, as Edmund says, you are the best quali- d . . ." Her voice was soft.

He looked at her. "Perhaps I am. But there are enty of others who will do a good job, Barbara, d who will enjoy it a hell of a lot more. I have

very serious responsibilities right here at home
consider—that gold you were counting only a fe
minutes ago."

"Oh, darling." She moved a little until she w
lying alongside him, her arm across his chest, h
cheek pressed against his shoulder.

"Do you realize that you and I have just abo
the only money-making plantation in the state
Virginia just now?" he asked. His left arm held h
close to him and his right hand began slowly to ru
the small of her back. "We can't possibly bo
leave it to go to New York together, and I will n
leave you again to carry on alone. And I have
duty to my children to protect their heritage; or
you are always telling me."

"Mmm." Barbara's eyes were closing and h
breathing had deepened. There was a spot on h
lower back she always found very erotic and I
knew it. He continued his rhythmic stroking.

"Let the other men do it. Let Robert run. It w
give him something serious to do with himself i
stead of racketing around Richmond pretending
practice law."

The sensations his hand was creating were hea
enly. "I think Robert misses the war," Barba
murmured.

"He ought to get himself married." Alan roll
her over and leaned over her, his hands braced
either side of her shoulders, his dark face ve
close to hers. "Making love to your wife can be

very time-consuming, not to mention gratifying, occupation."

He wasn't even touching her, yet she was totally his. "You certainly devote enough time to it," she whispered.

"I'm working on a daughter." Their eyes locked together. "Kiss me," he said, and she raised her head a little to meet his mouth. Their bodies still apart, they kissed deeply. Still holding her mouth with his, he shifted his weight to his side and pulled her along with him. Then he began to push up her nightgown. Barbara opened for him like a flower opening before the warmth of the sun.

"You really gave some thought to the Senate position, didn't you?" she asked later as they lay drowsily in each other's arms.

"Yes. I reckon I do feel a sense of obligation. After all, I worked so hard to convince the Virginia Assembly to ratify the constitution, it seemed churlish not to be willing to serve when I was asked. But I will continue to serve in the Assembly. That will have to do."

Unseen by him, Barbara smiled. The note of finality in his voice was clear, and Alan was not one to change his mind. She had him—she and the children. "It was such fun this morning, the hunt. We must take the boys again," she said.

"Yes. I'm going to teach Ian to jump five feet."

He felt her stiffen for just a minute and then she

relaxed. "Oh, all right. Have it your way. You always do."

"I like to try." He kissed her hair. "I surely do like to try."

They drifted off to sleep to the sound of the rain.

About the Author

Joan Wolf is a native of New York City who presently resides in Milford, Connecticut, with her husband and two young children. She taught high school English in New York for nine years and took up writing when she retired to rear a family. Her previous books, THE COUNTERFEIT MARRIAGE, A KIND OF HONOR, A LONDON SEASON, A DIFFICULT TRUCE, THE SCOTTISH LORD, and HIS LORDSHIP'S MISTRESS, are also available in Signet editions.

*er lips were still warm from the imprint of his kiss,
*t now Silvia knew there was nothing to protect her
*om the terror of Serpent Tree Hall. Not even love.
pecially not love. . . .

ANDREA PARNELL

vely young Silvia Bradstreet had come from London
* Colonial America to be a bondservant on an isolated
*and estate off the Georgia coast. But a far different
*te awaited her at the castle-like manor: a man whose
*s moved like a hot flame over her flesh . . . whose
*entless passion and incredible strength aroused feel-
*gs she could not control. And as a whirlpool of intrigue
*d violence sucked her into the depths of evil . . .
mes of desire melted all her power to resist. . . .

Coming in September from Signet!

27 million Americans can't read a bedtime story to a child.

It's because 27 million adults in this country simply can't read.

Functional illiteracy has reached one out of five Americans. It robs them of even the simplest of human pleasures, like reading a fairy tale to a child.

You can change all this by joining the fight against illiteracy.

Call the Coalition for Literacy at toll-free **1-800-228-8813** and volunteer.

Volunteer Against Illiteracy. The only degree you need is a degree of caring.